Jobless Recovery

L.C. Evans

Llumina Press

Copyright © 2005   L.C. Evans

All rights reserved. No part of this publication may be reproduced or transmitted in any form or by any means electronic or mechanical, including photocopy, recording, or any information storage and retrieval system, without permission in writing from both the copyright owner and the publisher.

Requests for permission to make copies of any part of this work should be mailed to Permissions Department, Llumina Press, PO Box 772246, Coral Springs, FL 33077-2246

ISBN: 1-59526-157-5
Printed in the United States of America by Llumina Press

Library of Congress Cataloging-in-Publication Data

Evans, L. C. (Linda C.), 1949-
 Jobless recovery / L.C. Evans.
    p. cm.
 ISBN 1-59526-157-5 (pbk. : alk. paper)
 1. Unemployment--Fiction. 2. North Carolina--Fiction. I. Title.
PS3605.V3683J63 2005
813'.54--dc22   2004029131

To all the true American Patriots who fight for their country each day.
You know who you are.

Chapter One

The radio announcer suggested that listeners enjoy lots of beautiful North Carolina sunshine and have themselves a good one. Dave Griffin maneuvered into an opening in the morning traffic and slotted his car into the right-hand lane. He figured he might be exposed to a bit of sun when he left the Markham-Hook Conglomerate's Pyramid Building at lunchtime, but he wasn't sure he'd be having himself a good one or even an okay one. A ton of work lay stacked on his desk in piles that only he could make sense of.

He swung his blood-colored SUV around a corner and joined the line inching into the company's lot for oversized vehicles. While he waited his turn to rumble down the ramp to the underground garage, he fiddled with the radio dials, trying to find a station that wasn't broadcasting air quality reports, as if people had any choice over which air to breathe. He'd just driven fifteen miles from his new home in the suburbs. He didn't need a voice coming out of his dashboard to tell him there was so much haze hanging over the city that the Pyramid on top of Markham-Hook's tallest building couldn't be seen from five miles away.

When he emerged from the garage, he squinted up toward the sky. No trouble seeing the building from across the street. The Markham-Hook Pyramid Building had won awards for everything except in-your-face audacity, and that one was probably in the works. The structure was fifty stories tall, besting by some thirty stories the next highest building in Avalon. The first five floors--main lobby, banquet hall, service floor, new accounts, and human resources--were all Markham-Hook. Floors six through twenty-four were leased to the most prosperous businessmen, lawyers, and doctors in the city. They--and their clients--rode up from the lobby in glass elevators that looked like futuristic space capsules. All the elevators in the building had been feng shueid, and people from Avalon Bonnie Blooms arrived daily to arrange freshly cut flowers in vases attached to the interior elevator walls.

Starting with floor twenty-five and ending with forty-five, Markham-Hook housed its own people--computer programmers, investment counselors, insurance and mortgage brokers, travel planners, administrative staff--all the thousands of workers required to keep the Markham-Hook economy humming. Floors forty-six through fifty were reserved for the top management. CEO John Victor Harris's office held the place of honor in the point of the pyramid where, it was rumored, he could see for thirty miles in every direction on days when the skies were clear.

Dave worked on twenty-five. He was a programmer with a workstation in the maze of cubicles that stretched across half of the floor space, from the front to the back of the building. He'd been here four years, hired straight out of NC State before he'd even stepped off the stage clutching his computer science degree. But he didn't rate one of the double-sized cubicles in a window row. In fact, his closet-sized cube opened onto the carpeted hallway leading from the elevator, so there was constant traffic scuffing back and forth. Someday, though, he'd move over a few aisles. He expected someday to arrive pretty quickly. He'd gotten his yearly review last week and scored above average in everything and superior in a few categories--problem-solving ability, speed and accuracy of his work, and willingness to work overtime when needed.

He wasn't working over today, though. Out of the question. He rode up to his floor on one of the employee elevators, a half-sized duplicate of the luxury cars provided to clients. The doors slid open to reveal the desk of his team's admin, Myra Hilton.

"Morning, Dave." She waved him to a stop, red-painted talons flashing, and looked at him over the top of her half glasses. "Ken wants to see you when you get a chance."

"Sure. Tell our esteemed supervisor I live to keep him happy."

"Just run by his office at some point in the next fifteen minutes, okay? Otherwise he'll think I forgot to tell you."

Dave rolled his eyes. Half the time Ken acted like he was too important to relay his own messages and the rest of the time he micromanaged the team. Dave thumped the top of Myra's desk as he moved past to peek around the corner. No sign of Ken. He turned and made a dash for his cubicle, bobbing and weaving between co-workers like a courier on his way to the CEO with the latest stock figures.

Mentally patting himself on the back after the narrow escape, Dave pulled out his desk chair. His triumph didn't last long. Thumping footsteps sounded behind him as if a troll had escaped from under a bridge and was loose in the building. Dave hunched his shoulders and tried to blend in with the gray walls.

"Dave, got a minute?"

With a sigh of resignation, he turned and pasted on a look of polite inquiry. Ken, the picture of a man with nothing but lard in his arteries, had clomped into Dave's cube breathing like a porn star in the middle of a hot scene. He stopped in front of Dave and pushed a piece of paper into his hand.

"You were supposed to come by my office." So this was one of the micromanage days. "Knew you'd forget to check your email yesterday, so I printed this off for you."

Dave hadn't forgotten, he just hadn't bothered with his email because anything Ken had to say wasn't all that important. Knowing it would annoy Ken, he read out loud in a voice he copied from his favorite doom and gloom newscaster. "Departmental meeting Friday morning in Conference Room 25. Nine AM. Mandatory. Major company announcement for all personnel. Cheers. Ken G. Archer, Team B Supervisor."

He crumpled the paper and pushed it into the breast pocket of Ken's wrinkled sport coat and patted the pocket. He wished his boss would let the coat die. It had long ago lost any ability to recover its shape after cleaning and hung from his shoulders like an old towel.

"Rumors were flying yesterday. I'd have to be brain dead not to know about the meeting."

"Dave, this isn't a regular announcement."

"Is it a surprise party for your birthday or something?" Dave held his watch up close to his eyes and pretended to be startled at the lateness of the hour.

Ken edged toward the hallway. "Just enjoy the day. You'll find out the bad news tomorrow."

Sure. Now that Ken had promised dire tidings, Dave was supposed to cheerfully knock out a pile of work and go home at the end of the day so he could curl up with a good book. Ken would probably recommend a nice success story, such as a biography of Bill Gates, that Dave could read while he munched on leftover pizza amid all the trappings of comfortable middle class life he'd managed to acquire in the last year.

Mandatory meeting. Bad news. Normally such meetings occurred so the CEO could announce another merger. Rah-rah. More profits for Markham-Hook Conglomerate. But this was different. Even if Ken hadn't come out and told him, Dave would have known by his lost dog expression. Probably a dip in the company stock prices. The party, after all, couldn't last forever, even though Markham-Hook had marched along making record profits while the rest of the economy staggered.

But Dave didn't have time to sit around wondering if the sky was going to fall on the company. He and his girlfriend Beth were going out to lunch later. And tonight they were having dinner to celebrate their one-month anniversary. Dave didn't have a clue as to what day he and Beth first went out, but Beth said it was one month ago today and a celebration was important to her. Dave would not disappoint. He put the thought of tomorrow's meeting out of his mind and picked up a work order.

Dave had made reservations a week ago at Pierre's Paris Cuisine, one of Avalon's finest restaurants. He didn't really care for the place, where private conversation with Beth was next to impossible because of constant interruptions from people she knew, people she was related to, people she thought she knew. But Beth had specified that only Pierre's would do for their celebration.

At exactly five-thirty he left work, barreled home through rush hour traffic, made himself presentable for an evening out, and reversed course back toward town to pick up Beth.

He parked his SUV a couple of blocks away from the restaurant and escorted Beth through the city's Harris Park. Dave couldn't help wondering how many millions of dollars had been spent on the park. It could have been a miniature replica of the Hanging Gardens of Babylon. Masses of greenery, some of it festooned with blooms in exotic hues of purple, cascaded over the sides of retaining walls. A solid mass of yellow tulips bloomed in huge concrete pots and in well-tended beds edging the walking paths meandering between patches of lush spring grass and circling a pond filled with giant goldfish. Wooden benches offered seating every few yards and trees, mostly oaks, provided shade for strategically placed street vendors.

Dave paused to draw in an especially deep breath. The smell of popcorn mixed in with cotton candy hung in the air and drew customers who swarmed to the vendors' carts like bees around fresh flowers.

Beth raised a questioning eyebrow. "What? You look like you've forgotten where we are."

"Nothing." He didn't want to tell her he was just thinking that if a person didn't know better, they'd conclude Harris Park was a movie set representing the center of some ideal town that could never exist in the real world. She might take it the wrong way, maybe accuse him of being jealous of John Victor Harris who'd donated half the building costs for the park.

They moved on, and he tried not to breathe in any more tempting food smells. They walked past a popcorn cart parked next to group of street entertainers gathered near the raised concrete platform that formed a stage. He'd read something in the paper about funding for the community theater being cut to almost nothing. Local talent had been given permission to perform at the park a few nights a week. He shook his head. Sad when people couldn't earn a living in their chosen field.

At the corner they crossed the street to Pierre's. He opened the door, and Beth slipped inside, trailing the scent of a perfume that reminded him of springtime in the mountains--sweet flowers and freshly mown grass. At a table near the door a squirrely guy with prominent teeth stared openly at Beth until the woman across from him frowned and rapped his hand with her menu.

Dave felt an inner glow of satisfaction. A couple of years ago he couldn't have imagined having a girlfriend like Beth--a beautiful, sophisticated, blonde goddess willing to go out with a guy who sometimes felt like an orange in a basket of apples. But that was one of the great things about his job. It supplied money, as well as a certain confidence that gave him the nerve to ask her out to begin with.

The restaurant's string quartet, which provided bland arrangements of pop music intended to promote pleasant moods and good digestion among the restaurant's patrons, launched their version of a Bruce Springsteen hit. Beth leaned lightly against him while they waited for the hostess, and Dave slid his arm around her waist.

As soon as Jason, their server for the evening, had escorted them to their favorite table, Dave ordered designer water and then picked up his menu.

"Dave?" Beth pushed the menu down. She drew a foil-wrapped box out of her purse and placed it next to the vase of white roses on their table. "I was going to wait until after dinner to give you this, but I can't stand the suspense."

A faint alarm buzzed in Dave's head. Did one month of dating bliss come with a special significance attached? Why hadn't he read some of the relationship books she'd recommended?

"Thanks, honey." Instead of opening the gift, he rubbed his chin, seeking enlightenment. When none came, he stuck the menu back in front of his eyes, though he'd already determined to order the freshly steamed vegetables with broiled salmon, which seemed a safe choice guaranteed to steer him clear of unfamiliar dishes such as escargot and artichokes. He wondered if he could get away with telling Beth he'd ordered her a gift from some far away, exotic emporium and it hadn't arrived yet, due to the inefficiency of some underpaid clerk. Probably not. That ploy was too obvious, and Beth wasn't stupid.

Before his racing thoughts could find a solution, the first of the evening's visitors stopped by their table to exchange air kisses and to remark on how beautiful Beth looked tonight. The visitor was someone who, Dave vaguely remembered, had gone to college with Beth. The rest of the Beth fan club passed by in a blur, except for Oxford DeWinters, who was too important to escape notice. DeWinters was Markham-Hook's second in command, a CEO understudy in case anything ever happened to John Victor Harris.

Dave stood and shook DeWinters' hand, noting that his grip was firm and dry. He'd met the under-CEO once before at a banquet for the programming staff, a formal affair where the drinks had flowed as if someone had uncorked a bottomless bottle.

DeWinters didn't look older than thirty-five, though Dave had heard he was forty-six. He always dressed as if he were on his way to pose for a photo shoot for the cover of a business magazine. His expression was unreadable, but Dave knew that was a good trait for a man in power. And Oxford DeWinters radiated power like a tanning bed.

"Good evening. Dave Griffin, right?"

Dave hoped he successfully hid his surprise that DeWinters had remembered his name. He was so low on the company depth chart that even Ken's boss didn't recognize him when they passed each other in the hall. "Nice to see you again, sir."

Dave had paid a lot of money for the coat he wore tonight, but now he felt his hands involuntarily slide over the dark material, smoothing out imaginary wrinkles and checking for snags or a dry cleaning tag left hanging.

DeWinters leaned down and brushed a kiss across Beth's cheek. "You look wonderful as always, Beth." His rich baritone sounded mellow notes like an aged cello.

"Thank you. Care to join us, Oxford? We haven't ordered yet."

"I'm just on my way out, but thank you for your offer. You two enjoy your meal." With a quick nod, he turned and made his exit.

Dave watched him leave. He wondered if he would ever develop such polish and charm. Probably not--if such a feat were possible, he likely would have shown promise by now.

He said, "I didn't know you were so tight with Oxford DeWinters."

"He's been a friend of my family for years, Dave. I'm sure I told you."

She probably had. Dave didn't always remember everything Beth said. He redirected his attention to the table. Beth chose that moment to blind-side him, picking up the gift box and thrusting it so close to his face he had to lean back to focus. "Aren't you going to open it?"

He shifted in his chair, his mind searching for the right comment. He could tell Beth he wanted to wait until later to exchange gifts. Then, while she was in the powder room, he could use his cell phone to call a jeweler or a florist and order something to be delivered to the restaurant STAT. But he had a vague memory that Beth had said she didn't like receiving flowers because that meant the giver had no imagination to figure out what she really wanted and besides flowers looked ugly when they died. And she said choosing jewelry for someone always worked out better if you quizzed the recipient's friends and family for clues as to their tastes. It wouldn't do, for example, to give someone a ruby if they hated red or if they really wanted an emerald.

He pulled his face muscles into a smile. "What's this? I'm sure it isn't my birthday."

"Silly. Open it."

Was it his imagination, or did Beth's gaze shift briefly to his coat pockets? Dave took his time tearing the foil off the box, waiting for inspiration to cry out to him, to say anything that would get him out of this without hurting Beth's feelings. Inspiration remained silent. Eventually the last bit of tape and foil fell free.

Dave lifted the box lid and peeked inside. Thank God. He'd been worried she might be giving him something elaborate or costly that he'd be hard-pressed to match on the spur of the moment. But the gift was a small book, one of those faddish paperbacks touting a set of rules that supposedly anyone could follow for a sure path to self-improvement and lasting enlightenment. This one was called, "Grab Yourself A CEO Spot. Ten Simple Rules." Beth had penned in purple ink inside the front cover, "With me helping you up the ladder, you're sure to succeed. Love, Beth."

"Thank you. I don't know what to say." Dave got up and kissed her and then plunked himself back in his chair.

He picked up the book and flipped through the pages. It shouldn't take long to grab a CEO spot. *Be alert for every promotion opportunity. Sell yourself. Don't let pushy co-workers take credit for your successes.* Every other page contained either a list or a flow chart.

He thought Beth should have known better than to try to give him a personality make-over, though. Dave's college professors had consistently referred to him as "a creative and innovative programmer with a gift for problem solving." But he'd never once heard any of them express the opinion that Dave Griffin was headed for stardom as a company manager or a corporate CEO.

Even so, he figured it was sweet of her to give him something, although she was destined to be disappointed if their relationship eventually progressed to marriage, and he was still sitting in a programmer's chair ten years from now. Especially if she'd spent those years prodding him from behind, and he hadn't moved up the ladder more than a rung or two.

He reached for her hand. "Beth, I know you're expecting me to give you a gift right now, but I'm not going to do that."

She was already launching her, "Silly, you didn't have to get me anything," response when the notes of the stringed quartet drifted across the room along with the garlicky scent of escargot at the next table. In that moment the inspiration that had eluded him all evening rose up to goad Dave somewhere deep in the get-a-clue center of his brain.

He said, "Your gift is a surprise. You'll find out after we finish eating."

Her eyes sparkled. She leaned toward him and put her hand on his arm. "What is it?"

"I said you'll have to wait."

"You're so mean. I hate surprises. When I was growing up, I used to bribe my sister to find out what I was getting for Christmas and tell me."

"But you know I'm too stubborn to give in, so you'll wait."

Beth sat back and pretended to pout. Dave made faces until she finally laughed.

An hour later, their multi-course meal finally consumed, and Jason their server well-tipped, Dave led her out of the restaurant. Arm in arm they wended their way back to Harris Park. The night was warm and a silver moon was visible low in the sky. He supposed a million stars would be visible, too, if the park weren't so well-lit that it had turned the sky from black to dusky lavender, but that was the price you paid for safety. He stopped at a front row bench in the park in front of the stage. He bowed from the waist and kissed her hand.

"Mademoiselle, please take a seat and enjoy the evening's entertainment planned just for you by the man of your sexiest dreams."

Corny, but Beth laughed. She pulled him down beside her on the bench. "What, no program?" she whispered.

"That would spoil the suspense."

A trio of folk singers finished a sad number about a man losing his hound dog on a lonely mountain where darkness tells no tales. Polite applause followed from the sparse audience and then a man wearing a tux and a blond wig, and a young woman with black hair and dark, expressive eyes, stepped forward. Another actor introduced them as "Benson and Lark."

The duo performed skits and told jokes. They finished with a scene supposedly taking place between a woman and her cheapskate husband.

Beth squeezed Dave's hand. "I never in a million years would have guessed my gift was a street performance. But I love it."

Dave released his breath in a sigh. Once again, he had come up with a solution.

Benson and Lark finished their act and then Lark, accompanied by a guitarist, sang a medley of Broadway hits. The crowd had doubled in size since Beth's and Dave's arrival. When the last song ended, Lark went to work collecting donations in a top hat. Dave fumbled for his wallet. He found two twenties tucked behind his credit cards, waiting like reserve units to be called in for special duty. He dropped both bills into the hat. Lark's dark eyes widened, and she mouthed a quick, "thank you," before she skipped away to the next bench.

Dave felt a pleasant warmth spread across his chest. He hadn't let Ken's warning spoil his evening. And who knew? Beth's book might somehow provide a magical power transfusion to lift him from the twenty-fifth floor to the top five floors, the executive office suites of the Markham-Hook Pyramid Building.

❦

Lark recited the lines out loud while she struggled to fit the last of the props into the trunk of her car. "What, you bought me a battery operated hairbrush for my birthday? Hey, I love it. Next time my hand gets tired from not lugging around that diamond ring I wanted, I'll still be able to do my hair." She wondered if she could have projected more sarcasm without going over the top.

No, she'd done fine, gotten a lot of laughs. The audience had been especially appreciative tonight, too. She slammed the trunk lid shut and walked around and got behind the wheel of her aging Nissan.

"Lark, wait."

Benson jogged up and grabbed the driver's side door handle. She rolled down the window. He poked his head inside. The faint aroma of Old Spice that always hung around his shoulders like an invisible scarf drifted her way, and she pulled back as far as she could without slipping out of her seat belt.

"I'm going to McDonalds for coffee. Want to come with?"

"Love to, Benson, but my dad will worry if I'm out late."

He scrunched his eyebrows into a single wiggly line and she knew that particular move signaled he was deep in thought, trying to come up with a clever line that would persuade her to change her mind. Poor Benson just didn't get it.

"Can't your roommate take care of him?" he offered finally.

"Jerry? He left a few days ago." Jerry hadn't been able to get along with her father and he'd left to take his chances with an elderly aunt who had an extra bedroom he could rent.

Getting along with people was sometimes hard for Lark's father, the way he was now. The two of them desperately needed another roommate to help with expenses. But even if Dad were on his best behavior, there was the neighborhood.

Benson was slow to react when Lark turned the key in the ignition. He hung there on her door as if he planned to let her drag him along the pavement when she pulled out.

"Benson?" She started rolling up the window as a signal.

"Oh, right."

He pulled his head out of the car and stepped away. At the end of the block, Lark glanced in the rear view mirror and saw him staring after the Nissan like an abandoned puppy.

At least she'd told him the truth about having to go straight home. Dad would wait up for her, pacing the floor and checking the time every few minutes until she was safely back in the house.

It hurt to compare the proud, competent father she remembered with the grim-faced, cynical man he was now. Dad was handsome, but his face wore a perpetual look of deep sadness. Lark remembered what he'd been like back when he was working. One of her girlfriends had told Lark that her father was charismatic, but dangerous.

"Dangerous?" she'd squealed. Her dad was about as dangerous as a hamster.

"Definitely," Fiona had said. "Joe Tremaine looks like he could handle any situation. Wouldn't work up a sweat, even if there were a dozen bodies on the ground afterward. A woman wants a sense of security, you know? Your dad--mmm, Lark, can't you see it? He wears an air of confidence that's burnt into his aura or something. He's like one of those movie characters you're not sure is really the good guy, but you root for him anyway because he's so damned cool. Like Clint Eastwood."

Lark remembered laughing and thinking that Fiona must have a crush on her father. But then all her girlfriends--and their mothers--loved her dad. It was her boyfriends who didn't get along with him. Dad, she admitted, liked to pick on her boyfriends. One after another they drifted away. She shrugged. None of the breakups had been that painful. She hadn't met a guy yet that was worth keeping. Besides, if they were such wimps that they wouldn't stick around because of a little teasing, then she didn't want them.

Lark had hopes that Dad would eventually be himself again, be cool again, if that's what he really was. And get over his depression and maybe even find a permanent job. That's all she lived on now--hope. Hope that she could land a decent job and hope that they could find another roommate and hope that Dad would recover his joy in life.

Chapter Two

Joe Tremaine didn't feel right the morning he went crazy. To begin with, his coffee tasted like sewer run-off and his head ached and throbbed, so he could barely see to dump the swamp-colored sludge down the sink. When he picked up the paper and tried to read about Senator Buford Drake's latest assault on American workers, the rattling of the pages thrummed against his eardrums like a swarm of bees and made him queasy.

He threw the paper down and jammed his hands tight over his ears. It was hot in the living room, so hot that the heat coming off the couch turned his skin red, and hotter yet in the kitchen where the pilot light on the stove waved its blue tongue as if to taunt him. He staggered outside and down the steps to the road. An early autumn frost still lingered on the grass like a veil of white lace. He scraped up a double handful to rub on his burning skin. Then he stood at the curb, his arms held straight out to his sides at shoulder level, and tilted his head back to catch the ghost of a breeze tantalizing his face.

He stood until the fire left him and then he started moving again, separating himself from the house and the source of the heat. The sidewalk melted as he walked, slipping into liquid under his feet. He ripped his gaze upward and away from the concrete sloshing around his ankles. When had the trees become so shiny? Someone, maybe one of the drug dealers on the corner, had polished the trunks so they shone like mirrors and the glare was coming in through his eyes and setting off fireworks to explode hot and noisy in his brain.

A woman burst out of a house and shimmered in front of him for a few seconds like one of the *Star Trek* crew beaming down to an alien world. Joe shook his head to clear the sparkles out of his vision and plunged forward, barely able to keep his balance as the earth tilted and spun, trying to shake him loose to send him flying into space. He ended up a block away at Oak Street Park where the air around him shattered without warning into a million pieces of colored glass. The breaking glass tinkled like wind chimes, and then the shrieks of children playing mixed in with the chimes and went to maximum volume in his head.

Children. The glass would cut their little bodies.

He flung himself from the pathway onto the grass and hooked his arms around the nearest child, a girl whose eyes had started to ooze down her face like melted ice cream, twin scoops of gooey chocolate.

"Get away. Run, little girl." The sounds came out in a pig's grunt and the girl he'd tried to save slipped out of his grasp and ran squealing toward the road.

Three women moved in front of him, positioning themselves to form an arc between him and the children. One of the women brandished a piece of wood, waving it like a battle flag. She swung at him, just missing his head. "Get out of here, you sicko." Dragon's breath flared out of her mouth.

Joe sank to the ground and curled his body, wrapping his arms around his head. His bad leg went into an agonizing spasm as each blade of grass turned into a tiny spear, and the spears probed his flesh, concentrating on the leg. He screamed and rolled onto his back.

Another of the women stepped forward and peered down at him, the skin of her face quivering like Jell-O, so he couldn't focus. "It's okay, Sondra. Looks to me like he's on some kind of drug trip."

She pulled something out of her purse, something small and silver-gray, a device with a metal stick poking out of the top. Joe couldn't remember what it was called. She jabbed the front of the thing with her fingers and put it to her ear, where it burst into flames that danced across her hair. Joe scrunched his eyes shut so he wouldn't have to see her burn up.

※

Joe felt something soft covering his body, lying over him like the lightest cloud. He let the fingers of his left hand glide across the softness. A blanket. His right hand was held tight and warm in someone's grasp, small fingers pressing into his palm, and he opened his eyes, blinking at the brightness of the light overhead. He made out a dim silhouette to his right and then a familiar face came into focus.

"Lark." His voice was a dry croak. Thank God, his speech had returned.

"Dad? You're in the hospital. I'll get your doctor." She pulled her hand loose from his and slipped out of the room before he could tell her he just wanted to go home.

He didn't need a doctor. The whole episode was just caused by stress. And who wouldn't be stressed if they had to live his nightmare? There was the move from Washington back to North Carolina and his job loss, finding out he wasn't worth two cents to the government or to anyone else. Lots of things, mitigating circumstances, coming on top of the fractured skull and the banged up leg that had cost him his job to begin with. He'd talk to the doctor, and then Lark could take him home.

Lark returned with an amiable-looking man wearing a lab coat over his street clothes. Mid thirties, maybe. Glasses, balding, about five-ten. Phony kind of smile--too many teeth and not enough eye involvement--but that's what you got these days when doctors were paid to run as many patients as possible through assembly lines.

"Hello. I'm Dr. Jefferson." He kept his hands parked in the pockets of his lab coat. "Well, Joe, you had quite an experience."

As if Joe had simply gone for a roller coaster ride to ease the boredom of sitting alone in the house day after day wondering if he'd ever find another job.

"What happened?" Joe sat up. He wanted to raise the head of the bed, but he couldn't find the controls.

"It seems you had a seizure."

"You mean like epilepsy? I've never--"

"A fractured skull can be tricky." Dr. Jefferson did something to the IV machine, changing the setting so the soft clicks slowed almost to a stop, and giving it his full attention instead of looking Joe in the eye. "A section of your brain must have gotten damaged back when you fractured your skull. If you don't like calling your experience a seizure, you might say it's a form of mental illness brought on by the injury."

Like mental illness was any better than brain seizures. Joe pondered, trying to get used to the idea of having something wrong with his head.

"Will it happen again?" he asked finally.

"Hard to say. I'm putting you on medication to prevent your neurons sparking out of control. The exact dosage may take some adjustment before we get it right, but it's a good drug, been around a long time. Does the job."

"How long do I have to be on this stuff?"

"It's safe to stay on it indefinitely." Grinning like a monkey. It wasn't Dr. Jefferson who had to find a way to pay for a lifetime supply of pills and deal with the inevitable side effects.

≈≈≈

Joe had one more seizure before he stabilized. The second was milder than the first, but worse, in a way, because Lark was a witness, and he hated that, would have avoided it at any cost if he'd had a way to know what was coming. He'd gone to the grocery store and he was in the bakery aisle trying to decide if he could afford a cake on sale for three dollars off. It would make a nice treat, and Lark sure deserved something. She'd slipped on some ice out front a couple of weeks ago. Cracked her wrist and was all down on herself because she couldn't work till it healed.

As soon as he tried to figure out how the cost affected the grocery budget, a voice in his head grabbed the numbers and started reciting a formula, making cash register sounds, sounds that went faster and faster, the figures astronomical. Immediately, he saw the implications. Adrenaline shot through his system, and it felt like something wet and cold squirted out the top of his head, so he put his hand up to feel that his hair was still dry. He had to hurry before someone stole his idea. His heart pounding in overdrive, he abandoned the cart full of groceries, leaving it sideways in front of the freezer section, and went to the front of the store for an empty cart. This he filled with boxes of salt and jars of instant coffee, paying with a check that would overdraw his account, but that didn't matter because the formula would make him rich. He kept the cart, speeding it home across the bumpy sidewalk and almost ramming a couple of kids on skateboards.

When Lark came home from a doctor appointment, Joe had already dumped all the salt into the kitchen sink and was poised with an open jar of Tasters Choice. His face felt like someone was holding a heating pad against his cheeks and, at the same time, ice water had soaked his clothes, running down his back and his chest, and he didn't know where it came from.

"Dad? Why is there a grocery cart on the front lawn?"

He waved her closer. "Sweetheart, you're just in time, we're gonna be rich after I get a patent on this invention. We're moving to a mansion. I'm getting you a new car and a closet full of clothes, anything you want, and I'll be famous, probably be on TV, all those talk shows, Montel and Jay Leno. Oprah. Just watch, just watch." He remembered his words had tumbled from his mouth like someone was pulling them out on a string, dragging them up through his throat and past his teeth, so he couldn't stop them.

"What are you doing?" She slung her purse across the room and stared at him like he was someone else, not her dad, and then she grabbed his arm. "Sit down. Please, just sit down while I call Dr. Jefferson."

"I invented a formula. It's so simple, I can't believe I'm the first one smart enough to think of making electricity this way. All those people who didn't want Joe Tremaine are going to be sorry. Soon's I add the coffee, the caffeine will react with the salt and the whole mess will start to glow like a Christmas tree, so all I need to do is hook up a wire and run it to the power lines outside the house."

"Dad, no." She lunged for the coffee jar.

He lifted it out of her reach and dodged past her, running outside where he pounded down the sidewalk yelling to everyone he saw about his invention. He crossed the road, hearing brakes squeal, and glimpsed angry eyes staring at him through a bug-spattered windshield. If he could just tell enough people, they'd understand and Lark would have to let him hook up the power. She'd have to, and then she'd understand and she'd be so proud of her dad.

Before the ambulance arrived, half the people in the neighborhood had taken in the freak show. Of course, Lark forgave him, but after that most people on Oak Street called him Crazy Joe. Maybe six months wasn't long enough for them to forget he'd ever been anything except what he was now, a useless specimen of humanity, drugged into what passed for sanity on Oak Street, and jobless because employers didn't even want healthy people, so what chance did he have?

***

Joe waited until the lone customer cleared the convenience store before he went in to steal cigarettes. The security camera only worked half the time, and the clerk, Howard Simms, always made sure that the down time coincided with Joe's visits. Joe would give him some of the stolen cigarettes later.

Howard glanced up from his newspaper. He raised his right hand in a halfhearted salute and pried himself from behind the counter to lumber down the narrow aisle to the back, his stocky body moving with the deliberate slowness of a man who'd given up and placed himself on permanent autopilot.

When Howard, former software engineer and now day clerk at the Quick Buy, returned to his station a minute later, Joe had already snared a carton of Marlboros and shoved them under his jacket. He fingered a Snickers bar as if trying to decide whether he wanted to part with seventy-five cents. He finally tossed the Snickers down on the counter and watched it skid to a stop next to a miniature Slim Jim rack.

"Still working, Howard?"

"I'm here, aren't I? And glad to have a job. I'm buried under a stack of bills a mile high." Howard jabbed the candy bar with his pudgy fingers. "That be all?"

Joe nodded. He paid with a handful of pennies and nickels that Howard didn't bother to count.

He collected his Snickers and walked outside like any paying customer, holding his head up and pretending he had places to go. He limped across the parking lot and paused next to the rusting gas pumps to squint into the distance toward the center of town. There was too much haze for him to see, but he knew it was there. Normally the soaring Pyramid Building owned by Markham-Hook Conglomerate dominated Avalon's skyline, poking heavenward to broadcast to everyone in North Carolina that Markham-Hook meant power. The building's architect had won an award for the design, a tower with a pyramid forming the top five floors, which he said was inspired by the pyramid on the dollar bill. But Joe thought that from a distance the silver pyramid topped by a golden globe made the building look like a NASA rocket with a giant wad of dirty chewing gum on top. He spat on the ground, just missing his left shoe.

He planned to go home and do his laundry, but there was no rush, there never was. He'd already washed the breakfast dishes, dried them, put them away, and swallowed his mental illness prevention pill this morning. He decided to reward himself for good behavior with a smoke or two.

Mental illness my ass, Joe thought, grimacing as he tripped over a bump in the sidewalk where tree roots had burst through the concrete. He was as sane as anyone. Saner, because at least he had sense enough to see what the politicians and their corporate campaign contributors were doing to the brain dead citizens of the country.

But his big mouth was part of the reason they'd cut him loose. No doubt if Joe had kept quiet about his political views and played the game their way, then he'd be sitting behind a desk pushing papers around and pretending to be important. He'd still be collecting his government paycheck instead of struggling to come up with the rent and the money for his medicine every month.

He hobbled a couple of blocks west, through a neighborhood that looked like what might happen if a giant ate a row of houses and then vomited the whole mess back up. Giant probably wouldn't be able to digest the bars on the windows. At the park, he settled himself on a bench, in a spot that promised sunshine when the sun rose a little higher. He pushed his long legs straight out in front of him and lit a cigarette, sucking in the smoke as if his life depended on a blast of nicotine. He'd sit here for a while watching things not happen and listening to traffic rumble past. Later he'd make his way down to the shelter on the corner and visit with the men and women who'd come by to check the jobs board. Everyone knew the jobs board was a joke and they just wanted lunch, the outdated bread and thin vegetable soup prepared by volunteers.

Oak Street Park, a strip of grass and trees left natural between two condemned houses, was deserted today. The benches were hard, damp concrete slabs coated with a veneer of greenish mold that rubbed off on clothes. None of the water fountains worked unless you counted the trickles of rusty water that grudgingly appeared when you pressed hard enough on the faucets.

Even the pigeons were out of work. They'd given up hoping for handouts in a place where people with the means to share their food were in short supply. The healthy pigeons had likely flown off to strut the sidewalks of more prosperous neighborhoods. The only birds remaining, the thin and the unfit, huddled near a trash can.

A squirrel appeared from behind a rock, turned a frenzied somersault and skittered up a tree as if afraid of catching whatever malady affected the birds. Joe heard footsteps approaching, but he didn't turn around. He recognized the scuffle of tired feet, as well as the squeak of Freddy's wheelchair.

"Morning, Martha. Hello, Freddy." He scooted sideways to make room for Martha.

He and Martha ran across each other two or three times a week at the park or strolling around the neighborhood. Martha used to own a restaurant east of town near the towel mill. But when Markham-Hook Conglomerate bought the mill and shipped the jobs to the third world, Martha's customers couldn't afford restaurant food anymore.

The wheels on the chair squealed when she parked it next to the bench. Freddy had a better chair provided by his church, a chair that didn't sound like ten mice with their tails caught in traps, but Martha kept the good one in the house so it wouldn't get ruined.

She sat next to him and massaged her knees through the thin cotton material of her dress. "Law, it feels good to sit down. My poor old legs keep telling me it's no fun toting around an extra fifty pounds." She chuckled, a deep throaty sound, and patted the roll of flesh on her midsection.

Joe handed her the Snickers, and she unwrapped it and passed it to her grandson. Freddy was twelve years old and he couldn't talk, couldn't do more than make garbled sounds that sounded to Joe's ears like he was saying, "fish food."

"Freddy says thank you," Martha translated.

"You're welcome, Freddy." Joe passed Martha a Marlboro and helped her light it.

She drew in on the cigarette, leaning her head back and closing her eyes. "You okay? I spotted you from a block away perched on this bench with your shoulders hunched up to your ears. Looks like you wish they'd shovel the dirt over you, put down flowers and a headstone and be done with it."

"That's pretty darn close. One day I'm in the service of my country. The next day they're dumping me out the door like month-old garbage."

"Not just you." Martha shifted on the bench as if that would help her get comfortable. "I survive, Joe. Life ain't as much fun as it used to be, but I keep on living. I'm grateful to the Lord for what I still have. You ever try prayer?"

Joe flicked his cigarette into the dust at his feet. "Only kind of higher power I believe in anymore is the power of a job and a steady income."

"Listen to me, Joe. Take your troubles to the Lord. I did and I finally got me a job. Praise him." Martha raised her eyes and studied the sky as if she hoped to see the Lord smiling down at her from somewhere just above the Pyramid Building where he probably hung out hoping some of the prosperity would rub off.

Joe snorted. "I heard down at the shelter about you getting work. What is it you call yourself--phone actress?" How many men who dialed Hot and Ready Babes realized they were talking to a sixty-year-old black woman who went to church three times a week?

Martha slapped his arm. "Don't you be so quick to put me down. I was facing foreclosure and thinking about having to live in the shelter, me and Freddy, fighting for space in a one-hundred cot room with a two-hundred people waiting list. The Lord told me he provided the job and I wasn't to take shame in it."

What would the Lord have said if Martha had been offered an opportunity to be an actual flesh and blood actress for Hot and Ready Babes instead of hiding behind a phone? But who was he to judge? After a year of frustration, he'd given up expecting a job to come along with his name on it. He'd learned a long time ago that the kids who owned the toys got to make the game rules. And Joe owned fewer toys every day.

By the time Lark was due home from her latest temp job--working for a caterer--Joe had hidden his cigarettes and cooked up a pot of spaghetti. The garlic and tomato sauce he'd made from scratch would help mask the odor of stale tobacco smoke.

She hated his smoking. She insisted the nicotine messed with his brain chemicals and it might upset the delicate balance of his medicine. Besides, they couldn't afford smokes. If she knew about the Marlboros, she'd know he'd stolen them, and they'd argue and then she'd find the carton and throw it out. None of those things had to happen if Joe could deceive her.

The sauce was bubbling like a potion in a witch's cauldron when he heard the quick tap of Lark's shoes on the brick steps. The front door swung open. Joe's heart ached when he saw his daughter.

Faint blue circles showed under her eyes, and her face was a pale, fragile oval. She was only a little thing, petite like her mother, though she had Joe's straight black hair and midnight eyes, and he liked to think she'd inherited her acting talent from him. If he could get a steady income, something better than the occasional handyman work he managed to scrounge, his little girl wouldn't have to exhaust herself lifting heavy trays and putting up with the demands of drunken men at the parties she worked.

The kitchen and living room were one open area, too tiny to permit walls. From his place at the stove, he watched her collapse in the chair closest to the door, a love seat with duct tape covering a ripped place on the faded cushion. She grinned up at him when he brought her a cup of the herbal tea she insisted on drinking. The stuff smelled like dried grass and probably tasted like it, too.

"Hey, Dad. Have a good day?"

"It went terrific, baby. I got a call from a man might want some rotten boards on his deck replaced. I'm going by tomorrow to quote him a price. And I fixed you the finest spaghetti you ever tasted." He made the announcement as though they rarely had spaghetti. But Joe cooked up a pot every week and made enough so they had leftovers for two or three nights.

"Didn't you have an appointment today? What did the doctor say?" She studied his expression.

"He says I'm doing great." He should have rehearsed. There was a hint of a stutter in his voice as he told the lie. He went to the door and pretended to busy himself checking the locks so she wouldn't see his face.

She wrapped her hands around her cup. "Any mail?"

"Bills. And a full color advertisement from some travel outfit wants to sell you a cruise to the Caribbean where you can feast your eyes on exotic locales and spend all your money on souvenirs and hot native men."

"Figures. Pathetic, daydreaming me hoped to open the mail and discover that the city had reconsidered about funding the community theater so I don't have to keep working for handouts in the park."

"You want me to fish that ad out of the trash and let you study it, maybe cut out the pictures and paste them on the refrigerator? That's about as close as you're going to get to that cruise or to funding for the theater, sweetheart."

"How does that go? 'Things aren't going to change until people pull their heads out of the sand and say they've had enough.'"

"Exactly. I've taught you well." He thrust out his jaw and took a pen out of his shirt pocket, holding it out to the side and pretending it was a cigar. "We must keep fighting, though the forces against us are way more than we should have to deal with. And when the battle is over, they will say this was their finest hour."

She laughed, as he knew she would. It was an old game of theirs from when she was a little girl--acting out scenes and mimicking the famous. At age five, Lark had been a terrific Shirley Temple with the tap shoes he'd bought her for her birthday.

"Your Winston Churchill has improved since last week, even though I'm sure you mangled the lines." She put her cup down and stretched. "God, I'm tired and still have to work tonight. Is the spaghetti done?"

"Go over to the table. I'll bring you a plate."

He went back to the stove to dish up the spaghetti, giving her an extra large serving of sauce. He was proud of himself. He'd successfully created a distraction to keep her from asking any more questions about the mail, which had also contained a notice about a rent increase. And she hadn't detected the lie about the doctor.

They'd cancelled his appointment. Due to cuts and trouble getting their money from the government, his doctor was forced to cut back on Medicaid patients. He was referring Joe to the health department clinic. Unless Joe directed otherwise, the doctor was sending his chart to his new doctor at the clinic. Now there was a caring health professional for you, made you feel all warm inside when he dumped you.

Joe rubbed his injured leg, trying to ease the pain and stiffness. It didn't take Madame Elana, the so-called psychic on the next block, to tell him his future. He hadn't had to go to the clinic before now, but he was out in the park and in the streets enough, so he heard stories. The doctors at the health department clinic were overworked and they were notorious for being stingy about seeing you when you needed them. They doled out expensive prescriptions as though money appeared magically in wallets whenever it was called for.

He ought to just let the ambulance cart off what was left of him to the hospital or the grave, he didn't care which, as long as it was a place where he could rest. But he couldn't give up because then there'd be no one to take care of his daughter. It took both his government check and whatever they were able to earn to keep them up, even in a neighborhood like this where people would fight each other over the gum in a dead man's mouth.

After Lark left for her second job, Joe cleaned up the dishes and settled into his second-hand armchair to read a newspaper he'd scrounged from the trash at the pizza place around the corner. It was yesterday's paper, but that didn't matter. News was always the same.

From somewhere a couple of blocks away shots barked out--two staccato bursts and then dead silence. Joe didn't look up. A lot happened on Oak Street. Most of it bad. Unless people actually saw blood or heard screams for help, they didn't bother to call the cops.

He read about more layoffs, a drug bust, and a new trade bill proposed by the powerful Senator Drake that would allow U.S. companies to import more "guest workers" to do the jobs that Americans "just couldn't or wouldn't do." Joe dropped the paper and let it fall to the floor.

The Senator wanted people to believe that Americans were spoiled, stupid and lazy and would rather starve than work. Senator Drake owned a mansion here in Avalon, a brick fortress big enough to hold half the city's poor, and used a friend's cottage along the river whenever he wanted to get away, though most people didn't know about the cottage. Joe had met the Senator, once in the line of duty and once when he was dumped from government service.

Joe knew his supervisor had already recommended that they retire him because of his injury. But if Senator Drake wanted Joe to keep his job, he would overrule the supervisor as easily as he signed his name on a check. Newly released from the hospital, Joe had humbled himself, reached deep inside and dragged up some defenseless part of his soul and showed it to the Senator. Joe said he'd take a desk job, he'd have surgery on his leg or even let them cut on his brain, anything they wanted. He'd gone so far as to remind the Senator he was one of the agents who'd saved him when he'd had his heart attack.

Senator Drake had looked Joe up and down with his piggish eyes, calculating, maybe deciding how best to give him the bad news. Then he reared back in his seat and rested his hands over his popped-out stomach, forefingers steepled and aimed at Joe's heart.

"I appreciate you saving my life, but sometimes, and it's sad, but sometimes, we have to put a sick horse out to pasture. I know you'll understand that as an elected official, I can't let favoritism interfere with my decisions. Wouldn't be fair to all my other constituents. No, sir, not fair at all."

What had the Senator ever done that didn't involve favoritism? A week later Joe was out of his job, and the Senator had introduced a bill, since passed, which cut Joe's pension and benefits in half.

Chapter Three

When he walked into his cubicle, Dave wondered if he had time to get any work done before the meeting. Probably not. The traffic had cost him twenty extra minutes, and Ken had made too much of a production over him being on time.

He picked up the phone and called Beth to thank her once again for the one-month anniversary gift she'd given him last night. She worked two floors up, on twenty-seven. Beth was technically a project coordinator, but she'd ended up as more of a social director and client liaison. Markham-Hook wanted its clients to interface with smart, gorgeous young women. Company policy. And there was no young woman in the company more gorgeous than Beth Winslow.

After three rings, her voice mail picked up. Ken suddenly appeared in Dave's peripheral vision, and Dave turned to see him glowering from across the hall, his eyes like twin lanterns signaling him to get a move on. Without taking time to leave a message, he put the phone down and trailed down the hall about ten yards behind Ken, so no one would think they'd walked to the meeting together. He found a seat at the front of the conference room, though he wasn't sure he really wanted such close exposure to Ken's sport coat of the day, a green plaid number that made Dave's eyes cross.

Someone had emptied the room of its long folding tables and substituted rows of chairs. They'd closed the vertical blinds covering the wall of windows, so the attendees were deprived of the usual panorama of the Avalon skyline, which from this side of the building included a nice view of the Avalon Grizzlies basketball stadium.

Dave's friend Michael, a tall, skinny black man, slipped into the seat beside him. Michael was breathing hard as if he'd run up the stairs instead of taking the elevator. He probably had. Michael used the stairs as a way to keep fit. He was always warning Dave about the dangers of a desk job where if you weren't careful you ended up with hemorrhoids and gout so you could neither sit nor stand without excruciating pain.

"Dave. You get my email about the weekend?"

Dave fingered the little holster on his belt to make sure his Mental Giant PDA was safely at his side in case he needed to take notes or play a game of hangman. "Haven't even had a chance to look at my computer."

"You and Beth want to go out to the lake with me and Rosie Saturday?"

"Can't. Beth's going to her high school reunion in Boston."

"Boston?" Michael made sympathy noises. "Poor Dave. Rich girlfriend and all."

Dave started to ask how Rosie was doing, but Ken cleared his throat. The low rumble of voices quieted. Like Dave, everyone else on the team was busy with the upcoming conversion to a new system. Dave wondered if his co-workers had any inkling that Ken was about to rock their world. They should, just from looking at him. Sweat was rolling down the sides of his face, and he wasn't making eye contact, unless you counted him focusing on the eyes of George Washington staring out of the painting at the back of the room.

"I guess the most efficient way to do this is to just skip the preliminaries and power up the video." Ken's usually ruddy complexion was pale, something like the color of an undercooked pancake, and he fumbled with his tie, pulling it away from his neck and wrapping it around his hand.

Dave felt a faint stirring of alarm. He'd checked the newspaper this morning and couldn't find anything about Markham-Hook, except for a story about a new food packaging plant they'd bought in Indianapolis. He cracked his knuckles. Ken was a dweeb, probably making a fuss over nothing.

Ken's usual opening to departmental meetings was a well-rehearsed, "We have to put our noses to the grindstone, our bodies to the wheel and our eyes in front of us while we dedicate ourselves to making Markham-Hook the biggest and the best company that ever existed." Ken always waved his arms expansively when he got to the part about the best company that ever existed, as if they were competing with corporations all the way back to the dawn of man when people presumably dealt in a currency of stone.

Today Ken skipped the opening and directed their attention to the TV and the VCR that had been brought in on a cart by a geekish youth who'd been billed as a junior programmer. He reminded Dave of himself when he'd been in school and teachers chose him to set up the AV equipment for educational films. Once Dave had substituted a video he'd stolen from his cousin, something about a liberated young lady called Lolli Pop, for the film on "All You Need to Know About Earthworms." The reaction from his classmates had made the consequences worthwhile, though he'd been permanently demoted from the AV setup job and he never did find out anything about earthworms.

Michael jabbed him in the side with his elbow, and Dave realized Ken had just asked him a question. He blinked and said, "Huh?"

"I said, how close are you to finishing your part of the test job?"

"Give me a week." Maybe less, if the test he was running today went through with no mistakes.

"Good. We don't have time to waste."

Now what did that mean? He was a month ahead of schedule already. Please, just let him get on with his work and make the bad news be nothing more earth shattering than a couple of dollars drop in the stock price that would mean a few weeks of overtime.

He didn't mean to come across as a geek, but he loved what he did, loved working with computer languages and putting systems together. There were times when he felt like a detective, puzzling out the best ways to communicate with the machine to get the desired results.

Ken punched the VCR power button and John Victor Harris, company CEO, appeared on screen wearing an expression that Dave immediately categorized as a combination of glee mixed with greed. Dave had never seen John Victor Harris except in pictures or on a video screen. Sometimes he wondered if the man actually existed or if he was a robot.

Cheesy intro music, something that featured a marching band heavy on the piccolo section, accompanied a shot of Harris posing in front of the company's Pyramid Building. Harris had his hands propped on his hips, and he'd planted his feet wide apart. The camera moved in for a close-up of his chiseled face. Carefully done lighting and make-up emphasized his light gray eyes, which gazed into the distance as if he were far seeing and noble, unlike ordinary men.

The camera pulled back for a shot of the building and slowly panned up the base all the way to the top. The music and the intro faded to another shot of Harris looking up from his desk in an opulent setting reminiscent of the Oval Office.

"Welcome Markham-Hook associates. I know you're all eager to get back to your desks, so let me begin without preamble. It is seldom that a corporation realizes the opportunity to maximize profits with minimal pain or negative consequences, as it were. But we now have that opportunity."

He paused to smile benignly at his intended audience, in this case the thirty programmers watching attentively from their seats in the meeting room. Good thing he couldn't see the junior programmer firing paperclips at Ken's back.

"Some of you are going to be disappointed by today's news. Some of you won't have seats on the rocket when the ship takes off. But that's progress, which I know everyone is in favor of. I'm sure you'll all find seats on a lesser rocket."

Dave and Michael exchanged looks of "What the hell?" Behind them a woman's voice called out, "This does not sound good."

Dave stole a glance at Ken. He sat facing them, looking at the floor and not at the screen, his fleshy hands dangling at his sides. Clearly, he'd previewed the video, knew what was coming, and had already conceded defeat.

"We, the leaders charting the course of Markham-Hook Conglomerate, have embarked on a new adventure. In the next few months thirty percent of our tech work is moving offshore."

Harris held out both hands, palms up, and grinned sheepishly, as though to indicate that the tech work had decided on its own to depart for a foreign locale, and he hadn't been able to rein it in.

On screen someone loosed a flurry of balloons in Markham-Hook's bright gold and silver colors. Several of the balloons drifted onto CEO Harris's head, and he brushed them out of his way as if he were shooing away a pesky fly. He skinned his lips back in a grin and turned his attention to the notes in front of him. "Markham-Hook Conglomerate is partnering with a company from India, Golden Orion Technology & Computer Help Agency. This company will supply the new personnel, both offshore and right here in Avalon. And, let me rush to tell you, this is a deal we simply couldn't overlook. Frankly, these Orion people are so cost effect...such good programmers, that we couldn't pass up the opportunity to avail ourselves of the talent, to take on the best and the brightest. Finally, Markham-Hook Conglomerate will have the good people it needs to achieve the prominence it deserves. All of you Markham-Hook Conglomerateers, I'm sure, recognize this as a proud and historic moment in the history of the world leader that started out twenty years ago as little old County First Financials of Avalon."

Harris paused in his delivery to beam once again into the camera and, no doubt, to give all the Markham-Hookers time to bask in the proud moment.

Dave's stomach was somewhere around his navel. He wished he hadn't eaten the high fiber cereal Beth had recommended for his breakfast. It felt like a dozen little wire brushes were trying to scrub their way through his intestinal wall.

"Lord, Jesus," Michael whispered, shifting in his seat. "Who stole that man's heart?"

Dave clutched his gut. Another minute or two of CEO Harris and he'd be forced to excuse himself to make a dash for the men's room.

"Some of you aren't going to be offered seats on the rocket." Harris lowered his gaze and pushed his lower lip out in a mini-pout, sparing a second of respectful silence for those who didn't rate a few extra gallons of rocket fuel. "You'll all receive packets outlining your fate with the company."

Anticipating his cue, Ken beckoned Myra Hilton. She marched forward bearing an armload of oversized white envelopes. It was no secret that Myra didn't care for Ken. But today she looked like she didn't care for anyone.

"This concludes our good news announcement," Harris said. "For any questions not answered in your individual personnel career planning packets, you can consult your respective supervisors."

Dave assumed Harris would finish by asking everyone to give three cheers for the company, and possibly order them to shed a little blood on their way out the door so Markham-Hook Conglomerate could best Avalon's other big corporation--King Energy and National Safe Trucking--in the annual county blood drive.

He didn't find out. Ken, for once showing good sense, pressed the power button on the machine.

The room erupted. The thirty programmers, minus Dave and Michael, who managed to get clear of the crush, surged forward sounding like a lynch mob on a B western. One shrill voice rose above the others. "This is a bunch of horseshit."

"They'll finally have good people?" Dave said. "What are we, trash?"

"Come on," Michael said, yanking the door open, "If he survives the question and answer session, Ken-Boy can give us our personalized career planning packets later."

"You mean our personalized career ending packets." Dave followed him into the hall. "It's been great working with you, Michael."

"Hey, dude, don't be like that. We might have tickets to ride the rocket. After all, you're dating the daughter of one of the biggest stockholders in the company. And I'm the token black man on the team, carefully selected to give Markham-Hook Conglomerate some diversity points."

Dave snorted. "Something tells me Daddy Winslow will go off like the laughtrack on a sitcom when he finds out I'm unemployed. As for you, being a black man won't help if they decide they'd rather keep the two black women, the visually impaired man, and the Latino man."

※

Ken stopped at Dave's cubicle shortly before lunch and dropped the envelope on his desk like it was a bomb. Dave shot a rubber band across the cubicle and watched it bounce off a spare monitor he'd scavenged from the supply room and left in a corner in case he needed it one day.

"Come to give me the tragic news? Don't like being the bad guy, huh? Guess it hurts your image of yourself as the ever-popular leader of Team B. Hey, don't worry, you'll still be my favorite bald-headed boss in plaid." He lounged in his seat, pretending he wasn't suffering internal panic.

Ken's face went blotchy, spots of red fighting for space with pale beige. "They told me yesterday afternoon in the supervisor's meeting. Who was riding the rocket and who wasn't, I mean. I get to stay on and supervise."

Ken lifted a Dollywood pencil sharpener off Dave's desk and turned it over and over in his hands until it popped open and shavings fell all over the front of his shirt.

Dave said, "You don't have to feel guilty because you didn't get fired."

Ken's expression remained glum, so Dave added, "I'm glad you still have a job." Ken might be a pain to work for, but Dave didn't wish bad luck on him and his family.

"Thanks. I can't tell you how relieved I am that I'm not losing...look, don't worry, Dave. You're a great programmer. You'll find something else."

"In this economy, I'll be lucky to get a ticket to ride a match."

"Don't take it like that. You do see, don't you, that the company couldn't afford to pass up this golden opportunity? These new people are sharp." Ken snapped his fingers.

Dave jerked upright in his seat and banged his fist on his desk. "Shut up, Ken. I mean it, man, don't insult me. It's lies and you know it. They're going to save a bundle of money on labor costs by shipping part of the work overseas and by bringing people here on work visas to undercut our wages. Ability has nothing to do with this whole rotten deal. It's all about cheaper labor."

"Try to see things from Markham-Hook's point of view." Ken couldn't meet his eyes.

"Yeah, right. Markham-Hook just announced record profits and a pay raise for Harris that makes God look poor. Naturally they don't have any spare change to spread among the workers who built this company to begin with. What about the eighty-hour weeks we put in to make deadlines and what about the error free conversions?"

"Dave, keep your voice down."

"Keep my voice down? I just lost my job because some greedy son of a bitch dumped me on the street like trash, so he can win a pissing contest with the rest of the heartless CEO's in corporate America. I'm supposed to give him a high five?"

"Bitter, bitter." Michael pressed into the cubicle.

Ken took the opportunity to slink past him into the hallway and scurry toward his office. Dave shot him a one-finger salute.

"Open your love letter yet?" Michael moved a pile of computer magazines off Dave's spare chair and plunked himself down. "Man, when you going to clean up this mess?"

Dave held up his envelope to the light. He inserted a pencil point under the flap and ripped it across. The letter was printed on watermarked, high-linen content paper. Only the best for Markham-Hook, even when they screwed you. He turned the envelope upside down and shook it. A contract spelling out his and the company's obligations fell out along with a letter.

The enclosed letter appeared under an embossed gold and silver company logo--the pyramid with the sun on top--and the company slogan, "Markham-Hook Conglomerate: Where Customers Share in the Prosperity. All Day. Every Day."

Whenever Dave encountered the company slogan, he was tempted to ask if customers were guaranteed a chicken in every pot along with the cheap pen and the handful of chocolate doubloons wrapped in gold and silver foil they received when they opened new accounts.

He read his letter.

Dear David R. Griffin:

By now you are aware of the unprecedented opportunity Markham-Hook Conglomerate has encountered. I am sure you rejoice at our good fortune and wish us every success in our leap forward into the global future.

Unfortunately, **David R. Griffin,** *you have not been selected to continue the journey with Markham-Hook Conglomerate. Your position with the company has been eliminated and will terminate on May 1st of this year. As part of your duties before you depart, you will be required to engage in knowledge transfer, making sure your replacement from India knows how to perform your job in a satisfactory manner. In addition, you must successfully complete all projects on your current work list.*

David R. Griffin, *we are pleased to announce that you will receive two weeks pay and access to our job search facilities in compensation for completing knowledge transfer duties. You will not be given the opportunity to apply for a position elsewhere in the company, since we do not currently have any positions that match the skill sets of* **David R. Griffin**.

We wish you the best of luck in your search for a new position. We are sure that the skills and the dedication to duty that you possess will make you an asset to any company.

With all sincerity,
Paul A. B. Curran,
Director of Personnel
Markham-Hook Conglomerate

Dave let go of the letter and it fluttered to the floor. "Crap." He'd known since the meeting what was coming and it still hit him like a kick in the face. Who did they think they were fooling? The tech bubble had burst last year. Jobs of any kind, let alone good-paying programming jobs with a solid company like Markham-Hook, were scarce to non-existent.

He picked up the envelope and looked inside. He frowned and turned it upside down, tapping the sides. This time nothing fell out.

"What you looking for, Dave?"

"Vaseline."

Michael chuckled. He pulled his own letter out of his pocket and handed it to Dave. "Guess they don't need a token black man anymore."

"Stop with the token black man stuff. You're one of the top programmers in this company, and they know it. But they don't care about that, not when they see dollar signs. They can probably import three or four programmers for what they pay you."

"Uhmm-hmmm. Guess what I've been doing since I opened my letter, which, as you can see, is exactly the same as yours, except they made it personal and plugged in Michael D. Hart instead of David R. Griffin. I got online, man, took a ride on that big superhighway out in cyberspace. Found out how it works. Listen to this, Dave. An American company decides to hire workers as cheap as they can. They bring people over here on work visas. Body shops from overseas provide the people, so the American companies don't even have to pay them benefits or bother with American labor laws about overtime, salary and such. Do you believe that? We train them, then most of them stay and some of them go back to do the work over there. Dirt cheap in those countries. I hear you can live like a king in India for about ten grand a year."

"That's nice." Dave dug both hands around in his thick, curly, dark hair, making it stand out from his head as if it had been electrified. "Jesus, Mike. I bought a house and an SUV and a bunch of other stuff. I've done nothing but stimulate the economy ever since I got this job."

"I hear you. I have bills of my own--new boat, pregnant wife and all. Okay, let's not panic. We have a month before we're cut loose. Then we get two weeks pay, plus our unused vacation and sick pay."

"You're right. Panic is just a knee-jerk reaction. The economy could turn around before we hit bottom. Any word yet on the names of the lucky rocketeers?" Dave's phone rang and he flipped a switch, turning off the ringer.

Michael nodded. "You were right about the diversity points. They're keeping one of the black women, the visually impaired man, the Latino man, and Chad, the junior programmer. I expect he's the cheap man."

"Four people? That's it?" Dave's voice came out in a high-pitched squawk. "I thought they said thirty percent."

"I asked Ken about that. He said every programming team is going to be affected. Some will lose all their people and some won't lose more than one or two. They're using guest worker visas to bring in replacement programmers, and there's not a damned thing we can do about it."

Dave hunched over, his arms resting on his thighs, and stared at the floor. He must look like he was sitting on the toilet, but who cared? Michael patted his shoulder and quietly slipped out of the cube.

Chapter Four

The clinic was just the way Joe had pictured it. Claustrophobic. And overcrowded with snot-nosed kids, pregnant women, and people who coughed too much or sat in defeated silence as if they'd waited for months and didn't care if their number ever came up. Whole place smelled of pee.

A janitor wearing absolutely no expression on his craggy face dragged a mop back and forth across the well-worn floor in front of the rest rooms. He'd put up a caution sign, but that didn't stop people from tracking through the water.

A baby stroller blocked access to the rack of public health pamphlets. That was okay. Joe didn't feel like reading about why he should always wear a condom when engaging in sex with strangers and how to avoid getting HIV from dirty needles.

He waited nearly three hours before they got around to calling him. An overworked assistant with a suspect yellow stain on the front of her uniform herded him through the lab and then over to the weigh in station before she ushered him into the presence of the doctor.

"I'm Dr. Whitman. Sit down, Joe." She didn't look up from studying his chart. Her glasses magnified her green eyes to three times normal size, making her look like something that had just stepped off the latest ship from Jupiter. "How are you doing on your medication? Have you had any seizures since the last time you were seen by Dr. Jefferson?"

"No." He knew the drill. He had to give the right answers, or they'd slap him in a locked mental ward. Non-compliance, they called it.

"Are you sure?"

Like he was two years old. "I'd remember."

"Are you taking your medication as directed? Failure to take your medication at the right time in the right dosage can result in seizures and irrational behavior, making you a danger to yourself and others and leading to hospitalization."

No kidding.

"Mr. Tremaine? Did you hear my question?" Dr. Whitman reached for her prescription pad.

"I peed in a cup. The nurse took blood. You don't have to take my word for it; just look at the test results."

He raked her over with his eyes. Snotty bitch was probably still sucking on a pacifier when he killed his first man, an action that had saved his country a lot of embarrassment. But doctors acted like it was his fault his brain circuits fired out of synch. If you had a broken leg, you earned a lot of sympathy. If something went wrong with your head, you got treated like a naughty child who'd pushed his teacher down the stairs just to see blood. And if you didn't have a job, you got double the amount of disrespect.

Damn them. Damn them all. He fought back the rage that surged up through his chest. If he didn't have Lark depending on him, he'd walk out of here and let them try to find him to ram their stupid pills down his non-complying throat.

"I detect a certain hostility in your manner, Mr. Tremaine."

He lowered his head and sighed deeply, humbling himself so she wouldn't call in the white coats to keep him in line.

"I'm real sorry about that." He let his words stretch into a lazy drawl. Almost, but not quite, Jed Clampett of *The Beverly Hillbillies*. "Had trouble paying the bills this month. It's real tough out there, real tough. Person gets frustrated."

He hadn't fooled her. Her magnified eyes were too easy to read, and they said, *Cut the crap. I've read your chart and your background and you, Mr. Tremaine, are a bitter man with a grudge.*

"Everyone has to deal with bills. It's part of life."

Everyone has to deal with bills. It's part of life. He mocked her in his mind. If Martha's god really existed, he'd come down and whack Dr. Whitman off her home made pedestal--starting by taking away her job and letting her see what it was like to have to worry over whether you could afford to buy a box of mac and cheese for supper.

"I'm changing your medication. We have an exciting new weapon in our seizure arsenal that promises hope for even the most difficult cases. Yes, there are side effects with Seizure-Out, but you owe a responsibility to society to keep yourself healthy and sane."

The drug companies must have scripted her little speech. Why else would any sensible person talk about exciting weapons in their seizure arsenal? Anyway, he was willing to bet the only excitement was on the part of the company that was going to earn billions from pushing their newest wonder drug. Seizure-Out. Real cute.

"I've been getting along fine with my medication, the one Dr. Jefferson prescribed. The dosage works, and I can handle the side effects."

"Just because you haven't had a seizure in..." she glanced at the chart. "six months, doesn't mean the medicine will continue to work."

"I'm adjusted to it. Why would you want to change something that's working?"

"There's a good chance your body will become so used to your present dosage that you'll develop tolerance. The new medication doesn't have that effect." She scribbled a prescription.

There was nothing he could do. Protest would only earn him a session with the shock-treatment boys in the basement of Avalon Hospital.

"Any other health problems, you be sure to let me know, and I'll give you a prescription."

Of course she would. He wondered if she had anything in her arsenal for a burning need to exact revenge.

When he talked to his pharmacist down at the CVS, he learned the really bad news.

"Lord, Joe, did you win the lottery?" Sherman read the prescription and then shook his head.

"What do you mean?" Joe was almost afraid to ask. Sherman's bassett hound face always made him look like he'd just come back from his best friend's funeral, but now he looked even sadder.

"This stuff is six hundred dollars for a month's supply. And that's just for starters. If it doesn't agree with you, you'll be back here in a couple of weeks with a fistful of prescriptions for more stuff to cover the side effects."

Joe rubbed his chin. "Is it any good?"

"Supposed to be. Test results are promising. Couple people I know are on it, and they think it's great, though one of them is complaining about stomach pains and nausea. Guess it comes down to how motivated a person is to keep their head working right. Sorry, Joe. I didn't mean to imply anything."

"It's okay. Just wait a few days on filling this until I come up with the money. I'll be back to pick it up."

"Sure." Sherman showed concern in his eyes. "Do you have enough of your old stuff to get by?"

"Plenty. Dr. Jefferson took good care of me."

The half-full bottle wasn't exactly plenty, but Joe could ration the pills out if he had to. Damn it, six hundred dollars was a fortune to a man without a job.

He called Dr. Jefferson's office as soon as he got home. The way he figured it, he could pay for his tests and his visits to Dr. Jefferson, and his old medication, and maybe even come out ahead when he figured it against the cost of the new stuff.

"Dr. Jefferson is vacationing with his family in Cape Cod," the receptionist chirped. Joe remembered her as a perky brunette with a ring in her nose.

"I just want to make an appointment."

"The doctor won't be back for two weeks. After that he's booked up until October and he's not taking new patients."

"I've been seeing him for months. You can check my chart."

"Mr. Tremaine, we've already turned your records over to the county clinic. That means you'd have to come back as a new patient. And Dr. Jefferson isn't taking new--"

Joe slammed the receiver down. This was it, the moment he should have known was looming in his future. Dumped by his doctor the same way he was dumped by the government and the same way he'd be dumped by society if he couldn't control his seizures. Now he had to find some way to come up with six hundred dollars for medicine that might kill him or make him sick as a lab monkey or he could do without and possibly end up slobbering in the streets like a rabid dog until the white coats arrived.

The Pyramid Building's main lobby was three stories tall. Dark wooden accent beams on all four walls narrowed as they neared the top, an effect that seemed to invite people to look up and see that the entire ceiling was covered with a giant mural of John Victor Harris. Harris was pictured sitting on a stone bench in a garden while small animals cavorted at his feet. Beth said she thought the mural was cute, in a Bambi-esque kind of way, but Dave thought it was creepy.

Dave slouched by the door and watched Beth step off the elevator. He knew his hair needed combing and his shirt was coming untucked from his trousers, but he made no attempt to neaten up. He waved to catch her attention, and she moved out of the way of the herd heading for the door, shoes tapping on the shiny black marble tiles and faces set in masks of concentration. Dave navigated the busy room, dodging the giant stone pots filled with greenery and cutting around the huge flowing fountain in the center.

Beth wrapped her arms around him. "Hello, sweets." She let go of him and passed her hands over his hair, pushing down the unruly curls.

"Come on." He linked his arm through hers and pulled her to the far corner of the room, next to an enormous potted palm.

"What's wrong? Don't you want to go to lunch?"

"In a minute." He turned her to face him.

"What?" Beth said, her blue eyes telegraphing alarm. "You've gone white as paper."

"Have you heard about the big screw job in the tech division? Importing cheaper programmers to take our jobs?"

"Oh, that." Beth put her hand on her throat and took in a long breath. "Wow. For a few terrible seconds I was on an emotional elevator headed for the basement. It's not that bad, honey, calm down."

"Not that bad? People are losing their jobs. I'm one of them. Out on the street like a sack of garbage, no more paycheck, no more American Dream."

"That won't happen to you as long as we're dating. Daddy's one of the biggest shareholders in the company. For that matter, Denton Harris is one of my best friends and, of course, there's Oxford DeWinters. My family has known him forever. I'll speak to Daddy tonight about finding you something on another team. If he won't help, Denton will. I mean, my God, his father is the company CEO."

"If I move to another team, I'll just be stealing a job from someone else and that isn't fair."

"Hush. You're creating a scene." Beth pulled Dave behind the palm tree so they were out of sight of the crowd. She pushed a frond out from between them and held it down. "There are plenty of programmers in this company who aren't half as talented and smart as you are. Why should they have a job instead of you? I'll talk to Daddy tonight, and he'll call someone first thing in the morning."

"That's not my way." Dave crossed his arms over his chest and leaned back against the wall. Surely, she ought to realize he wouldn't stomp on somebody else to get to the head of the line. Besides, a chill had passed through him when she added the phrase, "as long as we're dating." Do as I say or my daddy will see that you get the chop? What kind of man would settle for an arrangement like that?

Beth put her hands on his and gently uncrossed his arms. "Let's have lunch. And let's not argue or spend one minute talking about what's happened with your job for the rest of the day. Deal?"

"Okay," he said.

They walked hand in hand down Avalon's Finance Street. Dave knew what Beth was thinking as surely as if she'd spoken out loud. She'd accused him before, during their not infrequent arguments, of being childish.

If Beth hadn't decided that the topic of his job was off limits, she'd say, "Only children worry about fair. This is the business world, Dave." Then she'd purse her lips and look at him like she was his first grade teacher trying to get him to color inside the lines, when all he wanted to do was draw robots and space ships.

Some days were destined to turn out bad, and even if you knew it was one of those days, all you could do was wait for a pallet of bricks to fall on your head. Maybe there was an evil demon of bad luck on the other side, a sort of reverse guardian angel, who'd decided this was *Get Dave Day*.

After work he drove home to one of Avalon's grander neighborhoods in his new Spectrum Motors Behemoth. He'd had it for only a month and he hadn't quite gotten used to all the gadgets--the compass, meant to keep him aimed in the right direction, and the thermometer that displayed the outside temperature, so he'd know whether to put on a coat or take one off before he climbed out of the climate controlled passenger compartment. The stereo system that made his CD's sound as if a live band were sitting in the back seat for his listening pleasure, and the sun roof that allowed golden rays of sunshine to bathe the top of his head if he so chose.

He used a remote to raise the massive door of the palatial three-car garage so he could pilot the Behemoth smoothly inside. The garage was empty except for the car. Dave had sold his lawn tractor. He hadn't been able to get the hang of making the neat crosshatched lines that seemed to be a requirement of the neighborhood covenants in Eden Acres. After one too many appalled glances from his neighbors, he'd called in a lawn service. He supposed he'd have to cancel them now that he was losing his job.

Dave went into the house through the door that led from the garage to the kitchen. He opened one of the double doors on his stainless steel refrigerator, the Ultra 2, which was half the size of the Honda he'd traded on the Behemoth. The salesman had assured him that any man who planned to get married one day and start a family needed a refrigerator that would stand up to heavy use, as well as hold a month's worth of provisions for a family of four.

Dave slammed the door of the Ultra 2 on the day's worth of provisions for a family of one. He picked up his phone and dialed a familiar number.

"Griffin residence. Ruby speaking." The voice drawled the familiar greeting as though the speaker wished only to serve and comfort.

"Mawmaw?" Something ached in his chest, and he had to clench his jaw tight to keep that something inside where it belonged.

"What's wrong, sugarbiscuit?"

"Mawmaw, I told you not to call me that. It sounds like the name of a horse. And what makes you think something's wrong?" He could hear the evening news with Tom Brokaw playing in the background.

"I know your heart is aching. I can tell by your voice, baby."

"Now you sound like you're reciting the lyrics to a country and western song."

He was sorry he'd called. He realized he really wanted to talk to his father and he didn't know why because he and his father hadn't had much in common and they'd never been into father-son conversations. Their usual interactions while Dave still had a father involved Daddy patiently trying to teach him how to hunt deer or raise cattle, while Dave daydreamed about computers and artificial intelligence. His parents had died in a car crash when Dave was ten, so as much as he ached to be able to talk to his father, it simply wasn't possible.

"Tell your Mawmaw what's wrong. And don't try to fool me, David Robert. You know I don't tolerate lying." He heard a click on the other end of the line and Tom Brokaw was silenced in the middle of a sentence about breadlines.

"I lost my job today--but don't worry. I'll be okay." One handed he flipped through the stack of mail on the counter in front of him. Bills and a bunch of flyers for stuff he didn't need.

"Oh, sugarbiscuit, what happened?"

He told her. He didn't mention Beth's offer to have her father step in and wave his rich stockholder wand to make everything all better. He knew she wouldn't approve.

Dave sighed. If he had a pet, a dog for example, it would have sensed his misery and flung itself across the room to sit beside him, pushing its snout into his hand and offering silent comfort.

"That CEO Harris already has hundreds of millions of dollars. I declare, I read in a magazine at Dr. Blake's office that Harris owns ten or twelve houses. Can you imagine such a thing? What kind of company is it that treats its own workers like they don't matter as long as the rich people at the top can make more money?"

"Mawmaw, I don't know."

"The Lord doesn't approve of any of this. I've got a good mind to take the bus up to Washington and shake some sense into people. But I'd be wasting my time. Did you know the towel mill here in Hidden Springs closed last month?"

"Jesus, Mawmaw, I didn't hear about that." Dave bit his lip. He should have known. Manufacturing and textiles were no less important than technology. He guessed he'd been too busy spending money and having a good time to worry about other people's troubles. "What are they going to do?"

"Don't take the Lord's name, David. They're going to do the best they can to survive and that's all anyone can do, but it sure seems like there ought to be some justice somewhere."

His grandmother told him some of the townspeople had to move away, some hoped to get odd jobs wherever they could find them, some were selling their land for money to live on. Floyd Larson had killed himself by stepping in front of an eastbound freight train, but then he never could handle stress since his wife left him a few years ago for a used car salesman over at Bryson City.

"I know you wouldn't do anything like that. You're my brave lion heart."

Sure. A lion heart in the body of a slightly bewildered computer jockey.

He studied his arms, concluding they didn't look one bit like useful fighting weapons, not that the management at Markham-Hook would agree to physically fight this out. Dave had his father's clear blue eyes and his curly dark hair, but not his size. From deep in his memories Dave summoned up an image of his father, a tall, solidly built man with a ready grin and an honest heart. What would Daddy tell him if he were here now? Dave didn't know.

Chapter Five

The deck repair job wouldn't take more than half a day. Joe figured he'd clear maybe a hundred bucks for his trouble, not nearly enough to pay for his new prescription. There was too much competition out there from men who'd lost their jobs and were willing to take on any kind of handyman work.

The glass door in front of him slid open. Joe's customer, a smug-faced man wearing plaid slacks and a lime colored golf shirt pulled tight over his gut, walked out and stood over him with his hands on his hips like a guard watching a chain gang bust rocks.

"I've got to leave to pick up a few things at Office Max. You going to drag the job out to take me for a few more dollars?"

"Being that you're paying me so God-awful much money, I'm going to finish by noon so I can still have time to get down to the bar and hoist a few with my low-life friends." The customer had deducted fifty bucks from his bid, knowing Joe would be forced to take the offer. He picked up another nail and touched it to the wood. "You've got nothing to worry about. We already agreed on a price."

The man's wife sashayed out of the house wearing a tiny tube top, flesh-eating slacks and gold-colored high heels. She tugged at her husband's arm. "Herb, don't be so rude. Look, Mr. Tremaine's got only a few more boards to nail on. You go to the store, and I'll pay him when he's done."

Joe slid his glance sideways, letting his gaze roam from her face down to her hips and back up. She was a lot younger than her husband. Probably a second wife, or even a third. Let Herb think he was interested, maybe even give him cause to wonder if it was safe to leave his young wife alone with Joe. Serve him right. It was a shame, though, that he couldn't let the idiot know who he was really dealing with.

A few minutes later Joe banged in the last nail. His thoughts raced through his mind seeking a way out and coming up against a million dead ends. More than once since he landed in poverty he'd thought about making money, a lot of money, by robbing banks or committing any of dozens of other kinds of crimes. He certainly knew enough about crime to be able to put a good plan together and he already had the knack of ignoring his conscience when it was convenient. He'd always thought he'd make a good con man. The main problem, though, and one he hadn't yet been able to get past, was that he stood out like a giraffe in a pen full of cattle.

Any mark would be able to describe him to the police. "Yes, officer, the thief was six feet tall and he walked with a limp. Dark hair, going gray at the temples. Small scar on his face near his left eye." Most of the people in his neighborhood would shove each other out of the way to collect the reward money.

Before he left, he pulled his cigarettes out of the glovebox and smoked one, flipping through his appointment book. It was blank for all the days after today, except for the phone number of a woman who wanted her porch repaired because of termite damage. He tossed the book down on the seat next to his binoculars, still lying where he'd left them after the last time he'd driven down to the river on surveillance.

His mouth twisted into a grimace. Surveillance, as if he was still worth a damn and still had a job to do. A million times he'd driven past the house and down as close as he could get to the river without trespassing or being seen. He'd hidden among the trees, watching Senator Drake, so motionless even the insects didn't know he was there. Pathetic, that he had to pretend he was still in the FBI.

⁂

Dave had updated his resume yesterday evening when he got done talking to Mawmaw. He wished Beth hadn't left town for the weekend, but maybe it was a good thing she had. Other than wanting to get her friends and family to intervene, she wouldn't talk about his lost job, but that was the only thing he could think about.

He spent Saturday morning posting his resume on the electronic job boards and sending it directly to companies that allowed online applications. By early afternoon, he'd emailed his qualifications to nearly a hundred companies, most of them with Internet pages touting their products and services. But the Internet job boards that even a year ago had held out the promise of gainful employment now listed few opportunities, even for those with a college degree and experience with the most in demand programming skills.

He made himself a peanut butter and jelly sandwich and sat at the breakfast bar in the kitchen, his bare feet resting on the rungs of his barstool. He was glad he'd paid extra for a model with a kitchen island and the breakfast bar. If they weren't there to provide a barrier between the line-up of kitchen appliances and the far wall of the den at the other end of the open living area, the hardwood floors and the long rectangular space would lend the appearance of a bowling alley.

He tried to ignore the prodding reminders his mind sent him every few minutes: "How will you pay for all this stuff? Why did you listen to the lies about the American Dream?"

Absently he rubbed his hand back and forth across his breastbone. He remembered his grandmother telling him more than once about hard times when she was growing up and how they always got by. Sure, that was fine when you owned a few acres of good land and a couple of chickens, but how could you manage when you owed Markham-Hook for your mortgage, your furniture, your credit cards, your car, and-- God, did Markham-Hook own the Foodarama, too?

The company had just put banking branches in all the Foodaramas. Maybe they even controlled his food supply. He'd blindly let Markham-Hook Conglomerate take control of all his finances, his whole life. The bastards.

He finished his sandwich and wandered into the den. The house was a former model and he'd bought it decorated. But he'd fixed up the den himself, in a style that Beth laughingly referred to as country masculine the one time he'd brought her here. He didn't understand her objections to the beige walls, bare of decoration except for a framed print of the Avalon Speedway with race cars roaring under the checkered flag. The racing print was a housewarming gift from Michael and Rosie, and he'd chosen the mirror because he liked the gilt frame.

Beth had teased him about the couch and the love seat, both upholstered in dark plaid, and the green curtains that she said didn't match. The cherry bookcases, filled with computer books and science fiction novels, didn't match the oak-finished end tables and maple fireplace mantle. The huge afghan in shades of blue that Dave's grandmother had crocheted for him was "too country." He kept the afghan folded across the arm of his black recliner, which Beth insisted was not black, but hunter green. And she told him the color of the afghan didn't match anything, either. The only thing Beth liked about the den was the massive entertainment center with the big screen TV.

Dave set the ceiling fan on high and the air conditioner on maximum cool. He grabbed the universal remote and plopped down in the leather recliner that he referred to as his command center. He powered up the TV to the movie channel and pulled the afghan off the back of the chair, wrapping it around himself like a cocoon, as he settled in to watch the afternoon movie. The movie turned out to be an Australian picture called *The Return of the Man From Snowy River*. The man from Snowy River was a horse wrangler whose horses got stolen by a banker, who also wanted to steal the man's woman.

Did the man from Snowy River sit around whining while his four-legged wealth got run into the next territory by a rich banker? No way. At the end of the picture the banker had gotten the crap kicked out of him by the man from Snowy River, who ended up with all the horses and the girl. Maybe if Dave's life were a movie, he'd have a chance of winning.

When the show was over, he ordered a pizza and sat out on his deck. The neighbors had mowed earlier, and the sweet scent of freshly cut grass drifted across to tickle his nose. He drew in a deep breath and gazed out over his back yard, his mini-estate, as the Realtor had called it. A wide strip of lawn led to a wooded area, his own small forest of oak and maple and pine trees on the one-acre lot. He wondered what the neighbors would say if he put in a few rows of corn and pole beans on the lawn, maybe planted some peach trees, and tethered a cow out in the woods. A dozen or so chickens in a pen on the deck would come in handy. He could feed them kitchen scraps and they would repay him by providing eggs.

A crow marched out from under the nearest tree and tilted its head at him. Dave broke off a piece of pizza crust and tossed it over the deck. Somehow the idea of a mini farm in his back yard didn't do much to ease the ache in his chest.

The men and women at the shelter hung around at the wooden tables even after they'd eaten breakfast and everything had been cleared away except for the odor of grease. The director had announced she wanted to have a few words with the community of the homeless on this fine Monday morning. She was going to tell them how they could shine in a job interview. They would need such skills. A new trade deficit mart was opening up across town in another month. It was on the bus line. They were hosting a job fair and women and minorities were especially encouraged to apply. The director smiled, showing way too many teeth for a woman who wanted to be taken seriously.

Joe snorted. He got up and read the notice posted on the bulletin board. Women and minorities. Oh, please do apply. That meant minimum wage and probably no full time work in case the employees managed by putting in more than thirty hours a week to qualify for insurance and other benefits.

He sat at a table in the corner and folded his hands in front of him. He wasn't here for either tips on how to shine in a job interview or news about the job fair. He could just see himself wearing one of those flattering little yellow smocks as he limped around the parking lot corralling shopping carts and pretending to care about the store's image. Even assuming he got hired, it would take him more than a month to earn enough for his new pills, and then where would he get his share of the rent money?

No, Joe was here to observe the growing crop of the unemployed and homeless. He picked up a lot of useful information just by hanging around and it got him out of the house.

He pulled a paperback, a western, out of his pocket and opened it. He stayed for a while, eavesdropping while pretending not to hear anything or to notice his surroundings, something he excelled at and something that was easy enough since no one in here seemed inclined to keep things to themselves. Besides, to them he was Crazy Joe. They wouldn't perceive him as a threat.

He learned about a planned drug buy, as well as a place where he could go to play video poker. Too bad he was out to make money, not lose it. Abruptly he shut the book and left, stepping out into a beautiful spring day and sucking in a lungful of tree pollen that made him cough. He had a plan for getting the six hundred dollars for this month's medicine. It was risky. More than risky, it was foolhardy and he probably couldn't get away with it too often. But he had only a few pills left and no other options. And the way he'd worked things out, he'd get the money or he'd end up dead.

Chapter Six

Dave hadn't expected the replacement programmers so soon. When he stepped off the elevator on Monday morning, he spotted a group of chattering strangers, a stressed-out looking Ken herding them down the hallway in the direction of the conference room. So they were here already. He shook his head and pushed past them.

Half of Dave's teammates huddled near his cubicle, deep in conversation around the bulletin board in the hallway. Dave saw that someone had posted a couple of new notices in a prominent position, right under an announcement about the company stock prices. He squeezed in closer.

The cause for the mini riot was a sheaf of papers labeled Labor Condition Applications, required by the government to show what the new programmers imported on work visas were earning. A surge of anger raced through him when Dave read the reports. He knew his own salary and he knew the senior programmers made more than he did, some of them nearly twice as much. The replacement programmers from India were earning less than half the amount he earned. How could this be legal? He turned around and caught Michael's eye.

Michael shrugged. "Told you, dude. See, the employer is supposed to pay ninety-five percent of the prevailing wage. But here's the catch-- the prevailing wage is anything the employer says it is."

"That sucks. Who made up such a stupid law?"

"Our elected officials, busters of the middle class, lackeys of corporate America."

"So how are we supposed to compete against a worldwide supply of cheaper labor?"

Michael held both hands out, palms up. "Don't ask me, ask the brain surgeons who thought up this plan."

Another programmer--Jarod Andrews--was practically foaming at the mouth. "I don't care whether it's legal or not. They can't make me train them." Andrews had worked his way up from computer operator to senior analyst and he reminded everyone in the department of this fact at least once a week. "I'll stick around 'til they throw me out, but I'm not showing these job thieves a damn thing."

"I'm with you. By the time I get done with them, this bunch is going to know less about programming than they did the day they were born." Loretta Greene stepped aside to let Dave into his cubicle. Like Dave, she'd just bought a new SUV. She looked like she was ready to paw the carpet with the toe of her fashionable leather shoe and charge headfirst into the next company executive who stepped off the elevator.

Dave plunked down in his desk chair, still hearing the angry buzz in the hallway.

"Harris has gone nuts if he thinks he's getting away with this. I oughta walk out of here right now."

"Man, I've got bills to pay and a new baby to take care of."

"If I don't take the severance, my kids don't eat. But that doesn't mean I have to show them how my system really works."

The general consensus was that there was no reason to help Markham-Hook Conglomerate by cooperating in training their replacements. Dave was not inclined to help Markham-Hook, either. A predictable mix of anger, dismay, and insecurity fought for dominance in his emotional center, and in the end he was left with a serious case of heartburn and an empty antacid bottle. He wished he were back home, curled up in his command center with his grandmother's afghan wrapped around him.

Ken appeared in the hallway. He cleared his throat and held up both hands until there was silence. "I know you're all still upset, especially after seeing the LCA sheets, but we've got a meeting to attend. People? Go in and get acquainted with the Orion group. I'll join you in a few minutes." He jerked his thumb in the direction of the conference room.

Dave picked up a pencil and wrote Golden Orion Technology & Computer Help Agency in block letters on a scrap of memo paper. He carefully underlined the first letter of each word. Then he shot to his feet and slung his chair backward. It crashed into the padded side of the cubicle, where it threatened to topple the wall and start a chain reaction that would take down every cube on this side of the room.

Somebody in the hall yelled, "What in the hell's going on?"

"GOTCHA," Dave answered.

"What?"

"Never mind."

⁂

The long tables were back in the meeting room, arranged end to end to form one big table. The curtains were open and the sun shone in as if all were well. Dave paused in the doorway and narrowed his eyes. The

GOTCHA programmers, presumably fresh off the plane from India, sat in a row on one side of the room, their backs to the window. They were dressed in nearly identical white shirts, dark ties and dark slacks. Their hands were folded in front of them on the table, ready to pick up the programming reins and make off with the jobs.

The rest of his co-workers had already taken seats opposite the GOTCHA people. The two lines of programmers projected an impression of a face-off, and Dave half expected six shooters to be drawn and ultimatums to be issued, with the final showdown to take place at high noon in Harris Park.

"Are you the moderator?" one of the Indians asked, looking at Dave.

"No, I'm one of the fired programmers."

"Excuse me. What is that?"

The GOTCHA people, all men, stared at Dave, expressions of puzzlement on most faces, understanding on others. Two of the men directed their gazes to the tabletop.

"Haven't they told you? Not everyone gets a ride on the rocket, hotshot. Those of us who are no longer of use to Markham-Hook Conglomerate will get tickets to the nearest unemployment line, like so much used and abused former company assets. But, hey, that's life working for the richest man in the country. Enjoy your job in the big conglomerate while you can, but don't let them tattoo a company barcode on your ass. And keep looking over your shoulder for the next wave of cheaper labor. Can anyone say Vietnam?"

Loretta started to applaud. After a few seconds, the rest of the American programmers joined in and Michael let out a shrill whistle. The Indians sat with smiles frozen on their faces and, Dave hoped, with awareness dawning in their minds.

He took a bow. Behind him he heard the door open with a sharp click.

"Dave, sit down."

Ken, clearly in leadership mode this morning, slipped into the room and strode to the head of the table. He pointed toward one of the last two remaining seats, at the far end. "Dave, please."

Dave, enduring the stares from the GOTCHA employees, walked to the chair and sat. God, this was awkward. He hadn't felt so stupid and out of place since running across Oxford DeWinters at the restaurant last week.

Ken placed a stack of papers at his own place at the head of the table. He pushed a wayward clump from his comb-over off his forehead and brought the meeting to order by reminding everyone that he expected full cooperation.

Points on for Ken for being aware that his former team might not be ecstatic over losing their jobs. On the other hand, Ken wasn't known as an aware person. He'd probably received instructions from someone in HR who was paid to hire and fire and soothe and praise as need be and, while they were at it, they'd given him a backbone transplant.

Ken passed out nametags and made everyone print their names and then stick the tags on their left shirtfronts. Dave stole a glance at the GOTCHA employee sitting opposite, a short, stocky man wearing black-framed glasses. The man's name was long and, to Dave, unpronounceable. He caught the man glancing at his own tag. He hesitated, wondering whether to introduce himself or to make a rude remark. Then Ken asked for everyone's attention and the moment was lost.

The rest of the meeting went downhill. Ken passed out handbooks with shiny gold and silver covers.

"Any comments or questions?" He set the lower half of his face in a toothy grin that made him look like a con man trying to gain your trust while he stole your money.

To Dave's relief no one so much as twitched. He thumbed through his handbook, noting lines such as, "You may be feeling overwhelmed." The copy read like one of those books about puberty that teachers forced kids to read in junior high. "Changes are a normal part of growth and are to be welcomed."

He sighed. Today was one of the company's twice-monthly paydays. Just two more paydays, then he'd be on his way with his severance and his unused vacation pay and sick days. He'd heard that the long-term employees were getting as much as fifty weeks' pay, but people like Dave who'd been with the company for five years or less had to settle for a whopping two weeks. After that, the unemployment line. Dave had read his career-planning packet yesterday. He'd be entitled to continue his health insurance coverage, but he'd have to pay the premium himself. Sure, that would work, but not if he wanted to eat. He'd have to drop coverage and hope he didn't develop gout or the hemorrhoids Michael had warned him about.

The meeting ended with Ken assigning each of them an Indian programmer. Dave scrutinized his trainee. This man, too, had a long, unpronounceable name. He was tall and well built, a handsome man with a pleasant smile and an air of confidence. He yawned suddenly, and Dave wondered if he was suffering from jet lag after the long flight from India.

"Uhmm, follow me," Dave said. God, what should he do next? Should he ask the guy if he needed to use the can or get a cup of coffee before they got started? Did Indians drink coffee? Maybe Ken should have passed out books on the care and feeding of your very own foreign replacement.

He was supposed to spend the remaining weeks of his employment performing "knowledge transfer." Dave couldn't imagine anything more demoralizing. Too bad there wasn't some method of brain to brain transfer, maybe something similar to a Vulcan mind meld like on *Star Trek*, so he could be done with this nightmare in a matter of seconds.

Dave led the way to his cube, resisting the urge to point out landmarks such as the water fountain, the hallway that led to the rest rooms, and the door to the room with the copy machines. The guy found his way here from India, let him find his own way around the twenty-fifth floor. He righted the chair he'd slung into the wall earlier and plunked it in front of his desk. He removed the stack of magazines from his second chair and invited the Indian to sit.

The Indian studied Dave's nametag. "Certainly, Dave. Perhaps you are having difficulty with my name. You may call me Rex."

"Yeah, whatever. Sorry I don't speak your language. No one told me I'd have a need to communicate with people from another land right here at my own desk while I give away my knowledge."

Rex frowned. "Are you having a problem, Dave?"

Dave put the magazines on the floor and collapsed in his chair. "Why do you say that?" He pointed to his chest. "Do I look like a man who is having a problem? Seriously."

"I have noted some tension in your manner and an air of discontent." Rex looked at him with an earnest expression.

Tension in his manner? Discontent? Was that what you called it when a person's world fell apart, and he couldn't quite manage to pretend he was giddy with delight?

"Let's get something straight, Rex. Nothing against you. You wanted a job in the United States; you got one. But did anyone tell you that you were taking my job? I've got damned little chance of finding another one with half the frigging corporations in the country stomping all over each other in the rush to dump American workers."

Deep frown lines appeared on Rex's wide forehead. "Surely that is not correct. We at Golden Orion Technology were told there were many openings at Markham-Hook Conglomerate for skilled computer programmers with college degrees. Surely, if you are losing your job it is because you lack the skills they are wanting."

Give him credit. He actually looked surprised and maybe a little dismayed. Dave stared at him, firmly resisting the urge to march up to the top floor in the point of the pyramid and tell John Victor Harris where he could shove the severance.

"Lacking skills? If I'm so lacking in skills, Einstein, what am I doing training you?"

"I had not considered--"

"Damn right, you hadn't considered. This is supposed to be a knowledge transfer, or haven't you heard? If you think you have so many skills, maybe you ought to be training me. What about that, Rex? Go on. Transfer some knowledge." He leaned forward and tapped the top of his head. "Put it right there, buddy."

Rex sat very still, his face a study in deep concentration. "Clearly I have offended you, Dave. I apologize. But I had thought there were many openings."

"The openings are only for you people from India and they wouldn't be there if a couple thousand of us weren't losing our jobs. You'll be earning a lot less than we earn, the company saves a bundle. Americans and those pesky American wages and benefits out the door. The rich get richer. Get my drift?"

"So you are saying you have lost your job, and the job has been given to me because I am earning less pay."

"I am saying that. You catch on fast, Rex." Wow, what a whiz kid. He wondered if the rest of the GOTCHA boys were this sharp.

"I am so dreadfully sorry. I had no idea I would be causing hardship for someone else."

"But not sorry enough to say, 'no thanks.'"

"Excuse me?"

"You do what you have to do to earn a living, right?"

"Back in India I have a wife and a son, of whom I am very proud. I must provide for them."

"There you go. You have a family to take care of; you took my job." Dave shoved the stack of magazines with his foot and the stack fell, cascading magazines in a line toward the door.

"You are angry with me, Dave."

Dave pondered Rex's statement. Rex wasn't here because he'd gotten up one day and decided to fly to North Carolina and take Dave Griffin's job. He went over and started restacking the magazines, and Rex got up and helped.

"No, Rex. I'm angry with the company and the whole rotten system. I don't blame you for wanting to do the best you can for your family and yourself. If I were in your shoes, I'd be the first one on the plane to the United States. Tell you what, we only a have a few weeks for me to show you my part of the job. That isn't much time. I'll give you all the documentation I have and I'll show you as much as I have time to show you. After I leave, you're on your own and I don't care what happens to you or to anyone else at Markham-Hook. Don't call me, don't write me, don't email me. Fair enough?"

"That is very fair."

"Let's get started."

During the morning's meeting Dave had wavered between walking out the door, pretending to cooperate, or actually doing what he'd been asked--train his replacement. The course he'd settled on was hard to swallow, but seemed the most practical, simply because he desperately needed the money from the severance and the final few weeks with the company. He would teach Rex, even though he might as well be cutting his own throat.

The job was complex enough that it should take six months or so to give Rex a thorough grounding. He didn't have six months. And, he found when he actually sat face to face with Rex, a man with a family and hopes and dreams, he didn't have the heart to cause trouble for him. Besides, it was clear Markham-Hook was committed to the change. If Dave didn't cooperate, they had other ways to get the replacement workers trained. And ways to give Dave a bad recommendation so he wouldn't be able to get another job. It was blackmail, but Dave was vulnerable.

The phone shrilled. Dave stopped in the middle of explaining his day's routine to glance at the caller ID.

"Break time," he said.

"Break time? What are you meaning, Dave?"

"Take a break. I have a private call."

Rex looked at him blankly. Dave pointed toward the hallway. "Didn't anyone show you the break room? Vending machines? Microwave and refrigerator?"

"Ahhh." Understanding lit Rex's face and he stood. "I will return after I have consumed a snack."

"You do that." Dave lifted the receiver and pressed it tight against his ear. "Hi, Beth."

"I can't meet you for lunch, but we need to talk."

"Those are words guaranteed to strike fear in the heart of any man," he said, and chuckled. "How was your weekend?"

"This isn't a joke, Dave."

"Of course not."

"Can we meet this evening at Avalon Castle?"

Avalon Castle was a restaurant. It was decorated to look like a medieval castle and even had a goldfish-filled moat between the parking lot and the building. Dave didn't like the décor, but the food was terrific, and Beth loved the place.

"We can, but wouldn't it be better to talk someplace private? My house, for example. I can make dinner, if you're in the mood for steak and salad and the finest wine Foodarama has to offer." He picked up a pencil and drummed it against his mousepad. He could guess what Beth wanted--he still hadn't agreed to let her influence someone to move him ahead in the job queue.

"If we meet at your house, that will cloud the issue. I want to talk on neutral ground." Her words sounded clipped.

Dave dropped the pencil and watched it land on the floor. He and Beth had had more than their share of arguments and disagreements, considering they'd only dated for a month, but they'd never had to meet on so-called neutral ground.

"Avalon Castle's okay. I'll pick you up."

"No, I'll meet you. Seven, okay? Love you," she chirped.

The receiver clicked before he could respond with the obligatory, "love you, too." Besides, Beth's "love you" had sounded like, "talk to you later" or even worse, "love you, mean it."

Dave rested his elbows on his desk and cupped his chin in his hands. Funny how just last week at this time, he was happily employed and earning a middle-class income, happily dating a beautiful woman, happily oblivious and working his ass off for corporate America.

When Rex came back from break, Dave was copying the last of an array of phone numbers into his Mental Giant. Rex looked over his shoulder at the computer monitor.

"Is this part of the Markham-Hook system, Dave?"

"No, this is a site that tells me now to contact my elected officials. See this--phone and fax numbers, mailing addresses, emails. These are the people who made the law that allows you to come into my country and take my job."

"If this law is causing hardship for American workers, your government officials must be very unaware."

"That's exactly what I figured. I thought I'd give them a little wake-up call about what's happening in the world of the working man."

"I am sorry for you, Dave, but I am happy the law favors me and my countrymen."

"Nothing personal, Rex, but not for long once they find out what's going on."

Surely, the United States government wouldn't knowingly make laws that put hard-working Americans in the unemployment line just so people like John Victor Harris could get richer. What was the point in dropping middle class people to the bottom of the food chain? Dave had read some background on the tech worker visas. The business world had screamed about a tech worker shortage and the elected officials fell for it. They'd been had. Dave would contact them and tell them the truth. Once they knew what was happening, how they'd destroyed Dave's career and the careers of so many other white-collar workers, they'd have to fix things for the good of the country.

Chapter Seven

Dave was half-afraid he'd be required to go to lunch with Rex. Rex was okay, now that they'd come to a sort of truce, but Dave had no wish for a stranger's company when he had personal problems to stress over. He was relieved when Rex joined the other GOTCHA men to troop like a line of ducks across the street to the closest restaurant. He hoped they liked Chinese.

Dave wasn't hungry. It was impossible to have positive thoughts about food while his stomach was churning like an overloaded washing machine. He walked to Harris Park a few blocks from the Pyramid Building. He settled on a bench in the shade of a giant maple tree where sunlight could filter between the new leaves of spring to gently dapple his skin without imparting an unpleasant glare. He picked up his cell phone and punched in the first number on his list.

Someone picked up on the first ring. "Good afternoon, U.S. Department of Labor comment line," said a bored-sounding female voice.

"Good afternoon." Dave repositioned himself on the bench. A couple of pigeons waddled up and waited hopefully at his feet, and he shook his head at them, hoping they'd get the hint. "Dave Griffin from North Carolina. I'd like to report that I lost my computer programming job because my company replaced me with cheaper labor imported from another country on work visas. Isn't that illegal?"

"Actually, it isn't. Anyway, the Department of Labor doesn't do enforcement." Her voice sounded flat and disinterested. Dave pictured her thumbing through a tabloid while she spoke with him, maybe reading about a woman in Ohio growing a twelve-hundred pound tomato.

"But I'm out of work," he protested.

"Uh-huh. You need training. See, the fees from the H-1B visas that bring in these workers pay to retrain Americans for other jobs." She read out a toll free number, so Dave could call and apply for training.

Dave copied the number into his Mental Giant. Then he held the phone out in front of him and frowned at it before he returned it to his ear. "You don't understand. I have training and a college degree, Miss...?"

"It's not miss, it's U.S. Department of Labor comment line."

"Okay, U.S. Department of Labor comment line. I have training. In fact, my company is making me train my replacement. Why is this happening? People ought to be able to get a job in their own country and not have to worry about their employer dumping them and importing someone cheaper."

"With the current economic expansion, we have restructuring of labor due to free trade and globalization. Corporate CEO's need to make companies competitive for shareholders. This involves global sourcing and wage compression as well as trade in services." She recited her speech in tones of disdain, as if Dave had been hiding under a rock for a year or so and had totally missed the good things the government had wrought.

"So what's the plan?" he shot back.

"The plan?" The voice was a full octave higher.

"Don't you people have a plan for the survival of Americans? How can big corporations demand the power and protection of the U.S. military, when they won't even hire Americans?" Dave paused to catch his breath. He had the sudden thought that he'd sounded patriotic and noble. He wondered if Nathan Hale had felt the same way when he'd given his life for his country. Probably not. Most likely he'd only felt terrified over his impending execution, despite his claim about wishing he had more than one life he could give up.

"I won't be able to pay my bills," he added, going for the sympathy connection.

"Sorry about your credit issues. I have to listen to calls like yours from people without jobs all day long. I'm not an economist, you know. Get some training or call someone else."

He bit back a remark she wouldn't have appreciated. Wait till the government decided to save money by offshoring *her* job.

"The president maybe?"

"Yes, call the White House, sir."

He dialed the White House. The president was unavailable to speak to Dave Griffin in North Carolina, so he spoke with the staffer manning the comment line. She had no idea about a plan for the survival of the working poor and the middle class. He got the same results from his senators' offices and his congressman's office. All the staffers responded as if reading from the same script and they spouted the same meaningless phrases, "education is the answer" and "trade creates jobs."

The pigeons had gone away disappointed, and Dave's jaw had clamped into an unhealthy tightness by the time he got around to calling the U.S. Department of Commerce.

"What education? How exactly does trade create jobs when all the trade is only flowing one way?" He realized his voice did not sound like the calm, cool, Dave-in-command he'd wanted to project and instead had grown whiny and maybe a little desperate.

"The economic stimulus will create jobs," said another phone voice in soothing tones.

"But the corporations aren't hiring Americans. Don't they teach you anything up in Washington?"

"Sir-er," the nasal voice said, making sir into a two-syllable word, "contact your local Employment Security Commission."

Click.

Dave had exhausted all his options. If there was a book called *The New Economy for the Completely Clueless*, he hadn't read it. But all evidence indicated no one in Washington had either.

He felt as if he'd been smacked in the teeth by robots spouting government double-talk. He tried to imagine a scenario where the fast-talking salesman who'd sold him the Behemoth had tried to woo him with statements such as, "Celebrate diversity and wage compression in your vehicle. Let no car be left behind in the race to global sourcing. The new free trade in vehicles will spur economic growth through increased auto production and new low interest rates to stimulate consumer confidence. So don't worry about downsizing, rightsizing, and offshoring of your current model. Education is the key to safe driving. Just call this toll-free number for training."

He'd have peeled out of the Spectrum Motors lot like a scalded cat. Why, then, had he not reacted when his own government dealt the equivalent of that speech to the American people, not once, but many times over? As long as the trucks kept bringing goods to stock the shelves of the discount marts and the Foodarama, he'd allowed himself to become practically comatose.

As an afterthought, he dialed the toll-free training number given him by U.S. Department of Labor Comment Line. The number connected him to a recruiting office for the United States Army.

"You're kidding, right?" Dave had noticed a trendy-looking couple staring at him from a nearby bench. They were probably named Wendy and Cole and were newlyweds who'd just moved into a townhouse with their wedding gifts that included a Lhasa Apso puppy and a fondue kit. He was sure they didn't appreciate his angry words carrying to them on the breeze to invade their secure little space. But he didn't make an effort to tone it down. It was time they learned what was really going on with the economy before it was too late and they ended up having to take their Lhasa Apso to the pound on their way to the homeless shelter.

"Hey, sergeant, let me ask you something. How come Americans are good enough to fight and die in the U.S. military, but not good enough for their government to make sure they can have jobs in their own country?"

"Do you want to join up or not, son?"

"Hell, yes. A little hands-on driving a tank or operating a machine gun, maybe some experience shooting enemy soldiers in the head is going to look really great in the skills section of my resume when I apply for my next programming job."

Click.

Dave shoved his phone in his pocket. How many government workers had he pissed off today? Ten? Twelve? Too bad they hadn't put him through to the higher-ups. Those were the people who ought to be hearing from Dave Griffin, not the poor staffers forced to answer the phone and listen to complaints from a fed-up public.

Joe walked home from the shelter, detouring around a sack of trash someone had busted all over the sidewalk, and found what he needed--pair of gloves, plastic bag, couple of lightweight blankets, sunglasses, and a dark wool cap he could pull down almost over his eyes. He hobbled downstairs to the basement and hauled out the box he kept locked in a storage cabinet. He opened the box and picked up the Luger, making sure it was loaded. He'd considered using a toy gun or one with no bullets, but had decided that once he made the decision to bring a weapon with him, he wanted one that was operational in case of trouble. But he wouldn't shoot anyone, except himself. He'd die before he'd let them lock him up. He went back outside and headed toward the house on the corner, the one with window boxes full of yellow and purple pansies, and the wooden ramp leading up to the front door.

Martha was probably inside, maybe working the phone. Must be, in fact, because Freddy's outside wheelchair was parked where Joe expected to find it, next to the porch. He pulled on his gloves and grabbed the chair handles. Hoping no prying eyes were watching from windows, he pushed the chair toward the street. Crappy piece of junk. The squeaking was about to drive him crazy.

He took it to his garage and oiled the wheels until they spun freely and silently, then folded the chair and hoisted it into the back of his truck. He put it on top of a tarp and folded the top piece to cover it--not that an extra few scratches would be noticeable among all the others. He took a long drive out of the city, opening the windows to enjoy the cool breeze while he could. Summer came early to Avalon and soon enough he'd be running the AC and smelling the stale smoke of his cigarettes circulating through the cab.

He passed lines of stores and eventually came to neighborhoods with houses filling every available patch of land. A few more miles and the neighborhoods gave way to the mill, a brick building sitting windowless and empty, smokeless chimneys reaching to the sky. Past that was a strip of shops he drove by every time he went to the river. Music store--couple of sun-warped guitars hanging in the window--thrift shop, and a day-old bread store. He sped by for another mile, rolling between condemned apartment buildings and duplexes that lined the road, and parked the truck in an alley a block away from another strip of shops. No one around, just like he figured. There wasn't much left on this street, only a car repair shop or two, a gas station, a dollar store and an appliance sales and repair store.

Joe chose the appliance store because there didn't ever seem to be many customers around. He'd scoped this place out in advance, hiding behind an abandoned gas station across the street and using binoculars. He knew there was always a small flurry of customers in the morning and again late in the afternoon, but business was slack the rest of the time, and there was only one clerk to man the register and help the customers. He hauled the wheelchair out of the truck and sat in it, arranging the blankets around his legs and putting the cap on, pulling it low to hide his hair, and then putting the shades over his eyes.

He wheeled down the block and up to the door. A sweet scent, some kind of flowers, floated on the breeze. Must have come from a long way off because there was nothing green around here where pavement was the only crop.

He started to push his way in, but the man inside must have seen him through the window. He was kind enough to open the door and welcome Joe inside.

"Help you today, sir?"

During the planning phase of this operation, Joe had decided on the accent he'd use. British. Different enough so that when the clerk talked to the cops later he'd remember and send them off looking for a handicapped guy who spoke the Queen's English.

"Yes, actually. I'm looking for a new refrigerator. Mine makes a rather dreadful groaning sound, and I'm afraid it's ready for the rubbish bin."

"Any idea what price range?" Gum chewer, leaning against the counter and not caring that his shirt was coming untucked from his shabby slacks. All the time in the world to wait on a customer.

"How much do you have in the register?" Keeping it polite and low-key, he even managed to smile pleasantly.

"What?" The startled clerk turned to glance at the register, then, realization taking hold, he looked back at Joe, his eyes wide and his face suddenly the same color of pale lemon as his shirt.

Joe pulled the gun out from under the blanket and pointed the barrel at the clerk's midsection. If another customer wandered in, he'd shoot himself before this was over. He wasn't going to kill some innocent slob who'd just been trying to do his job. Joe's life wasn't worth living anyway and it would be no loss when he limped toward the light--if there was a light. The way things were going, that was debatable. Lark would have to find it in her heart to forgive him one day.

"All of it please. Put it in this bag and give it to me. Don't try alerting anyone." He jabbed the air with the gun, causing the clerk to grab onto the counter for support.

His victim grabbed the bag and scurried to the register. Joe wheeled up close so he could watch the man's hands. The hands shook as they picked up the money.

Joe took the bag from him and dropped it in his lap. "Put your hands up and keep them there. You have a storeroom, I presume?"

"Yes, sir. You're not going to hurt me are you? Hey, I got a wife and a kid. Son's almost ready to start school. Jesus, man, just don't hurt me." He was blubbering now, tears running down his flabby face and slime coursing out of his nose, his hands still in the air.

"I'm going to lock you in the storeroom. First empty your pockets."

A wallet, a set of keys, and a cell phone landed on the counter.

"Ah. It would have been very naughty of you to call for help from inside the storeroom, now wouldn't it?"

"I won't do anything. Please, man, have a heart."

Joe picked up the keys. "Key to the storeroom?"

"The big brass colored one."

"Lead the way." When the man turned his back, Joe put the gun in his lap on top of the bag and pushed himself along in the chair behind the stumbling clerk. They went straight down the wide aisle between lines of refrigerators and freezers and then turned right. The storeroom was a large closet filled with shelves.

"Go inside and get face down on the floor. There's a good fellow. I promise I won't hurt you."

"Oh, please. Thank you, Jesus."

The poor son of a bitch was so upset and then so relieved to be escaping death that Joe felt like a good Samaritan for not hurting him. He slammed the door and locked it.

This had taken a lot longer than he'd figured. He'd taken a hell of a chance, pulling something like this in broad daylight. Odd, though, that he'd stayed so cool. Or maybe not so odd. The memories, all the moves were still there, only now he was on the other side of the law.

As soon as he was out of the store and around the corner, he hid behind a Dumpster that smelled like it was filled with rotting meat, and slipped out of his disguise. He made his movements smooth and economical and kept his senses on full alert so as not to leave a speck of evidence. He wished he could leave the wheelchair, but it would be traceable. Besides, Freddy needed it.

He went back to Oak Street by a roundabout route, taking an extra twenty minutes to cruise into downtown Avalon and past the Pyramid Building, before he swung back toward home. He parked in the garage to count the money. A little over four hundred dollars. More than he expected from an out of the way place like the appliance shop. He locked the money and the Luger in the wooden case.

Martha was standing in her front yard, hands on her hips, when Joe wheeled the chair back. Her expression could have scared off Attila the Hun. Joe felt his stomach clench.

"There better be a real good reason for you to have that chair, Joe Tremaine."

He took a second to compose his expression. "Found it over near my place. And I found this on the seat." He flipped his wallet open and drew out a twenty, holding it out to her.

Martha snatched the money and shoved it down the front of her dress. "Ask and ye shall receive. I've been on my knees praying that the heartless thief who stole Freddy's chair would bring it back, so I could take him to the park this afternoon. He's been fretting something awful about being stuck inside, and you know I don't want to ruin his good chair. Umm-hmm. The Lord answers all righteous prayers."

"You didn't by any chance ask the Lord to wreak vengeance upon the chair thief, did you Martha?"

"Vengeance belongs to the Lord." She gazed at him steadily. "Thanks for bringing the chair back. You stay out of trouble."

"That's the plan." He started down the sidewalk and then turned to look back at her. "Martha? I oiled those wheels for you. Least I could do."

"You're on my prayer list, Joe."

Chapter Eight

Dave chatted with co-workers waiting for the elevator, most of them from his team, telling them about his unproductive lunch hour calling Washington.

"Okay, Markham-Hook is still going to dump us, but maybe if we make our voices heard, they'll think twice about doing the same thing next year or the year after."

"You're tilting at windmills, Dave." Norah McCabe looked at him with sorrowful eyes.

Norah stood in front of the others, but now he saw they stood on one side of the mirrored hallway and he was alone opposite them. They fixed him in a collective stare. If he didn't know better, he'd think he had vomit dripping down his face.

"Don't any of you get it? They did this to us because we let them."

A faint flush spread across Norah's face and she turned her back. A chime sounded and the elevator doors slid open, revealing yellow roses in the wall vases, the flower of the day. When the others boarded, the elevator wasn't full, but Dave stepped away. He waited for the next one and rode up alone.

He'd always considered himself as patriotic as anyone, maybe more so than most. Didn't he have a miniature American flag flying from the top of his monitor? And a flag lapel pin that he wore at least once a week? A flag bumper sticker on the Behemoth? Why did his co-workers act as if there were something wrong with disagreeing with laws that you believed were bad? Wasn't it better to do your own thinking than to let the government tell you how you ought to feel, the way they did in those countries ruled by dictators?

Dave straightened his shoulders. Yeah, you had to walk the path you believed was right, even if it was a lonely and unpopular walk. He'd show them. Right now, he didn't quite know who "they" were or how he was going to show them, but people were going to know one day that Dave Griffin had stood up for what was right.

He knew something big was going down when Ken's boss's boss, Art Mahaffey, paid a visit to his cubicle in the middle of the afternoon. Rex, murmuring apologies for unintentionally causing him grief by taking his job and promising to be on time in the morning, had just left to attend a meeting for new hires in one of the other company buildings. No doubt Mahaffey was well aware that Rex was not around to serve as a witness.

Dave stood, and they shook hands. His skills of perception had definitely sharpened since Friday's announcement about the mass firing. He'd have to rank Mahaffey a nine out of ten on the "looks like he's going to rip some poor slob a new one" scale. Besides, Art Mahaffey was too high up to pay social calls to regular programmers like Dave. Alarm signals raced to his fight or flight center and his body received a jolt of adrenaline that made his leg muscles cramp up.

"Let's take a break and step into my office for a few minutes, Dave, if you don't mind."

Of course he minded. He'd rather take the stairs down all twenty-five floors to the lobby than go with Mahaffey to get chewed out.

"Sure," he croaked. Amazing how he could still manage to speak even though his mouth was as dry as rotted leather and the muscles across his shoulders were locked into a hard bar.

He marched down the hall after Mahaffey. His arms and legs were so stiff they swung forward like sticks, threatening to bang into anyone who got too close. He searched his mind, trying to come up with a reason for the summons to the big corner office at the end of the hall. Had Rex complained about his knowledge transfer skills? Maybe Beth's father or Denton Harris had interfered. If they had, he wouldn't take the job if it meant a co-worker were replaced. Otherwise--well, he supposed it was okay to keep his job if another spot were added. No, if they'd decided they wanted to keep him, they wouldn't have sent Mahaffey.

Mahaffey pushed open his door and motioned Dave in ahead of him. A woman--short, big-haired, middle-aged--sat in a chair next to the desk. The cloying scent of her gardenia perfume had settled on every surface, and Dave tried not to breathe. Ken sat next to her, picking non-existent debris off his jacket, his fingers wriggling like fat earthworms against the dark plaid. He didn't look up.

Mahaffey performed the introduction. The woman was Sandra Brewster from personnel.

Dave sat where directed, in a cushioned chair by the door. Mahaffey perched on the edge of his desk and cleared his throat. It sounded like he had a wad of mucus the size of a golf ball stuck somewhere behind his tonsils.

"The reason we've called you in, Dave, is that we've had a report that you've been, ah, calling government officials, things like that."

Mahaffey said, "calling government officials," like he might say "peeing in the lobby fountain at lunch time." He pursed his lips and walked his fingertips back and forth across the front of piece three of his three-piece suit.

"Yes, I called some people," Dave admitted, acid washing up his throat. "This is your business because?"

Jesus, what a nightmare. How did they know about the calls? Did the government rat on you to your employer if they didn't like what you said? Had the U.S. Department of Labor called John Victor Harris and said Dave Griffin needed his ass kicked?

"Well, Dave, here at Markham-Hook Conglomerate we don't like trouble and we don't like troublemakers. Wouldn't you say that's a reasonable way to do business?"

"Well, yes, Art, I feel the same way."

"I'm glad to hear that. Really glad." Mahaffey nodded about fifty times, his head bobbing mechanically. "You see, with all the transitions we're undergoing, we like things to run smoothly. You understand that, don't you?"

He was using a telemarketing technique, asking obvious questions to get the potential buyer to keep saying yes. *Well, Mr. Griffin, every home needs energy efficient windows so all the expensive air-conditioning isn't sucked out into the environment. Wouldn't you agree that's a true statement? Like every American, you want your home to look good and be energy efficient, agreed? Now may I set you up for an appointment with our most persistent and annoying salesman, Mr. Griffin?*

"I understand you don't want people raising a fuss about losing their jobs and making the company look bad." Dave chose his words carefully.

Mahaffey slid back on his desk and steepled his fingers, before tapping them gently against his chin. "Dave, this is a done deal. Trying to stir up opposition, especially here in the very halls of the Pyramid Building, could prove extremely costly to you."

Someone at the elevator when he came back from lunch had told on him. He didn't think it was Norah. She was the type who minded her own business. It was probably the pinch-faced guy standing behind her wearing an expression that made you think someone was twisting his nipples. He was an assistant team lead from the forty-first floor and maybe he thought that made him an executive. Dave supposed he'd never know. He should have kept his mouth shut, instead of rattling off like an overexcited fifteen-year-old talking about a bully in gym class, but how was he to anticipate that Markham-Hook Conglomerate would react as if he'd committed high treason? Especially here, in the very halls of the Pyramid Building.

"I didn't look at it as stirring up opposition." He resisted the urge to bite his nails by shoving his hands under his thighs.

"That's good, Dave. I'm glad to hear that you didn't have negative intentions." Mahaffey slid off the desk and turned to Ken and to Sandra Brewster from personnel, and they were quick to nod their agreement.

Oh, happy day. Dave Griffin did not have negative intentions. Okay, bad ten minutes in the principal's office. He'd be sure to stop stirring up opposition, especially since his co-workers were too wimpy to join in, and at least one of them was a narc. He stood, and Mahaffey held up a hand. Mahaffey was not wearing a you-are-dismissed expression.

"Just one more thing." He picked up a paper from his desk. "We need you to sign something before you leave my office."

"Sign what?" Dave glanced at his watch. If he didn't get back to his desk and put in some work on his project, he'd be late getting out of here and he'd get caught in traffic, all of which would make him late for his meeting with Beth. "You want me to sign that I understand my right to remain silent and anything I say can and will be used against me, is that it?"

Twin red circles appeared high on Mahaffey's cheeks. "It's just a promise to keep your views on company policy to yourself while on company property and on company time. And a loyalty oath for our files."

"A loyalty oath?" His voice cracked.

He took the paper from Mahaffey and studied it, bringing it a couple of inches nearer his eyes to decipher the fine print. He'd never seen anything like this. He was sure it had been especially crafted for him, probably by a company lawyer with a dozen degrees in corporate law.

If he signed, it meant that he agreed to refrain from complaining about company policy, he would accept the terms of his severance without disclosing them to anyone, and he would refrain from discussing Markham-Hook Conglomerate employment policy with government officials or the media. Forever. There was a lot more about how he recognized that no employer was perfect, but in the interests of smooth business operation and the common good, he would not encourage anti-corporate, anti-business, anti-government viewpoints.

They couldn't be serious. They couldn't really expect him to sign away his rights to freedom of speech and freedom of opinion or any other freedoms guaranteed to him by the U.S. Constitution.

Dave looked up to see Sandra Brewster waving a silver and gold Markham-Hook Conglomerate pen at him. He'd like to tell them what they could do with their loyalty oath, but he was too close to exploding.

"No," he said softly. He ripped the paper in two. He turned from side to side hunting a trash can and when he didn't find one, he crumpled the paper and stuffed it in his pocket. No one was going to be able to accuse Dave Griffin of littering.

Ken winced and screwed up his face so that he looked like a baboon that just bit into a rotten orange. Mahaffey shrugged. Dave realized with a jolt that Mahaffey had known all along he wouldn't sign. They wanted to get rid of him for causing trouble, and he'd just given them the excuse they needed. But this wasn't a communist country--he could express whatever opinions he wanted.

"I'd like that back, please." Mahaffey pointed to Dave's pocket.

Dave dragged out what was left of the loyalty oath and handed it over. He could see why they wouldn't want him keeping it. He might give it to a reporter who'd write up a story that embarrassed Markham-Hook when word got out that they tried to force an employee to sign away his constitutional rights.

Sandra Brewster quietly left the room. Dave moved half a step to follow her out the door, and Mahaffey told him to wait. A roaring sound filled his ears, and he felt wobbly enough to have to collapse back into the chair.

"I'm sorry, Dave. Your position with the company is terminated as of this moment. Wait here until the security officers arrive to collect all company property from you and escort you out of the building."

"Why the extreme measures to keep me quiet?"

"We're not trying to keep anyone quiet." Mahaffey looked at Ken Archer in feigned surprise. "But these days an employer can't be too careful with disgruntled employees. Surely you know that."

"Disgruntled?" Was disgruntled a Markham-Hook euphemism for angry, betrayed, and disbelieving? "Are you afraid I'll bring in an Uzi and shoot the place up or something?"

Mahaffey darted his eyes from side to side. "Of course not. We didn't think anything of the kind."

"If I was going to do something like that and I'd signed your stupid agreement, I still could have come in tomorrow and made Swiss cheese out of this building. But then I guess you could add that to the list of charges when they hauled me to jail. 'Last, but not least, Mr. Griffin is charged with violating an oath of loyalty.' What's the prison term on that anyway? Think the cops would offer me a plea bargain if I signed an oath and promised to behave?"

"I think you've said quite enough. Security's here. Let's go."

They did everything but handcuff him. Mahaffey led the way back to his cubicle, marching in front of him with his back held stiff. Two burly security guards flanked him on either side and Ken followed a few paces behind, his head bowed. In addition to his shoes swishing against the carpet, Dave could hear Ken sighing deeply every few seconds, sounding like an air mattress being gradually deflated.

As they passed the cubicles of his co-workers, all activity stopped. Stares from eyes widened by disbelief burned into him. Dave thrust out his jaw. Mahaffey could have waited till the rest of the team left before they paraded him down the hall like a captured spy. But then that would have cost Markham-Hook the deterrent value inherent in letting the other inmates see what happened to a rebellious employee. Now none of them would dare to even sneeze without company permission.

He had to turn in his security badge and his key card. Then they let him collect his personal property and dump it into a cardboard box one of the guards scavenged from the recycle bin in the break room. He gathered his briefcase, his computer magazines and books, his pencils and pens, his Dollywood pencil sharpener, and framed pictures of his grandmother and his parents. When the box was full, he picked up his miniature American flag and taped it upright to the front of the box so it was still flying proudly when he left the building with his escort. The guards didn't try to prevent him from using a hunk of company tape. Probably, when they thought about it later, they'd slap their heads and feel stupid that they hadn't ripped the tape out of his thieving hands.

Dave could muster only one positive feeling as he drove the Behemoth out of the parking garage for the last time--he was glad he wouldn't have to train his own replacement. It hadn't felt right from the beginning and it had felt even less right when he actually tried it.

◦◦◦

When he strode into Avalon Castle that evening, he stopped near the hostess station to get his bearings. Beth was already there, settled at a table for two next to a massive stone fireplace in a back corner of the room. The room was dark, the only light coming from candles flickering on the tables and in wall sconces. Tunic-clad minimum wage serfs quietly bussed tables while lords and ladies wearing costumes representing the finest in medieval attire took orders from hungry diners. Madrigal singers accompanied by lute players strolled the room making themselves heard over the clink of silverware and the hum of a few dozen conversations.

Beth stood when he got to the table and her welcoming kiss was so brief, he almost couldn't feel her lips brush against his own.

He put his hands on her shoulders and stepped back to study her expression. "You feeling okay, Beth?"

"Of course. But we do have something to discuss, don't we?"

At least she was getting right to the point. He liked that. He couldn't see that there was anything to be gained by dancing around the subject while trying to down a multi-course meal, maybe waiting even longer if Beth decided to visit the "Damsels" to freshen her make-up.

"If I didn't want to give us a chance, we wouldn't be meeting tonight. Besides, I think it's tacky to break up over the phone, if that's what it comes down to."

Break up? He wanted them to be at his house where he could tell her that he got fired an hour ago, and the company treated him like an especially nasty disease, shaming him in front of everyone on his team. He wanted to be home where he could cry on her shoulder, and she could stroke his hair and tell him, "It's okay."

Instead, he had to get through yet one more nightmare scene in a day that could have been scripted by his worst enemy. His face burned as he remembered each second in Mahaffey's office.

"I've ordered Evian for myself. Call the waiter over and tell him what you want to drink and ask him for menus." Her eyes were cold, the dark blue having mysteriously turned to a color somewhere between steel and winter rain.

For God's sake, she didn't have to tell him how to place an order in a restaurant. He didn't want to eat and drink anyway. They sat, and he put his hand over hers, hoping she didn't notice the chill flowing from his fingers. After a moment, she slid her hand free and rested it in her lap.

That bad. He could delay the news about the job until they'd eaten or until they'd hashed out their relationship problems, but that wasn't his way. His grandmother was fond of telling people that her Dave was born under the sign of Leo, not that she believed in that pagan nonsense, and he had the heart of a lion.

"I got fired today."

Beth turned to look at him, a glass of lemon-wedged Evian halfway to her mouth. "Fired? As in you're unemployed right this second instead of in another month?" She lowered the glass and pulled her lips into a tight line.

"Exactly."

"What did you do?" The words came out separated by little spaces as if each were its own sentence.

Dave watched the play of emotions across her face. Why did she assume he'd done something? Why couldn't it be, "What's the problem with those bastards at Markham-Hook?"

"My crime was to call government offices to complain about Markham-Hook's dumping American workers. Then I told some people waiting for the elevator what I'd done and I guess I suggested they do the same. Workers of the world unite and all that."

"How stupid." She rolled her eyes. "What were you thinking?"

"I was thinking I was in the United States. I was thinking I could speak freely without a bunch of thought police reporting me to their superiors." He wanted to get up and pace, but he fought the urge down. "Apparently it's against company policy to do your own thinking."

"So they just walked up and fired you?"

"Not exactly. They asked me to sign a loyalty oath."

"Did you?" Her eyes bored into him.

"Don't you already know the answer to that?"

"I guess I do. Mr. Truth, Justice, and the American Way had to prove he cared more about some stupid ideal than he does about his own girlfriend."

"It's not a competition between you and my ideals."

"Then what is it? I don't want you to think I'm shallow. But I've been thinking really hard since Friday. None of this had to happen with your job. Daddy or my friends would have helped if I'd asked. But now--well, you have to see, even Daddy can't get you another position at the company after what you did. You had a choice and you wouldn't do what was best." She ducked her head to stare at the tabletop.

"Beth, be reasonable. I don't have to keep working at Markham-Hook Conglomerate for us to keep dating."

"Yes, you do."

They were going in circles. He gripped the table edge with both hands until his knuckles ached. "You can't control me. I'm not a toy that your daddy can get for you and that you can toss out when you're done playing date-the-hick."

He knew from the subtle change of expression around her eyes he'd gone too far. If she slapped him right now, he wouldn't have blamed her. But Beth's face was a wooden mask.

"You're accusing me of using you. But isn't that exactly what you did to me? Weren't you proud of yourself for moving up the social ladder when I started going out with you last month?"

He blinked. The words cut, and yet he had to admit, she was at least partially right. His heart wanted him to apologize, to say he should have let her family or friends move him ahead of someone else on the job list, but his mind wouldn't let him. A man needed his self-respect.

"It's over. Not because you don't have a job, but because you didn't care enough about us to let me help you stay on at Markham-Hook. And now we both see that what we wanted from the relationship was two different things."

"I'm sorry." He reached toward her and then let his hand drop to his side. He didn't want to leave her alone, but Beth had turned her back and was already digging her cell phone out of her purse. He knew she'd call one of her friends or maybe even her parents. Beth wasn't the one who was going to end up alone tonight.

Chapter Nine

Dave didn't wake up the next morning, he merely rolled out of bed. You couldn't honestly say you woke up if you'd never been to sleep in the first place, he mused as he stared at his crumpled face in the mirror over his bathroom sink. He didn't need to shave or shower this morning. Why should he when all he had to do was spend the day on the Internet looking for a job? But what if someone came to the door selling magazines, and he was still wandering around the house in the middle of the afternoon wearing a tee shirt and boxers, his face a stubbled picture of defeat? He forced himself to get cleaned up and slap on a pair of jeans and a golf shirt.

He dragged the phone off its cradle and called the North Carolina Employment Security Commission, finally getting past a busy signal on his tenth try. They gave him an appointment for the following Monday. His unemployment pay would be nothing compared to what he'd been earning and not half enough to cover his current expenses. But he could buy groceries and gas and pay his utilities.

He'd have to put his student loans on deferment. God, it had cost thousands to get his degree, money he'd planned on paying back from his earnings in the field of computer programming. He felt stupid, as if he'd fallen for a con man's trick.

Step right up and get your high tech degree. Don't worry about the cost, just sign on the dotted line. Hot tech field, plenty of good-paying jobs. Education is the key.

Late in the afternoon he wandered into the kitchen, realizing he hadn't eaten anything all day except for a handful of stale Cheez Its he'd found in a box under his desk. The refrigerator offered only some questionable Hamburger Helper and a bowl of something well-fuzzed with a thriving mold colony. He tossed them in the trash and drove the Behemoth a couple of miles to the Foodarama.

"Bananas, apples, oranges, lettuce, potatoes," he muttered, piling fruit and vegetables into his cart. Mawmaw always said fresh fruit and vegetables were the best nutrition value and he definitely needed to get best value if his unemployment were to stretch out for months. He turned a corner, still muttering the names of produce that had made the cut for a place in his cart. Metal clashed against metal and he realized he'd collided with a cart piloted by a familiar figure.

"George," he said, smiling at his former co-worker as if they hadn't seen each other for months. Had it really been only yesterday when George had stood outside Dave's cube griping about how he wasn't going to train foreign imports to take his job unless hell froze over? "How's life in the big conglomerate?"

George's grip tightened on his cart handle. His knuckles whitened until they looked like a row of oversized teeth. He darted his glance to the side, where a sign offered a buy one get one free sale on rutabagas and then, with obvious reluctance, redirected his attention to Dave.

"Fine. I'm in a hell of a hurry. Wife's parents are visiting. Got to bring home the ingredients for a cook-out."

Dave's stomach clenched. "I'm not contagious."

"No offense meant."

"Well, plenty of offense taken. How do you get off treating me like I'm a disease? You're the one who got suckered into training your own replacement. Guess hell froze over since yesterday morning. If you and all the rest of the programmers who are being so accommodating would raise a fuss with Washington and then tell Markham-Hook where to stick it, they couldn't replace you because the new people wouldn't have a clue how the system works."

George raised one hairy paw as if to whack Dave out of his way. His face went crimson. "It's pretty easy for you to talk. You've got only your own hide to worry about. I've been at Markham-Hook for more than twenty years. I get almost a year's pay as severance. You want me to go home to my two daughters in college and my wife who can't work because she has Lupus and say, 'We're going to live in the car because I've turned down the severance and I won't train my replacement?' Listen, you self-righteous jackass, I'll do whatever it takes."

He backed his cart loose from Dave's and rammed it into the only available space, doing a hit and run on a box of Corn Chex before he swung around a corner.

Dave stood where he was for a good five minutes until an elderly woman told him he was blocking her access to the Raisin Bran. She shook her finger at him. "Either decide on a cereal or move on, young man."

"Sorry," he muttered.

He shoved his cart forward, following the aroma of fresh baked bread. He didn't feel hungry anymore, but he picked up a loaf of Italian bread and ordered himself to finish shopping. When he crossed paths with George again in the check-out line, George did everything except hold up two crossed fingers in a hex-busting sign. Dave knew that in his position he'd do exactly the same--take the hush money and pray for a miracle.

He told himself he had no reason to feel shame, but he kept his head down, his gaze trained on the conveyor belt looping endlessly toward the end of the counter. The scanner beeped the final item through and the cashier rang up his total with a cheery, "Find everything okay, sir?"

"Yeah, debit." He pressed the yes button for amount approved, all the while wondering how he'd manage after the last direct deposit from Markham-Hook went into his account and he used up the last of his savings and unemployment money. Would alarm bells go off when the amount wasn't approved? Would the cashier call security to escort him empty-handed from the grocery while customers with cash clutched their wallets to their chests and shot him looks of disgust?

Once he'd seen a woman with three pale-faced kids in tow get turned down to cash a check. She'd said she'd lost her job. She'd quietly left the Foodarama, and Dave had stared after her like all the other shoppers at the checkout.

Heat streaked up his face at the memory. She'd only been trying to score some milk and cereal for her family. Why hadn't he stepped forward and given her a few dollars, so she could feed her kids? Now he understood. It wasn't enough to just say you were sorry when someone lost a job. And until you'd been there, you couldn't know the feelings of worthlessness and failure, the sleepless nights, the depression and the hopelessness. And this was only his first day of unemployment, his first day of wondering if his life would ever be more than a day to day struggle to belong in a work world that didn't want him any more.

"Sir? Sir?"

Dave jerked his attention back to the present. The cashier was eyeing him like she might be wondering if he'd lost his mind somewhere back in aisle three among the canned goods.

"Paper or plastic, sir?"

"I don't give a...I mean, plastic is fine."

Dave checked the job boards every day. By Friday, there'd been no new programming jobs posted, and there were no bright spots in his first dismal week of joblessness. Not unless he wanted to make thousands every day from the privacy of his own home using only his computer and the knowledge supplied by a company that sold dog food through multi-level marketing. Not just any dog food, you understand. Fido Banquet would make any canine shiny, healthy, smart, and obedient. It probably also cleaned your carpet if Fido had an accident, and Dave could get in on the ground floor, if he acted now to commit to purchasing a mere three-hundred bucks worth of product monthly and signed up only twelve new distributors.

An email with "good jobs here" in the subject line caught his eye. He didn't recognize the sender until he read the message. Rex, his trainee from India, had sent him a list of headhunters and job boards from the Internet, sites that Dave had already hit multiple times. Pretty basic stuff that everyone looking for a job knew about, unless they were brain dead.

Rex had written he was very sorry Dave had to leave, especially since Rex was not getting on well with George, who was not so informative or so polite as Dave. He hoped Dave found the list productive in his job search.

Dave was glad he'd just swallowed the last mouthful of his coffee or it would have shot across the table and sprayed the kitchen wallpaper patterned with red roosters strutting on a sunny yellow background. He thought about sending back an email telling Rex he'd already found a job and was making a gazillion dollars a year, but something inside him was touched. Maybe Rex wasn't really serious about feeling sorry for him and maybe he didn't care for one second whether or not Dave found a job. But Dave chose to take Rex's attempt to help at face value. He emailed his thanks.

Still, he didn't think there was any hope. He'd seen ads on the net for H-1B or L-1 visa programmers only--for jobs in the U.S. So much for having to give Americans first crack at the jobs or pay an American wage like all the newspaper articles claimed. You'd think reporters would get the facts straight before they printed up corporate lies.

Dave had already decided not to make a house payment this month, as well as to skip the payment on the Behemoth because he didn't want to use up his cash until he started to collect unemployment. He guessed he might as well consider he'd missed on the credit card, though it wasn't due yet. If he got a job, he could pay the penalties and catch up on the back payments. If not--then bankruptcy and a return to the mountains to live with his grandmother were his only options.

He cringed inwardly at the thought. Returning to the mountains was something he'd avoid until they pried him loose from his house and tossed him in the street. Why burden his seventy-two-year-old grandmother?

⁂

Joe bought a month's supply of Seizure-Out, thanks to the money stolen from the appliance store added to what he'd earned fixing a porch. After that, he didn't know. Maybe a job fairy would put in an appearance before he was forced to commit another robbery. He turned on the tap at the kitchen sink and filled a glass with water. Today was his second day on the new pills. So far he couldn't detect any problems, other than a headache that came and went. One kind of poison or another, there was no free ride. His first medicine, as if he didn't already feel bad enough, had depressed him so that he'd have eaten a bullet if it weren't for Lark. At least the Seizure-Out hadn't compounded the problem. Not yet, anyway.

He knew that--long term--robbing stores was going to get him caught or killed, but what the hell else was he supposed to do? The tires on his truck had only the barest hint of tread left and the engine was running rough. Back when he had a job, he could have bought a new truck if he wanted, but now mechanical problems meant disaster and another step down the short road to homelessness.

⁂

Dave set his alarm to get him up early Monday morning. He dressed in business clothes and scrounged a tie from the back of his closet. At least his appointment was late in the morning, so he'd miss the rush hour.

The parking lot at the state unemployment office was filled to overflowing with cars, bicycles and even shopping carts crammed with empty bottles and aluminum cans and pushed up close to the crumbling red bricks at the side of the building. Dave circled the block twice and finally gave up and cruised into a metered lot. Before he got out of the car, he stared through the windshield, past the closely jammed buildings lining the expensive real estate of Avalon's Financial Street and toward the horizon where gray clouds formed in the darkening sky. Rain for sure. Oh, well, the Behemoth needed a good washing and he couldn't afford to pay for a car wash.

He joined a mob of other jobless people pushing into the unemployment office and sat on a hard wooden bench to listen for his name to be called. The air in the room smelled of nothing identifiable, just something stale, as though nothing were ever new in this room, not even the sad stories about loss of income and lives shattered. A couple of times he caught a whiff of cherry flavoring. He finally turned around to look for the source and spotted a child sucking on a piece of candy, red coloring running down her chin and onto her pink T-shirt.

She grinned at him, and he grinned back. The kid was clueless. She didn't know her mom was out of work and that she was clutching what might be her last piece of candy for a long while. He'd read somewhere about a kind of meditation called being in the moment that was supposed to make you happy and calm because you weren't thinking about the past or worrying over the future. Seemed to be working okay for the kid. Maybe he ought to try it. His nerves were twanging under his skin, and it was all he could do to keep from getting up to pace between the bench and the window.

He cut his eyes sideways and looked at his benchmates. Some, like Dave, were dressed in business clothes. Others wore faded, shapeless outfits that could have come from the thrift store. A few places to his right he spotted a guy he was sure worked for Markham-Hook. He was a middle manager in charge of the insurance programming teams. Used to be, anyway.

"David Griffin."

He jumped and looked up to see an attractive woman standing in front of the bullpen and scanning the crowd.

"Yes." He waved his hand, made eye contact, and she nodded.

"I'm Mrs. Cartwright." She motioned for him to follow.

They walked down a long hallway, past cubicles filled with unemployment counselors and their clients engaged in earnest conversation, and past bulletin boards dotted with yellowed sheets of paper announcing job vacancies from two years ago. The threadbare carpet, once blue, but now more of a gray-brown if it was any color at all, was showing concrete floor in places where it was worn through.

Mrs. Cartwright occupied the last cube in the building. They'd ended up in a dark corner with three empty cubes between them and the next employment counselor. Despite the surroundings, she'd made an attempt to fix her place up. She'd hung pictures of kittens on the wall in front of her desk and a vase of artificial flowers--blue and yellow and red--rested on her file cabinet.

The odor was different here--cinnamon, with maybe cloves mixed in. The source was an unlit candle next to the flowers. He'd already eaten, oatmeal topped with a sliced banana, but suddenly wished he had a cinnamon bun and a cup of coffee.

Jobless Recovery

"Take a seat, Mr. Griffin."

She indicated the rusty folding chair beside her desk. Dave sat and felt the chair tilt under him. Mrs. Cartwright sat in the other seat, a crooked desk chair with the stuffing coming out of the back. Nothing a little duct tape wouldn't fix.

"So you used to work for Markham-Hook? We've gotten a lot of their people in the past few weeks." She pawed through a stack of file folders on her desk and pulled out a set of forms clipped together at the top.

Dave adjusted his tie and tried to get comfortable on the hard metal of his chair. The chair tilted again, and he noticed that one of the rubber tips for the legs was missing. "Ex-people."

"Excuse me?" Mrs. Cartwright didn't look amused.

"Sorry."

She was obviously a busy lady, and besides, he just wanted to get this show over with. The worn-out building, the jobless crowd in the waiting room, the expressions of despair, made him feel like going out and lighting a candle in the nearest church.

While she entered his personal information into the system, the tension that had him wound up like newly tightened guitar strings went even tighter. He had a college degree and this was the United States. Why didn't someone wake him up and tell him it was all a terrible dream?

"Oh." Mrs. Cartwright's brown eyes narrowed, and then she pursed her lips.

Dave's fifth grade teacher used to take on that same expression just before she announced that she knew who'd permanently attached her lunch bag to her desk with Super Glue, and the culprit--usually Morgan Sipes, a kid with poor impulse control--was destined for disciplinary action. Dave slunk down in his chair as though a ruler were about to descend on his head.

"It says here you were terminated from your last position." She looked at him with disapproving eyes.

"Terminated?" Dave tried to wrap his thoughts around the word. Terminated sounded like what happened to unwanted dogs and cats down at the animal shelter. He forced a smile and launched an explanation. "That's right, they eliminated my position. Markham-Hook replaced American programmers with cheaper foreign programmers."

"Markham-Hook Conglomerate has reported that you were terminated for insubordination. Firing for cause means you don't qualify for benefits."

"But--all I did was refuse to sign a loyalty oath. Then they escorted me out."

"I really am sorry." Mrs. Cartwright took off her glasses and placed them on her desk. The corners of her mouth drooped.

She did look sad, he had to admit. The real cause might be that she found her goldfish belly up in its tank this morning, but right now he didn't care. The checks he'd counted on to help him get by while he looked for work weren't going to materialize. You'd think a huge company like Markham-Hook would be too big to exact petty revenge against a former employee who hadn't fallen into line with the rest of the sheep.

The way things were, you played the game Markham-Hook's way and you lost your job. You played the game Dave's way and you lost your job sooner. Same outcome, only less money. At least he didn't have to suffer through the demoralizing task of transferring his knowledge to the man who replaced him.

"You still qualify for training and for access to the job bank." Mrs. Cartwright's expression brightened. She reapplied her glasses and poised her fingers over her keyboard waiting for Dave's next move. Very professional, Mrs. Cartwright.

"Training?"

"The government collects fees from the H-1B visas and uses the money to train former programmers so they can get jobs. Let's see." She hit a few keys. "We have PC technician. That should help you get back into the computer field. Or would you prefer network specialist?"

Dave bit back a rude remark, one that would earn him a serious lecture from his grandmother if she ever heard him say such words. It was not Mrs. Cartwright's fault that his elected officials decided to turn a highly-skilled, highly-educated, American programmer into a network specialist, a job which required only a high school diploma and a minimum of training.

"So are there actually jobs in those fields?"

"Well, no. And the waiting lists are unreal." Mrs. Cartwright didn't bother to punch in another search. "But you can take the training." When Dave didn't respond, she went on, "If computer classes don't suit, we have hairdresser, funeral counselor, and restaurant specialist. Of course, those classes are all full, but I can put you on the waiting list, and we should have a spot for you in nine or ten months."

He frowned. "Restaurant specialist?"

"That means, you know, food prep and so forth."

"In other words, the government will collect fees from the visas they used to import workers to take my computer programming job and use the money to teach me to make sandwiches."

"Sandwich making is not that bad." Mrs. Cartwright beamed at him. "Do you know it's recently been reclassified as manufacturing so it no longer has the stigma of being labeled low-skill?"

"Yeah, and the government can claim we've added millions of manufacturing jobs. Do they think we're that stupid?"

Mrs. Cartwright was no longer beaming. "Do you want the training or not?" She glanced at her watch.

Dave hauled himself out of his chair. "I'll let you know in a few months--if I haven't starved to death by then." He wondered if he should look into leaving his body to science to spare Mawmaw the funeral expenses after he starved.

Dave exited the unemployment office and stepped out into a downpour. Yellow pollen, what Mawmaw called nature's gold dust, floated on top of the water pouring into the storm sewers. Cars splashed by on the road in front of him, the drivers oblivious to the problems of the jobless. And why should they care? He'd been exactly like them a week ago.

Chapter Ten

Now in his second week of unemployment, Dave sat on the edge of his bed and mindlessly plucked the strings of the guitar his father had left him. He'd been awake for hours, his mind churning in panic. The thought came to him that other than the phone calls he'd made to Washington on the day he was fired, he hadn't done much about his situation.

Sitting in his house shooting off resumes and calling headhunters to beg for a job had not gotten him one step closer to gainful employment. All he had now was a dwindling savings account and damn little hope. He pondered his next move. If people in Washington were going to make laws that prevented Dave Griffin from keeping his job and getting a new one, then maybe it was time he paid them a visit. It couldn't hurt, could it, to give them some feedback?

In the morning, he made a series of calls to Washington. He'd imagined that since the voters were the ones who put people in office, the voters would have a little clout. But no one had time for him, except for Senator Buford Drake, who was up for reelection in the fall. Senator Drake, it turned out, had regular weekly meetings with voters from his district. Usually these meetings were booked up, but someone had canceled, so Dave was penciled in for Thursday afternoon.

The only thing was, his grandmother was planning to visit on Thursday. He suspected she wanted to talk him into returning to the mountains. Dave couldn't do that. He was not going to be a parasite, living off his grandmother's social security. He called her to reschedule.

"Senator Drake? You're going to meet with a real United States senator? That's something, sugarbiscuit. Wait till I tell Millie and the rest of the ladies in Sunday school. When are you going?"

"That's the trouble, Mawmaw. Thursday is the only time he can fit me in."

"Oh." Long pause. "I sure was looking forward to seeing you. You know I need to see for myself that you're eating right."

"Can you come next week instead?" He hadn't seen his grandmother since before he lost his job, but if he didn't talk to Senator Drake this week, he'd have to wait at least a month. He heard her draw her breath in sharply.

"Sugarbiscuit, I've got the best idea. I've always wanted to see the Lincoln Memorial and the Washington Monument and Arlington. We could see all those places and more, if I go with you." She sounded like a little kid excited over Christmas, but Dave was shaking his head as if she could see him over the phone lines.

"I'm not so sure that's a good idea. I mean, Mawmaw, I don't need a babysitter. What kind of impression would that make?"

"If that's your excuse, David, then it's no excuse at all. I can wait outside or go visit a museum or something while you're in the Senator's office."

"Sure, I guess that would work." Trips with Mawmaw had been few while he was growing up and had usually involved budget motels and the embarrassment of watching his grandmother lay down the law to strangers she thought were out to cheat her. But this might be Mawmaw's only chance to see the nation's capitol. Dave would manage.

Short of robbing a bank, Joe didn't have a way to get enough money to replace his truck tires. He knew of a store that might have cash in the register, an electronics place at the end of an isolated street. The owner did mostly repairs, but he ought to have a few hundred around. Lark was working. He could drive clear into the next county, rob a store, and still have time to clean the house and cook supper before she got in. She'd never suspect.

He got his blanket, his gloves and his hat, and tossed them into the truck. He'd get the Luger out of the cabinet when he got back from Martha's with the wheelchair.

At the end of the block, a couple of drug dealers who lived across from the park--a guy named Arthur, who called himself Wolf, and his brother, Bubba--were conducting a roadside sale with a woman in a banged-up Mercedes. Joe leaned against a tree to wait for them to move on. His heart was thudding with the same kind of excitement he used to get when he was working and he was about to make an arrest. Adrenaline, he guessed. You got the same jolt whether you were muscling a couple of bad guys into custody or you were on the other side of the law, scaring hell out of a shop owner and then making off with his money.

Bubba was leaning into the car, then Arthur shoved him out of the way and leaned into the car and finally they must have made a deal. Arthur took something out of his pocket, exchanged it for a wad of bills handed to him by the passenger, and then the Mercedes sped down the block. Joe peeled himself away from the tree, moving like he had a million years to waste, and watched the brothers disappear into their shack.

He left the sidewalk and set a diagonal course across Martha's grass-poor yard. The chair was parked against the porch--with a length of shiny chain looped through the wheels and padlocked to a porch column. Joe picked up the chain and felt the heavy links slide across his hands. He could snap the links in about two seconds with a bolt cutter. Or he might be able to jimmy the lock to keep from ruining the chain.

He wouldn't, though. He sensed her before he saw the front curtain twitch and then he made out a faint silhouette in the window. What was she up to, anyway? Martha knew he'd taken the chair the first time. Did she think she was protecting him from himself, maybe trying to be his keeper? Fool woman needed to get back to her phones and let Joe worry about Joe.

He went back home and sulked in his recliner for an hour. Revenge would be sweet. He could burn up the chair or come for it during the night. He could--what was he thinking? He rubbed his forehead. Look at him. Pathetic, thinking about burning up a poor person's wheelchair. He'd been feeling better since he started on the Seizure-Out, but today was definitely a setback.

Maybe Martha had done him a favor, given him a kick in the butt. He'd been thinking for a long while about finding an alternate source of income, and this might be just the time to find a new career. He had an idea, not a great one, but better than anything else he'd come up with during the bleak night hours, when his mind, recently so dull, had seemed to move into third gear. He felt good, better than he had in a long time, and he'd rediscovered his creative edge.

He had a window repair job and when that was finished, he headed directly to the nearest library, not taking time to get lunch, though he was hungry and on the verge of a headache. He followed a sign directing him to a back room behind the adult fiction and was relieved to find an Internet machine available with no waiting.

He logged on and Googled his way to a site that promised quick results for those who wanted to change careers. He skipped the promotional materials--he'd already made up his mind. Anyway, just thinking about getting his new degree made his heart pound faster and that aggravated the throbbing in his head, so he wanted to get home and lie down. He killed half a dozen pop-ups and then filled in the form to take divinity classes. Fifty dollars was a lot of money, but not when he figured how much he'd rake in after he graduated in a few days.

He still had to find an assistant and borrow the start up costs for the church. He knew Lark would gladly offer to help, but he didn't want her to give up her acting. It was the only piece of her dream she had left. As for borrowing the money, he knew where he could get what he needed when he had all the other pieces of the plan ready to go. After that, he'd have to make the church work so he could pay off the loan and stop the clock on the interest. No doubt about it--being poor was just one big sorry adventure after another.

Dave didn't want to look like he was off the farm for the first time as they strolled along in front of the Washington Monument. Silently he lectured himself--don't stare at the Capitol Dome or the Lincoln Memorial. Pay attention. Know where you're going.

He'd taken Mawmaw's advice and put on a suit this morning. He hoped his outfit made him look like a businessman who belonged here, but he kind of doubted it. Maybe the way he ogled the big elephant in the Smithsonian was a clue to anyone who wanted to assign him to the tourist category.

He stole a glance at his grandmother, marching along at his side with the aid of a stout wooden cane. A disposable camera hung from her neck by a cloth strap, and she'd slung a black purse the size of a Rottweiler over her shoulder. She probably had a week's worth of snacks, an entire first aid kit, and an arsenal of home remedies in her bag.

She caught him looking at her. "Isn't this fun?" She lifted her camera and aimed it for another shot of the Capitol Dome. "I'm going to have myself a whole picture album full of memories."

"Sure, Mawmaw." So far she'd only told off a guy who tried to sell them wax replicas of the Lincoln Memorial for a price she claimed would have bought them both lunch at a sit down restaurant. Dave was nervous as a caged cat in a roomful of dogs, but just watching her take so much enjoyment from being in the nation's capital made him feel better. He figured she'd planned it that way.

When it was time for him to go into the Senator's office, Mawmaw insisted on waiting outside because her ankles were starting to swell. "Anyway, I'm happy to sit on a bench and enjoy the weather. It's a beautiful day, sugarbiscuit. The Lord has blessed us with perfection. And, like you said on the phone, you sure don't need a babysitter."

Dave swiveled his head from side to side. The sun was bright, but not fierce, the cloudless sky was a pure Carolina blue, and hoards of people tramping by would ensure that no one tried to drag his grandmother off if he left her unattended for a few minutes.

"I'll be back soon. The Senator only sees people for a couple of minutes."

"His time must be very precious. Goodness, I almost forgot his gift." Mawmaw backed up to a bench and sat, dropping the cane on the ground and undoing the clasp on her purse so it yawned wide, looking like a giant cloth clam.

Gift? Dave winced. Please don't let it be one of her homemade "tonics," something oily and foul-smelling that ensured the recipient would develop a close acquaintance with the bathroom for a few days. He stood with his hands behind his back and watched her rummage. She pulled out a change purse, a bag of pretzels, a dozen or so neatly folded handkerchiefs, a tin of Altoids, and finally, a needlepoint in a wooden frame. She thrust the frame forward. "Look here, it says, 'Liberty and Justice for All' and there's an American flag smack in the middle of the picture."

Dave grimaced. The last thing he wanted was to sashay into Senator Drake's office with a piece of needlepoint. But it was fine workmanship and it was made by his very own grandmother. He thanked her and tucked the frame under his arm.

Ruby watched her grandson stride up the steps. Her poor sugarbiscuit was so sorrowful since losing his job. He looked like somebody stole his last nickel and then knocked him down and spit in his face. Not that she blamed him for being upset. Goodness, it was just that he took things so hard. When he was still in grade school, he used to stand up for all the younger children who got picked on by those awful Sipes kids, the school bullies. More than once, he'd come home with a bloody nose or a black eye, his clothes torn to rags. She'd warn him to be careful.

"But, Mawmaw," he'd say, his blue eyes flashing. "If nobody does anything, then bullies will keep on doing what they want."

"Hush, biscuit. Just because you're the same age as Morgan Sipes doesn't mean you're big enough to fight him."

He hadn't paid her the least bit of mind. She'd finally gotten so tired of patching his scrapes and bruises and listening to his tearful rages that she'd signed him up for karate lessons.

After that, sometimes he won against the Sipes kids and sometimes he didn't. She'd tried to get him to stay out of fights, but secretly she'd been proud of her grandson's crusade against the county bullies. She'd even told him he was her lion heart, a fighter to the end, though the bullies were still out there waiting to do their nasty work.

Now she wished she hadn't. Maybe if she'd done like Sue Ann Cooper, who punished her grandkids for getting into fights, he'd have learned to take life a little easier and let someone else do the fighting.

More than eight hundred computer programmers, he'd told her, along with fifteen hundred call center operators, had lost their jobs when Markham-Hook went with cheaper foreign labor. Not one of them, as far as Ruby Griffin knew, had even opened their mouths to say, "This is not right to expect Americans to buy your products and fight for your interests, but you won't let them work for you in their own country." Not one--except for her lion heart.

Here he was in Washington, daring to tell a U.S. senator what had happened at Markham-Hook. David was a smart boy. But Ruby knew as sure as she knew that tender green grass came up in the spring, Senator Drake didn't care one bit for all the people out of work in this country. Oh, he said he did. But he'd been in office too long and he wore the hypocritical look of a man who'd convinced himself all the lies out of the mouth of Markham-Hook's CEO were straight from the Good Book. If he wasn't raking in cash from John Victor Harris and calling it campaign contributions, then Ruby Griffin wasn't a seventy-two-year-old woman from Hidden Springs, North Carolina.

She could have told David, could have told him what he was up against, but he wouldn't be her lion heart if he didn't have to go see for himself. She'd enjoy the sunshine, let it tickle her face and warm her bones, and she'd watch the tourists tramp by chatting about the scenery like it was all that different from what they had back home, while he went in and rammed his head into a brick wall.

Then they'd drive back to North Carolina in his big car with the seats that smelled like a saddle shop, and she'd soothe his wounded feelings, tell him how much she loved him and how brave he was. And she'd pray he'd find another job soon, so he could help her out. She didn't dare tell him about the tax bill for the farm, how a sewer line was going in for a new development of vacation homes for rich people and how she had to pay a special assessment, but she didn't have the money. Sugarbiscuit sure didn't need more troubles on his young shoulders.

A male staffer, who introduced himself as Douglas, ushered people in and out of the Senator's inner sanctum with practiced efficiency, his manicured hands signaling and his well-modulated voice giving quiet instructions. He had the system down to a fine science. Door opened, visitor out. Signal next visitor. Door closed. Wait five minutes. Repeat procedure.

When it was Dave's turn, Douglas took the needlepoint from him and examined it millimeter by millimeter, as though he suspected Dave might have concealed a time bomb among the stitches. When he finally handed it back, Dave was sure he could detect a smirk forming on the man's ferret face.

"My grandmother made it for the Senator," Dave said.

"Sure." He signaled for Dave to step into the room where the Senator stood beside his desk wearing a toothy smile.

Senator Drake was a short man, small except for a paunch. He was middle-aged and balding and his pants rode low on his narrow hips under the stomach that threatened to upset his balance and send him toppling forward. His complexion was an unhealthy shade of pale beige with blue overtones. A prominent roman nose, deep-set eyes and a mouthful of long, pointy teeth made him look predatory. In fact, the Senator's way of holding his arms bent out from his body made them seem unusually short, so he reminded Dave of a miniature tyrannosaurus rex.

They shook hands, and the Senator invited him to take a seat. He did so, but first he awkwardly held out the needlepoint. "My grandmother made this for you, Senator."

Senator Drake took the gift, turning it over and over in his squarish hands as though he didn't know which way was up. Finally he said, "Liberty and Justice for All. This is going to look just dandy on the wall of my office. Thank you. And thank your grandmother for me."

"I will, Senator Drake. She'll be pleased to know how much you like it."

Dave glanced around. He wondered if the Senator meant to hang the needlepoint in this particular office, where the walls were plastered with award certificates and diplomas interspersed with expensive looking oil paintings of hunt scenes.

The Senator dropped the needlepoint on his desk and collapsed into his leather-upholstered armchair, where he breathed heavily for a few seconds before he said, "Now what brings you to my office?"

Dave knew he had only a matter of minutes to get his point across. He'd made notes and mentally rehearsed. He spoke quickly, explaining about the work visas and the mass firing of programmers and call center operators at Markham-Hook Conglomerate and at other corporations throughout the country.

"I'm sure you didn't intend this when you voted for those trade bills, Senator Drake," he finished respectfully.

The Senator reared back as if Dave had slapped him. He clapped his hand over his heart and said, "Why, I've been taken advantage of by unscrupulous business interests."

Dave let out his breath and felt the knot in his stomach take a first step toward breaking up. "I'm glad you see that, Senator. I knew that you'd--"

"Next time I'm going to look things over a lot more carefully, I can assure you of that, Mr. Griffin. It was nice meeting you. You keep in touch and let me know if there's anything else I can do for you. Be sure to stop by the front desk on your way out and have my secretary give you an autographed picture and explain how you can send in campaign contributions."

The Senator stood and extended his hand. Dave blinked. Was this what he'd driven hundreds of miles and spent scarce dollars for?

He kept his seat. "Wait a minute--isn't there anything you can do about repealing the law that's costing so many Americans their jobs?"

"Repeal?" The Senator looked startled. "No, Mr. Griffin. You see, trade bills can't be repealed. Thanks for coming by, though, and I'll surely keep you in mind."

"That's not enough," Dave said. "Didn't you hear what I said about people losing their jobs and their careers?"

"Of course, of course. But you have no concept how the government of this country works."

"I've started to get a pretty good idea. What makes you think the people of this country are going to let you stay in office once they find out what you've done?"

The Senator's expression darkened. "Is that a threat, Mr. Griffin?"

Before he could answer, a sharp rap sounded on the door, and then Douglas burst into the room and assumed the position of a fencing master about to do combat--right arm raised and pointing forward, left behind his back, except that he held a clipboard instead of a sword. He looked at Dave and jabbed his thumb in the direction of the exit. His expression said he'd heard Dave getting snotty with the Senator, and Dave had about fifteen seconds to get out of here before security showed up with weapons drawn.

Dave got up and snatched the needlepoint off the Senator's desk. He stumbled into the hall, bypassing the suggested visit to the secretary to pick up an autographed picture. His legs felt like they belonged to someone else. He sensed cameras recording his every move as he made his way through the building, past endless security checks, and back to the door.

He saw his grandmother looking at him as soon as he stepped back into the light. She waved from her bench under a tree, shading her eyes with one hand. He sighed and made his way down the sidewalk trying to think up a good lie.

"How'd it go, sugarbiscuit?"

"Just fine, Mawmaw." He used all his acting skills to project happiness and good cheer, the smile of a man who'd just accomplished something in his nations' capital and was on his way to better things thanks to his own initiative and good sense.

Mawmaw's face darkened and she drew her eyebrows together. So much for his acting skills. Besides, he'd forgotten about the needlepoint, still clutched in his hands. That was a major clue that things hadn't gone well.

She pulled herself up from the bench without the aid of her cane. "I should have gone in with you and given that ignorant man a piece of my mind." She shook her fist.

"Settle down, Mawmaw. That wouldn't have done any good." He handed her the needlepoint, and she tucked it back inside her purse.

Thank God, he hadn't insisted she come in and sit in the air-conditioning and meet Senator Drake. She'd probably have pulled a pointed umbrella out of her bag and poked the Senator's paunch.

"What'd he say that's got you looking like a freshly neutered tomcat?" Her blue eyes stared from behind the lenses of her glasses and her jaw was thrust out, squared up, so she didn't look like a sweet little old lady in her best Sunday dress anymore, she looked like a bulldog itching for a fight.

"About what I should have known he'd say. Mawmaw, he doesn't care about people and their jobs." He studied the ground where someone had dropped a couple of dozen cigarette butts in the grass. He used the toe of his shoe to try to grind one of them out of existence.

He'd been too trusting, a naïve kid to think Senator Drake cared what happened to him and other American workers. Norah at Markham-Hook had been right when she'd told him he was tilting at windmills.

Mawmaw linked her arm through his. "You forget about what happened in there and finish taking your grandmother sightseeing."

Oh, sure, he felt like experiencing a few more hours of fighting crowds to gawk at monuments. At her insistence, they hopped a trolley and rode back to the Lincoln Memorial. Mawmaw waited on a bench, while Dave climbed about a million steps to stand at the feet of the marble Lincoln.

Here was a man who cared deeply about his country, a man who got things done. As Dave stared into the giant face, he felt an ache in his soul that hurt worse than any pain he'd ever experienced. He cared just as deeply about his country, but, unlike Lincoln, he was not a man of destiny and there was precious little one man could do.

A few hours later, after they'd made what seemed to be endless circles of the major attractions in a series of sightseeing trolleys, they found themselves once again in front of the Senate building. Dave consulted his watch.

"Mawmaw, let's grab something to eat and then call it a day." He squinted back at the building and spotted Senator Drake leaving with an entourage scurrying behind him at a respectful distance, stopping when he stopped, walking when he walked. The Senator strutted like the only rooster in a yard with a hundred hens. Dave thrust his hands into his pockets and curled them into fists. "There he is, that hypocritical son of a..."

"David." His grandmother grabbed his shoulder and yanked him around to face her. "There will be no ugly talk in front of a lady."

"I can't help it, Mawmaw."

She raised her chin. "You can and you will, young man. Ugly talk is not going to hurt Senator Drake, but it is going to upset your grandmother. Just take this incident as proof that the man is totally out of touch with ordinary people. Wait for another opportunity to show what you're made of and pick your fight."

She let go of his arm and tromped down the sidewalk ahead of him, her new sneakers bought special for the trip thunking against the pavement with every stride. A long strand of white hair that had worked free of the clip on the top of her head whipped back and forth against her neck like the tail of an angry lioness.

Dave caught up to her. "What other opportunity?"

She kept walking, swinging her cane out to the side, so it threatened to bash him across the legs if he got too close. "We can't always pick our opponents, sugarbiscuit, but we can pick the way we're going to live our lives."

"Mawmaw, what does that mean?" She could be so exasperating when she spouted off this stuff that sounded good, but never seemed to solve any of his problems.

"It's what my mother always told me. Somehow everything has a way of working out." She plowed ahead, the cane scattering strangers on either side while Dave trotted in her wake.

He hoped to God things worked out soon. He didn't know about picking opponents. So far he hadn't done any winning when it came to doing battle against big corporations or politicians and they were the only enemies he had. He ought to set his sights a little lower, maybe somewhere around the level of his neighbor's Jack Russell. Yeah, that was it. The next time that yappy little beast came over to crap in his yard, he'd wave his arms and yell and it would run off like it had seen the gates of hell open up and it didn't like the looks of the fire.

Chapter Eleven

Dave hadn't had a single response to his broadcasting of two thousand resumes, his networking calls, his applications to job postings in classifieds throughout the country. That wasn't surprising. According to the online forums, programmers who'd lost their jobs before he did were out of money and out of hope. They were, if they were lucky, cleaning offices or driving taxis.

The stack of unpaid bills on his desk grew taller, toppled over, and spilled onto the floor. Despite the fact that he wasn't even a month late on his payments, Dave had to screen his calls to weed out bill collectors who'd grown increasingly persistent and rude.

"Mr. Griffin, what are you going to do about this obligation?" They always talked about obligations as if he would be suddenly motivated to pay because calling a bill an obligation made it sound so much more significant. "We have to have a payment by next week."

Or what? Had the government reinstated debtors' prisons? Would the Behemoth turn into a pumpkin if he missed another payment on his obligation?

He pretended the harassment didn't matter, but when he saw an online ad that a jewelry store at the Wonderland Mall north of town was hiring, he took a bus to the mall to put in an application. The Behemoth sat in a corner of the garage like an abandoned toy. The SUV slurped up high octane like a camel at an oasis, and without an income he could barely afford to drive it. After he dropped off his application, he was lucky enough to catch another bus right away, even though this one only went to Church Street, a few blocks from Harris Park. No matter. Wonderland Mall had deteriorated sharply in the past year. Armed criminal types lurked in corners. Carjackings and muggings were now an everyday occurrence. Dave didn't think there'd be enough left of him to scoop off the sidewalk if he waited at the bus stop more than five minutes to catch a bus that went all the way into town.

He stepped off at Church Street, intending to walk to Harris Park and get a bus home. He paused to check out his surroundings. Nice neighborhood of small shops and businesses. A red and white sign over the door of a two story brick building caught his eye. Avalon Plasma Center and Lab.

A thought drifted through his head. He didn't like the sight of his own blood--who did? But a person needed to earn money to survive--and to meet their obligations--and he'd heard that you could get as much as two hundred dollars a month for plasma.

He veered right and marched up the brick steps to the building, where a couple of pots of overgrown ferns flanked the outer door. He went inside. The black and white floor tiles gleamed under at least ten coats of wax, and the scent of orange room deodorizer almost masked the disinfectant smell that stung his nostrils.

Chairs were lined up in an L shape around two walls of the room and every chair was occupied. Dave stepped up to the desk and got the attention of the receptionist, a twentyish redhead reading a tabloid. She finally frowned up at Dave and lowered her magazine to the desk.

He leaned on the counter and beamed her a winning smile. "Excuse me. I'd like to sell plasma." Not quite the truth. He didn't like to sell plasma, he liked to earn money.

Her expression stayed fixed in a frown. "Sorry. We already have people totally crawling out of the woodwork, you just would not believe. I mean, there's only so much plasma we can process." She pointed to a stack of forms on her desk. "You could add your name to our waiting list and if we get an opening, we'll call you."

"You mean like in case one of your present donors gets a real job or dies?"

"Whatever."

Sad day when you couldn't even get a job letting people stick needles in your arm to take out your blood. He turned down her offer to get on the waiting list. He was tired of waiting lists and he was sure he wasn't the only one. Waiting lists for government services, for training, to put in job applications, and now to sell plasma. Maybe someone should contact the spin doctors in Washington, have them work on the problem. No time at all and people would learn to say, "Would you like to sign up for our opportunity success module, Mr. Griffin?"

As if getting turned down by the plasma lab wasn't enough, when he got to Harris Park to wait for a bus, he spotted Beth strolling out of the Pyramid Building with Denton Harris. They looked like a couple of prototypes for America's new privileged generation.

Thank God, Dave had seen them first and ducked behind a maple tree, even though for a moment he'd been mistaken for one of the street entertainers by a group of actors running through a skit. A pretty, dark-haired girl, looked in his direction.

"Come to enjoy the evening's entertainment?" Her smile was welcoming.

"Not tonight." His face burned. He wouldn't admit he had no job and no money to put in the hat. Funny how being without an income made you feel like you weren't a real member of society, like there was something terribly wrong with you.

"That's too bad. We're premiering a new show tonight and I'm sure you'd like it. By the way, I'm Lark and these are my friends--Joanie, Benson, Emma, and Steve." She pointed to each of her friends in turn, and they said their greetings.

"I'm Dave." He glanced back toward the building across the street. Denton had left, but Beth wasn't alone. Oxford DeWinters, of all people, stood beside her. Damn. The sun chose that moment to slip a few millimeters toward the horizon, sending its rays at the exact angle to flash a halo of gold off DeWinter's hair and reflect it toward Beth.

Dave tore his gaze away. Lark was putting on some kind of makeup that made her eyes look huge. She'd definitely caught his interest. Maybe he ought to make an effort to see her performance. "What other evenings do you perform?"

"Usually Mondays, Wednesdays and Sundays. Whoops, they're getting started without me." She waggled her fingers at him and slipped away to join her fellow actors.

He counted to ten and peeked out from behind the tree again. No sign of Beth or DeWinters. He turned and scuffed down the path toward the bus stop, where he could catch the last bus of the day outward bound for the suburbs. Man, what had he become? Not only was he hiding from Beth, instead of walking where he wanted to walk, but he'd met a beautiful woman and all he could do was slink off like a whipped dog.

※ ※ ※

Joe's headache pounded and his heart seemed to be pumping at double the normal rate. For a few seconds the images hitting his vision center shimmied, and he experienced panic until they settled back down. Must be that the new medicine, the Seizure-Out, wasn't strong enough. He didn't have another appointment at the clinic until next month, but he couldn't see anything wrong with increasing the dosage on his own. Besides, unlike his old medicine, the Seizure-Out didn't depress him, it made him feel pretty good, so more could only make him feel better. The only problem was the cost if he had to take extra pills. But soon money wasn't going to matter. He had the answer; all he needed was the financing, and then he and Lark wouldn't have any more worries.

He got out of his truck and looked across the gravel parking lot to get an overall view of the structure he'd chosen. The building used to be a fitness center until the owner moved to a bigger place, but it might do. It was rectangular to fit the long, narrow lot, with the narrow end facing the road. It had a skin of metal siding painted dark gray with red trim, and a couple of big windows in the front looking into the reception area.

He'd seen prettier, but this was okay. The location was perfect, for one thing. The building was situated halfway between the godless and the clueless--in the thin commercial area separating the playgrounds of the criminal element from the well-kept suburban neighborhoods of people who didn't know and didn't want to know. The ladies who'd attend his fundraisers wouldn't risk coming any closer than this to the bad side of town, where they'd be prey for people without souls. And they wouldn't want a bingo hall in their backyards.

He'd called the owner in advance to say he was interested. A lowslung blue truck pulled up beside him, the engine rumbling. The driver parked and jumped out, hand outstretched.

"Mr. Tremaine? Bill Coffey. Real happy to show you around."

"Excellent. I hope the interior is as fine looking as what I see out here." Joe had donned his best manners. Bill Coffey's voice held more than a trace of a Midwestern accent, so Joe morphed his own accent from his normal drawl to the flat tones of the Midwest. Even if Coffey didn't notice they had something in common, the similar accents and cadence in their speech would register in his subconscious, and he'd be more inclined to like Joe and want to give him a good deal. Psychological tricks were one more bit of training he could thank the government for. Your tax dollars at work.

Coffey unlocked the door and stood back for Joe to enter first. "Nice lobby, wouldn't you say? Small, but that gives you more space for fitness equipment in the next room and the mirrors are already up. Buildings been vacant almost a year. I could give you a decent price." He jittered around touching the mirrors and poking at the light switches. Pretty eager to close the deal. All the better.

"Fitness center? Didn't I tell you? I'm looking for a church building." Joe clapped Bill Coffey on the back. "I'm a man of the cloth, ready to spread the good word."

"Well. I had no idea." Coffey blinked at him.

"Most people don't. I try to present myself as a regular person just like everyone else. And that's what I am. The only difference between me and the next guy is that I carry a Bible instead of a briefcase."

Joe moved past him, ignoring the sharp pain that zipped across his head. He studied the big room. The mirrors would be a distraction, but he'd probably leave them up to save the bother of taking them down.

They finished the walk through of the main room, the changing rooms and the showers, and the two rest rooms at the end of a long hall. Coffey opened the back door and led Joe around to the back of the building, showing him a murky pond overcrowded with Canada geese.

"I gotta say, Reverend Tremaine, you can't go wrong with this place. I'm picturing Sunday school, Bible study, couples groups meeting in the evenings, maybe a nursery school. Call it the education center. What do you say?"

Joe was picturing a bingo hall, money coming in, and eventually a move to a house in a decent neighborhood. Call it the parsonage. He'd finally turned things around. Senator Drake would fall out of his chair if he could see Joe now. The man he'd thrown away was back--better, a new improved model.

"Let's talk money, Mr. Coffey. What kind of a deal can you give to a charitable organization?"

Dave fixed a ham and cheese sandwich for supper and sat in front of the big screen watching a speech by Senator Drake. The Senator was in Raleigh campaigning. He'd made it clear to Dave that he wouldn't do anything about stopping the corporations that were taking over the country. But maybe since Dave's disastrous trip to Washington, the Senator had seen the light about the state's economy and he'd do something to help the unemployed.

At least now, after his visit to Washington, Dave wasn't still stupid enough to believe that Senator Drake had finally realized what the lopsided trade and labor laws he'd voted for had done to his constituents. He already knew.

Senator Drake gave an emotional speech, eyes rolling heavenward at intervals, fists banging on the lectern to illustrate points, as he insisted he was all for the working people who had lost their jobs because of government trade laws. His teeth looked like miniature knives in his mouth, flashing as he talked.

A woman reporter at the back of the room waved her hand and was recognized. "In all this talk about textile and manufacturing, let's not forget another segment of workers. What about white-collar workers losing their jobs to cheaper imported labor? That seems to be quite a big issue."

Senator Drake's fixed smile remained in place, but Dave saw the muscles around his right eye start twitching as if they'd been hooked up to a battery. "Well," the Senator said. He waved his arms, revealing patches of damp around his armpits. "Clearly, our educational system has failed to prepare American workers to compete, by golly it has. Until taxpayers vote for the dollars to upgrade our workers' skills, we've got to import people to maintain American tech superiority. Why, I've just introduced a new bill that asks for increased funding for education. Those tech workers who want jobs, those who want to work instead of complain, will take advantage of the training, so they'll have employment even during the current jobless recovery. I'm tired of racist American tech workers complaining when people from China or India get the jobs Americans can't do."

Dave rocketed out of his chair, flapping his sandwich back and forth like a cardboard church fan. "You weasel. You lying dog. You put us out of work and then you have the gall to tell us to stop whining because we're having a jobless recovery? What the hell is a jobless recovery anyway? Excuse me, while I run down to the bank and deposit my moneyless paycheck." He clamped down hard on his sandwich and bit his finger. He howled and shook his hand. Chunks of ham plopped on the floor.

"And returning to blue collar jobs." The camera panned back to the reporter. "What about textile and manufacturing in this state? Those jobs are just about gone."

"Didn't I just answer that question, ma'am? Upgrade skills. Get an education in the booming tech market." The knife-teeth flashed. "Next?"

"A lot of workers, both tech and textile, have been out work for a year. Any chance of increasing unemployment benefits for them?"

"Current laws do not provide for such increases. However, rest assured, I am deeply saddened by their plight and if they will just get educated they will be able to compete."

The station cut to a commercial, and Dave powered off the set. He was too sick to finish the last of his sandwich and too angry to watch any more of Senator Drake.

The hypocritical bastard had the nerve to stand up in front of reporters on national TV and claim he had the best interests of workers at heart. And, hey, according to the Senator it was the workers' own fault they lost their jobs. They didn't keep up their skills or they didn't get educated in the first place. Win-win situation for Senator Drake and the rest of the Washington mob. And then there was the crack about "racist" American tech workers. Oh, sure, Americans would gladly give up their jobs, their homes, everything they ever worked for if only the jobs were going to Europeans instead of to Chinese or Indian workers.

Dave sat for a few minutes, adrenaline still pumping uselessly through his body, probably burning up brain cells that he badly needed. All his nerves screamed, "Hey, Dave, time to put up a fight, buddy. Pick this one." The trouble was, as he'd found out the hard way, there wasn't any way to change the situation and not a thing he could do. Sometimes Dave wished he were a dog, so he could lie around all day with his nose on his paws and not have to be aware of impending poverty.

The phone rang and the caller ID came up Markham-Hook Conglomerate Consumer Credit. Bloodsuckers wouldn't leave him alone. Dave let the answering machine pick up.

"This is Miss Dunn," whined a nasal voice. "Please call Markham-Hook Conglomerate Consumer Credit as soon as possible."

Let's see--starve or make a car payment? Maybe he should stop being selfish and consider Miss Dunn's feelings. The poor woman probably wanted to spend a quiet evening at home, maybe reading hot sex scenes in romance novels, instead of calling Dave Griffin to insist that he do something about his obligation. Her fingers were probably worn to stubs from punching in his number.

Soon, though, he had to do something about transportation. After they repossessed the Behemoth, he'd have no way except the bus to get to the store or to a job interview if he ever got one. He had to make a plan, but somehow making plans didn't come easily anymore.

The Dave who'd met everything head on, had given way to a where's-my-next-meal-coming-from creature with dark hollows under its eyes that stared out of his bathroom mirror at him. He couldn't even look directly at the grocery cashiers anymore in case they could see inside him and know that someday soon the electronic beast at the register was going to flash back not-approved when he pressed debit.

The doorbell chime sounded. Dave jumped. Here he'd just been thinking about Miss Dunn and now he had the thought that it might be her standing on his doorstep, demanding that he either pay up or surrender the keys to the Behemoth. She'd be a tiny woman with big gold hair sprayed and teased into a spiky cone on top of her head, mimicking the top of the company pyramid, and she'd stare at him with the cold yellow eyes of a lizard. A couple of club-wielding thugs would accompany her, ready to crack his kneecaps if he decided to talk ugly to Miss Dunn.

He padded down the hallway barefoot to peek through a front window. It was already dark out, so he turned on the porch light and spotted a heavy-set figure on his front steps, leaning against a porch column.

Henry Crane. Architect. Dave's neighbor from across the street. Dave opened the door.

"Substitute postman left your mail in my box." Crane held out a handful of envelopes.

"Thanks. Uh, want to come in and have coffee?"

He was just being polite, but Crane said he'd love to and stepped inside. Dave was forced to lead him to the kitchen and put on a pot of coffee.

He set the mail on top of the microwave and pawed around in a cabinet until he found a couple of mugs. He couldn't remember if Henry Crane had ever visited in the past. Probably not. They'd usually talked in their front yards if they happened to be outside at the same time.

"Dave?"

He said, "Yeah?" without turning around. He had a sugar bowl around here somewhere. He figured he ought to offer doughnuts, but he didn't have any. Henry might like Fritos. No, he didn't have those either. He doubted Henry would go for bread heels or leftover rice.

"I was going to come see you next week. Then your mail showed up at my place and I figured this was as good a time as any."

Now Dave looked at him. Clearly, Crane was about to say something he knew Dave wouldn't like. Funny how his ability to sense bad news had sharpened since he lost his job.

Dave wouldn't make it easy for him. The smug bastard had everything he wanted. "You're here to offer me a job? Thank God. Man, for a while there I was starting to think I'd end up living in a box under an overpass."

Crane's complexion deepened from tanning bed orange to brick. He studied his well-manicured hands. "I'm head of the homeowners' association and we've, ah, we've noticed that your lawn hasn't been mowed in, ah, more than a month." He forced a laugh. "Another inch or so and you'll be able to bail that stuff and make hay."

Dave assumed the expression of someone who might have just discovered a hundred dollars on the sidewalk. "Wow! Great idea, Henry. I don't have a lawn mower or money to hire anyone to cut the grass. Selling hay should be just the thing to lift me out of poverty."

"Sorry." Henry's face flushed. "I know you're out of work, but I'm just doing my job. According to the neighborhood covenants, you're required to keep your lawn clipped to a height of no more than two and a half inches."

Dave bit back a remark about rulers and the grass Nazis of Eden Acres. Why bother? Crane didn't feel good about coming over here rubbing his face in his problems. Besides, Dave knew he worked for Avalon Architectural Services, and they'd just announced upcoming job cuts. Henry Crane might soon be joining the unemployment club. And he supposed Crane had had the unenviable task of making visits to other pitiful cases who didn't keep up appearances. In recent weeks Dave had noticed "For Sale" signs sprouting on neighborhood lawns like dandelions.

Wordlessly, he poured them each a mug of coffee and brought the mugs to the kitchen table. He picked up his mail and sat across from Crane, opening the overdue notices in front of him, sure that Crane had already flipped through the stack and seen for himself.

When he was done going through the mail, exploring for good news that didn't appear, he ripped the bills in two and pushed them aside. "Henry, I don't like the way my yard looks any more than you do. But unless I get a sharp pair of scissors and cut it blade by blade, it's going to have to stay that way."

"I'll report to the association that I spoke with you about the problem. You understand? No hard feelings, Dave. I know it's not your fault, but rules are rules."

"It's okay, Henry."

Yeah, no hard feelings, just the tough reality that you couldn't live in Eden Acres if you didn't have a job.

Phase one of Joe's plan for getting the church had fallen into place like a quarter dropping down the chute of a slot machine. Coffey had made him a good price and promised to hold the building for a month. Joe was back.

He'd said he be around to finalize the deal and sign the lease as soon as he got his accounts set up. Joe made it sound like he was new in town and money was just a matter of talking to the bank. But he knew he could sit in front of a bank loan officer and talk until his vocal cords developed calluses from overuse and he wouldn't get so much as a quarter to buy a cough drop.

An ironic fact of being unemployed was that you didn't have credit and if you didn't have credit, everything cost more. And sometimes you had to deal with the type of people who'd serve their own grandmothers up as the main course at a barbecue if it would net them a profit. He knew how to locate such people.

Joe already knew all about the city's leading loan sharks. But high interest wouldn't be a problem. The money would pour in and maybe Joe would even get religion for real--he certainly felt like things were finally happening for him after months of dragging around like he was fatally wounded. That bitchy lady doctor at the clinic had done him a big favor switching him to the Seizure-Out that made him feel so good. He'd finally gotten an idea, a way out of this mess, and there were lots of other Internet courses he could take, maybe even get himself a few doctorate degrees, and soon everyone in Avalon would join his church to hear him speak and they'd play bingo to raise money for the poor. Joe Tremaine was going to be famous. Maybe even as famous as Billy Graham.

The reception Lark had worked this morning had been hell. Why people insisted on partying outdoors when it was already as hot as summer and it rained every other day, she would never know. As if she weren't sweaty and tired enough, she somehow managed to drop half a tray of glasses. They shattered at the feet of the guest of honor, splashing dregs of half a dozen different drinks over the legs of his tux and scratching the finish of his shoes. Some men would have tried to soothe her feelings, but not this one. He'd looked at her squint-eyed, as if she'd tried to murder him with broken glass. If she hadn't started crying, he probably would have insisted that Kathie fire her.

The heat and the mishap had left her drained and the air had cut out in her car again. She'd given a coworker a ride home, and all he did was whine until she wanted to scream.

"I hate my girlfriend. She doesn't understand me. My cat has fleas. Hey, watch out for that guy on the bike! Don't you know how to drive? If I'd known you didn't have air, I'd have asked Kathie for a ride."

"I wish you had." She jammed on the brakes in front of his apartment building and practically shoved him out of the car.

Thank God, she wasn't working tonight. She'd stay home and read a book, maybe a novel about kids in high school whose lives revolved around going to the prom and finding just the right zit concealer. Or maybe one of those historical romances where Lord Rakehell had to enter a marriage of convenience with a prim governess.

She flung open the front door and saw her father standing near the stove cradling a manila envelope in his arms like a baby. The grin stretching his face could have won him a job modeling tooth whitener. Her stomach flip-flopped. He'd been depressed for months, but lately he seemed to be going in the other direction, and Lark wasn't sure that was a positive step.

"Bring that envelope over here and fan my face, Dad," she said, pretending a light mood. "I'm melting."

"Sweetheart, I have really good news."

She clasped her hands over her stomach. He'd been okay for months. Why now? Please, don't let him tell her he'd figured out a way to power a rocket to Mars using only a few ounces of cinnamon and oregano combined with orange juice. She couldn't take it. Not today.

A tear slipped down her cheek, and he crossed the room and reached his arms out to her. "Baby, don't worry." He hugged her tenderly. "I know just what you're thinking. I'm fine, honest to God. I just want to show you what came in the mail today. We're celebrating tonight, ordering a pizza. See for yourself."

He handed her the envelope, and she opened it and drew out what looked like a diploma. It was a diploma, she decided on closer inspection, depending on the definition of what constituted school. She studied the words penned in bold calligraphy. Doctor of Divinity. Joseph Dennis Tremaine. Graduate in good standing from the school of the Sweet Jesus Church of Love. It was signed by the Reverend Albert LeMay Carter. Dot Com.

"Dad." She shook her head. "What were you thinking?"

"Nothing but good, Lark. I know you didn't have any idea I was so into the God thing. But there's a lot about your father you don't know."

"Cut the crap and tell me what's going on."

"I'm just being a good citizen. Every day I read articles in the paper about how Americans who lose their jobs are supposed to get training in hot new fields. They've got lines out the door down at the community college. So I got on the Internet and got trained in case a preacher job opens up. Aren't you proud of me?"

"Stop playing around and tell me the truth. I will not have you scamming people, especially not innocent people who place their trust in God." She'd met cats who were more religious than Joe Tremaine. "I'm in no mood for this, Dad."

"I swear, I'm not scamming anyone. For a few days, I had a purpose in life and a reason to get up in the morning. This diploma didn't come easy. I had to read the Bible and study and pass tests. You know how hard it is to pass tests after you've had your skull broken in half a dozen pieces? I'll tell you, it's like climbing Mount Everest in a bathing suit. I'm going to frame my diploma and hang it in my room and study the Bible in my spare time. That all right with you, Miss Josephine Lark Tremaine?"

Now he was trying to push her guilt trip button. Lark didn't believe for half a second that he'd gone to "divinity school" for the fun of passing tests. But if he was up to something, she wouldn't find out until it was a done deal. Her best course was to wait and then deal with the problem when she knew what form it had taken. At least he wasn't delusional this time.

"Go ahead and order the pizza," she said kicking off her shoes. "I'll have mushrooms and black olives with mine."

Chapter Twelve

This time the mailman left the envelopes in his box instead of Henry Crane's. More bills. Polite letters thanking him for applying for the position from companies that weren't going to hire him.

Your credentials are indeed impressive. However, we have already filled the position. We will keep you in mind should another opening occur.

He'd just gotten off the phone with Mawmaw. She'd called to tell him she was moving from the farm into a one-bedroom trailer home.

"The trailer is the cutest little thing. Got yellow curtains on the windows and a box by the front door to plant flowers. You know I'm too old to keep up a farm, sugarbiscuit," she'd said.

"What about Mr. Baker?" Mawmaw loved the farm. She'd been born there and she'd always said she was going to die right in the same room where she first saw the light of day. She would not be doing this just because she'd gone silly over a trailer home with yellow curtains. "Doesn't he rent acreage from you anymore?"

"Ed says he's too old to keep farming. He retired down to Florida a few months ago."

A light flipped on. Mawmaw needed Baker's rent money. She couldn't manage on her pension check. Dave flopped into his command center and said, "Mawmaw? You're always getting after me for trying to lie to you. Why are you really leaving the farm?"

He heard her catch her breath. "David, it's rude to accuse your elders of lying."

"Then tell me the truth. Isn't there someone else who could rent the land?"

"I've had a few offers, but no one's willing to pay as much as Ed Baker paid."

"You can't afford to take less?" His head was spinning. Why hadn't she told him about Baker leaving back when he still had money and a job?

"Not really."

After he prodded for a few more minutes, she told him about an assessment for sewer lines and higher taxes. There was no way she could handle the assessment as well as the increased taxes.

"Don't worry, sugarbiscuit. I'll have the money from the sale of the farm and I can use it to help you out if you don't find a job."

"I don't want you to sell the farm and I don't need your money." His voice rose in pitch. "You always said the farm was my inheritance. Well, I want it, Mawmaw. I want my inheritance."

"You'll have the money instead of the land. That's the same thing. Now promise me you'll calm down and stop making a fuss."

He'd promised. But the money was not the same thing as the farm. He wouldn't take money from his grandmother. Besides, if he didn't get another job, he might have to turn to farming to keep from starving. What was it called? Subsistence farming. He doubted that the lot for the trailer home Mawmaw planned to move to was big enough to plow.

He returned his attention to the mail. Surely, somewhere in all this paper, one person wanted to hire him, give him prize money, or even send him a card saying he was a nice person. Didn't he deserve one tiny moment of joy today? At the bottom of the stack he found a card from Markham-Hook announcing the annual programming staff appreciation party along with an invitation requesting Dave's presence.

"Love to go, Mr. Harris. Love you to death. Love the whole damned company. To death." He crumpled the invitation and tossed it in the direction of the trash, watching it miss the bin and skitter along the floor toward the dishwasher.

They'd outsourced human resources to a company that in turn had offshored to Mexico, or maybe it was China. Such delicate touches as removing the names of former employees from the party list hadn't happened yet. Too bad they'd been so quick to remove him from the payroll.

He'd attended the festivities last year when he was still a valued member of the Markham-Hook family. It had been rumored that John Victor Harris himself was going to put in an appearance to personally meet the "fine people who had put the company on the map." But the closest they got to seeing Harris was watching him on the giant screen up on the wall of the banquet room.

Dave should have known the company CEO wouldn't be there in person. Some new guy he'd sat with in the break room the day before had bragged about helping to set up the video equipment on the third floor. Videos at Markham-Hook usually meant Harris on tape and, sure enough, that's what had happened. Harris had starred in a video that showed footage of Markham-Hook's worldwide presence. Oxford DeWinters had stood in for the absent Harris, shaking hands and giving praise to the members of the programming staff who had "made it happen." Dave had won an award, a glass replica of the Pyramid Building, for bringing a project in six weeks ahead of schedule.

Harris's voice narrated as shots of gleaming factories, state-of-the art farms, and brand new financial centers, both here and abroad, appeared on the screen one after another. Was there any industry Markham-Hook wasn't involved in? Dave had groaned out loud when Harris concluded by remarking that the sun never set on the Markham-Hook Empire.

A lot had changed since last year's party. For one thing, Dave had time, now that he was unemployed, to cruise the Internet and read about the real world. He felt like he'd missed the get-a-clue train by not educating himself sooner. The video shown by Markham-Hook was nothing more than propaganda, probably supplied by a company specializing in deception.

By now, Dave knew the gleaming factories were a figment of someone's imagination, probably shot on a back lot of the cheapest movie studio on Earth. The real factories were sweatshops in third world countries, the state-of-the art farms were pesticide contaminated hellholes worked by dispirited serfs, and the financial centers charged killer interest rates to those who didn't have resources of their own. Did earning profits mean you had to enslave people and turn the world into a cesspool?

He'd love to show the partygoers the real Markham-Hook story. It wouldn't be that hard to put together a little video of his own. The footage was readily available on the Internet.

Half-formed thoughts fought each other for prominence in his mind:.
Impossible to get to the video room, you dope.
No, it isn't.
You'll be caught and arrested.
Yeah, but what great publicity. Up till now Markham-Hook's gotten away with ruining people's lives. Call them out. Show people what's looming in their own futures if they don't wake up.
I don't want to go to jail.
Hey, three squares a day and no more bills.
You make jail sound like the Holiday Inn.
Okay, it would be hell, but you'd be helping humanity.
I couldn't do anything that would hurt Mawmaw.
Mawmaw will understand. You are her lion heart.

Dave presented his crumpled invitation at the door and was granted admittance to the banquet hall, where the price of the decorations alone could have fed him for a year. Of course, none of the guards who waved him through suspected he was armed with a videotape hidden inside his rented tux.

As soon as he was safely in the room, he drifted across the marble tiled floor to the buffet table, drawn by the scent of little meatballs on sticks. He devoured a dozen or so. They made a nice change from the bread and cheese he'd been eating all week.

He glanced around, keeping his chin low. The banquet hall was the size of a football field. Across the room near the live band, he spotted Rex standing with Ken and some of the other Indians. Go team. He turned quickly and pretended he was trying to decide between the miniature sandwiches packed with salmon and cheese or the bite-sized cakes frosted in silver and gold. He finally selected a handful of the little cakes and popped them into his mouth. Chewed and swallowed. He edged farther along, putting a group of people he didn't know between him and Ken's group. He came to a punch bowl and helped himself to a cupful of the pink liquid. The cakes had been drier than they looked.

He moved through the room, nodding at the few strangers who made eye contact. When no one challenged him, he started slipping through the crowd toward the door to the back hallway.

As soon as he was through the door, he spotted Art Mahaffey walking out of the men's room with a cell phone plastered to his ear. Crap. Mahaffey's last memory of Dave Griffin was the exit scene where Dave had left the building with an armed escort. All Mahaffey had to do was look straight ahead and Dave was busted.

He glanced around wildly. Damn these bare hallways. Plenty of expensive flocked wallpaper decorated with original artwork, but no handy cabinets or even a water fountain to squat behind. There were only doors that might or might not be locked. He turned the handle of the first door on his right and darted inside. Mops. Buckets. Brooms. The smell of pine soap.

A woman dressed in the shapeless gray jumpsuit and white sneakers of the Markham-Hook janitorial staff locked gazes with him, a roll of toilet paper clutched in each hand.

"Sir, the men's room is down the hall. Past the elevator. Says Men's Room on the door."

"Right. Thanks for setting me straight." He didn't move.

"Sir? Do you need help?" Growing alarm in her voice and a paleness to her complexion that hadn't been there a minute ago. Obviously, she'd concluded the toilet paper wouldn't make much of a weapon if he turned out to be a mad killer loose among the Markham-Hook people.

Dave shook his head as though clearing it of mental cobwebs, raised his hand in a half wave, and about-faced. He pulled open the door and peered out. Mahaffey was gone.

He stepped into the empty hallway and scooted toward the stairs at the end. Before he opened the door, he glanced back to make sure the woman from the utility room wasn't watching. Hallway clear. He slipped into the stairwell and climbed up to the third floor, his footsteps echoing too loudly on the concrete steps.

He didn't expect that the setup from last year had changed. If it had, he'd stick around for a few minutes, maybe snare as many hors d'oeuvres as he could and pretend he thought he'd been invited on purpose, then quietly make his exit. If not, he'd go ahead as planned.

He strode up to the conference room door and pushed it open, projecting the confidence of someone who was supposed to be there. The video equipment was set up, the room wired to beam the picture to the giant screen for the viewing pleasure of the Markham-Hook crowd.

"Hey, what's up?" A guy Dave recognized as a company technician was sitting in a chair with his feet propped on the nearest conference table. He put down his magazine. His brow furrowed.

Dave hadn't known whether the room would be empty, but he'd rehearsed in case it wasn't. "You're wanted downstairs." He gestured toward the door with his thumb. "Mr. DeWinters needs to see you."

Dave hoped DeWinters was in attendance, shaking hands and making the programmers feel like they were important to the company.

"What's he want?"

"Oxford DeWinters doesn't share his thoughts with me. You going downstairs or not?"

"I'm not supposed to leave the stuff unattended." An expression of uncertainty appeared on the technician's bony face. He put his hand protectively on the nearest piece of company equipment, a computer monitor.

"I know. He told me to wait up here and keep an eye on things till you get back. That a *Sports Illustrated*?" He pointed to the magazine on the table. "I haven't seen this issue."

"Help yourself."

Dave watched the poor sap shuffle out of the room in search of Oxford DeWinters. As soon as the door shut, he pushed a chair under the handle to block it from opening. He wished he had a key, but they'd surely have a duplicate, so a locked door might not buy him much time.

He moved to the VCR and hunkered down to bring the front to eye level. He pressed eject. Nothing. Damn. Where was the tape? Then he saw that the machine wasn't even hooked up.

They had to be playing a video this year. It was tradition. He got up and studied the pile of machinery and wires in front of him. Sweat beads popped out on his forehead. Move, move. Video boy could be back in just a few minutes if he found DeWinters right away and realized he'd been duped. But Dave was still no closer to running his tape.

He walked behind the table and picked up a tangle of wires. These he separated, following each to its end. The wire leading to the banquet hall screen was plugged into another machine, a shiny, silver DVD player with Markham-Hook Electronics stamped across the front under a barcode.

Dave sat back on his heels. He should have known they'd go with DVD. They'd just bought a factory in Michigan and outsourced the work to China, leasing the property back to the city to be converted into a homeless shelter. Videotape was out, and DVD was this year's hot new thing.

He ran his hands through his hair. The wires were still here, just waiting for his command. All he had to do was plug them into the right sockets. He went to work, unhooking the DVD player and wiring up the VCR. He thought he heard a door slam somewhere down the hall, but he couldn't be sure and he couldn't take the time to investigate.

He turned on the conference room TV to monitor the broadcast and rammed the tape into the VCR. He pressed play and sat back to enjoy the movie.

Children slaved away at Markham-Hook looms in textile factories halfway around the world. Pregnant women, looking like they were ready to fall out of their chairs from exhaustion, assembled electronic components. Workers trudged home to shantytowns where raw sewage bubbled in gutters and smokestacks belched pollution into brown skies.

He'd made up the script from what he remembered of last year's movie and he'd narrated the film himself. "And here we have the finest in worker facilities as promised by Markham-Hook." Shot of an open cesspool buzzing with flies. "Environmental laws strictly enforced." Shot of pesticides being dumped in ditches next to the homes of the poor. The trade laws that favored Markham-Hook's outsourcing didn't make mention of either the environment or worker's rights.

"Next we see comfortable homes for workers. When Markham-Hook comes into a village, you can count on an improved standard of living and jobs for all." Shot of tumble-down shacks with thin, big-eyed urchins sitting in dirt yards and playing with sticks.

"The company grows like a kudzu vine, twining and twisting and putting down deep roots and a dark impenetrable layer wherever it touches down. Other companies, smaller and weaker, are absorbed or crushed out of existence, hidden forever behind the maze of holding companies and reams of paperwork and false trails. Welcome to life on Planet Markham-Hook."

Dimly he heard pounding on the door. Another few seconds and the movie would be at the best part, the part showing pictures of all twelve of Harris's homes.

He got up and flung himself across the room, throwing his weight against the door. The chair scraped on the floor and started to give way. He heard his voice on the soundtrack say, "Finally, take a look at the rewards earned by the man who made it all happen for Markham-Hook and the company's happy workers worldwide: These are the palatial mansions of John Victor Harris. Because he deserves to be richer than God."

The chair popped loose, cracking Dave across the shins and then spinning across the room to land under a table. The door flew open. Hands grabbed him, forcing him face down to the floor. He tried to hunch his shoulders, but they wouldn't move.

"That's enough. Bring him to my office." The smooth cello of Oxford DeWinters' voice somehow soothed Dave and lessened the wild pounding of his heart.

DeWinters exited ahead of them, his gait so smooth and unruffled, he could have been on his way to a family birthday party.

Dave lay panting on the floor until two of the guards yanked him to his feet. He dusted himself off. This was it. DeWinters was going to have him arrested. He wondered if the cops would make him put on one of those orange prisoner outfits or if they'd let him wear his tux for his mugshots. If they tried to interrogate him, he'd tell them he was lawyering up, the way they did on TV dramas. Except he couldn't afford a lawyer, and they'd have to appoint some overworked public defender to handle his case.

Dave had never been in Oxford DeWinter's office. It was on the forty-ninth floor, one floor down from the top of the Pyramid Building. The room could have been the lobby for a world class hotel. Royal blue carpet that looked like velvet seemed too costly to walk on. Dave was tempted to take off his shoes to keep from leaving dirt marks. The scent of fine tobacco and something else, some kind of cologne, hung in the air. It smelled like a combination of cedar and a sunny day.

"Please take a seat."

DeWinters' voice never changed. Dave wondered if he talked to his wife the same way. *Please get in bed, dear. I'm ready to make love to you.* Then he remembered that Oxford DeWinters was divorced. *Please don't let the door hit you on your way out, dear.*

"Dave?" DeWinters raised an eyebrow ever so slightly.

Dave collapsed into the indicated seat, an oversized armchair that made him feel small. He'd been all fire and fight a few moments ago, ready to do or die for his cause. Now, seeing Oxford DeWinters standing in front of him like the right hand man of God himself, made the fire flicker. Dave sent himself a command to get a grip, take slow deep breaths. The deep breaths made him feel dizzy.

DeWinters sent the guards to wait outside the door and walked over to stand in front of Dave, staring down at him with an expression of curiosity in his eyes.

"What did you hope to accomplish by pulling that childish stunt?"

Dave shrugged. "Publicity. It's way past time people knew how this company got where it is and what's in store for them before it's all over." A note of defiance had crept into his voice.

"Publicity? How old are you, Dave? I've known kids in junior high who were more savvy than you are. What publicity are you talking about? Local newspaper? Owned by Markham-Hook. Local TV stations? The same. National media? Even the ones not owned by Markham-Hook get too much advertising money to be in a hurry to cause trouble for this company."

"I was so hell-bent on doing something other than sitting on my ass, I did the only thing I could think of. I wanted to show people what Markham-Hook is doing to workers all over the world."

"I suppose it's a good thing you don't own an army tank."

"I'd never do something violent. Doesn't it bother you that you're second in command of a company that tramples over the top of people to get anything it wants?"

"Not at all." DeWinters looked undisturbed by Dave's implication that he was one of the masterminds of the heartless giant. "I don't have the clout to change Harris's mind on any of this, even if I wanted to. He makes the decisions. I'm smart enough to position myself to profit. End of story. Except for the problem of what to do with Dave Griffin, who insists on fighting against impossible odds. What do you expect to happen now?"

"That's easy. You finish telling me off. Then you have your guards cart me to jail." He studied a speck of lint on the carpet near his feet. "I pay a fine or spend a few months as a county guest and after that I go away forever, having learned the lesson you taught me--resistance is futile."

"So you've thought ahead. You may have really put yourself into a no-win fight, although there's nothing wrong with your logic. But I'm going to surprise you. I'm going to have my people escort you back to your car. No arrest."

Dave searched DeWinter's face for signs of deception. "Why?"

DeWinters waved a hand as if he were shooing an insect out of his personal space. "For one thing, I don't want to cause further embarrassment for Beth. For another, you're so insignificant that you may as well not exist. Sending you to jail would just make you angry and even give you the opportunity to sell your story to some fool tabloid. This way we can run you off and deny the whole thing."

"Yeah, I lose." Dave chewed on his lip.

As if he weren't humiliated enough, DeWinters had to add one more dig. "I expect you're still out of work."

"You know the job market sucks." He wasn't a mouse to be toyed with by a smug cat. He'd go home and hunt up some comfort foods when all this was over, but he didn't need DeWinters to twist the knife by pointing out that he couldn't even earn a living.

"We have a position open at Markham-Hook. I know you'll work hard, but the position also requires someone with polish, a quality you've demonstrated you don't have. Of course, I can help you acquire that skill."

Yeah, DeWinters was all set to send him to charm school. Why did Dave get the feeling he was about to get taken down again? Still, the prospect of a job after all this time, when things looked so grim...his heart pounded in his ears. He could pay the taxes on the farm, so Mawmaw wouldn't have to move into that trailer home that boasted yellow curtains on all the windows and not much else.

"Why would you help me?"

"I've already given you the reason--avoiding more embarrassment for Beth. You'll like the pay. A hundred and twenty grand a year to start and bonuses and stock options after six months."

Avoiding embarrassment for Beth? What did Beth have to do with this? But Beth had told him Oxford DeWinters was a family friend. Putting himself in DeWinter's place, Dave supposed a friend might want to spare Beth from the reminder that she'd once dated a total loser.

"What's the catch?" he asked cautiously.

"No catch," replied the hypnotic voice, "just an opportunity to be a player in this company. I'll even put it in writing."

"Is it a programming job?"

DeWinters almost showed some expression. The corners of his mouth pulled together into what could be taken for a smirk. "You ought to know by now we can get programmers a lot cheaper than that. The official job title is Global Management Specialist. We'll relocate you permanently to our New York office. You'll travel overseas a few times a year to line up programmers and engineers to come here and do the work that's currently being done by Americans."

Dave's heart slammed in his chest and blood rushed to his head. He sputtered helplessly for a good ten seconds before he said, "You mean you want me to help this company hire more sweatshop labor to replace Americans? No thanks." He pushed out of his chair.

"Angry with me, Dave? My, my, that is hypocritical. A minute ago you were all but ready to sign on with the company. The same company that owns all those third world sweatshops you showed us tonight. Apparently it's okay to enslave people in factories overseas. You just don't want to be the guy who recruits high tech people to take jobs from white-collar workers."

"That's not true. You tempted me, I admit that. But I wouldn't go back to work for this company even to save myself from starving."

"Serious words, but have you thought that through? This is your last chance. You walk out that door and the offer disappears forever."

Dave said, "I don't want your job."

DeWinters rubbed his chin. "Okay," he said. He'd gone back to wearing an unreadable expression.

He opened the door and spoke softly to the guards. One of them, a bearded and overmuscled type who looked like he ate lead weights for breakfast, stepped into the room and motioned for Dave to follow.

Dave's hands shook as he walked down the hall. The guards had him get onto the elevator first and then stood one on either side of him breathing heavily and, no doubt, secretly wishing he'd try to get away. The elevator finally bumped to a stop on the first floor, and Dave was whisked out of the building through a side door. They escorted him off the property with a warning not to return. Like that would be a problem. He expected DeWinters to post his picture in strategic locations throughout the building, maybe even put a price on his head if he dared to show up.

Chapter Thirteen

Dave sat on a bench in front of the mailbox center across from Harris Park with his boxes and bundles arranged at his feet. He'd held a giant garage sale, the only choice remaining to him after Markham-Hook, apparently as a result of his abortive attempt to embarrass the company, moved him to the top of the foreclosure stack the day after the programmers' banquet. All he had left were his guitar, his laptop and stereo, his clothes, and a boxful of his favorite books and CD's.

But when he thought things over, he had everything he needed, as long as he didn't count food and a place to stay. If he could get a job, any job, he'd find a way to manage.

In a few minutes he'd muster the energy to drag himself inside and arrange to ship his things to Hidden Springs. Henry Crane had been kind enough to give him a lift into town, since Markham-Hook had repossessed the Behemoth, another move to the top of the repo list. Crane was probably relieved to get him out of the neighborhood so that pesky lawn could finally get mowed.

After he shipped his stuff, he'd take a city bus over to the Greyhound Station where he could buy a ticket to Hidden Springs. He hadn't told Mawmaw he was returning. She'd have insisted on finding someone to come to Avalon to pick him up, and he didn't want to cause even more trouble for her.

At least he wasn't coming home empty-handed. The garage sale had netted him pennies on the dollar if he wanted to add up what he'd paid for everything back when he still believed the good times were going to last forever. But he'd taken in enough to pay the tax bill on the farm. He hadn't asked his grandmother's permission, he'd simply sent the payment to the tax collector.

When he showed up at the door with his last few hundred dollars, he'd tell her the farm was safe and then he'd say that as long as they had the land to grow crops, they'd be okay. He didn't know the first thing about farming, but Mawmaw could teach him how to coax vegetables out of the ground.

He heard a car door open and glanced up. A pale blue Nissan with a UNCG bumper sticker in the back window had just pulled into a parking space halfway up the block, the driver wedging it neatly between an SUV and a Lincoln. A young woman dressed in blue jeans and a pink blouse slid out of the car. She slammed the door and dropped the keys into her purse.

Dave couldn't take his eyes off her. Lark. The actress from the park. As if sensing him watching her, she swung her gaze in his direction. She waved and yelled, "Hey."

He waved back, and Lark turned and headed in his direction, the slight breeze catching her black hair and whipping it back over her shoulders. "Dave, right?" she said.

"Lark. The star of Harris Park." Then, realizing how it sounded, he said, "I didn't mean that as a put down."

"No offense taken." She pointed to his guitar case. "I hope you don't think this is a stupid question, but is that a guitar?"

"It's not a stupid question. After all, I could have a machine gun hidden in here, part of my plan to take out my frustrations on the park's pigeon flock."

"Do you? I mean, should I be warning the birds?"

"It's a guitar." He'd considered selling it, but it had belonged to his father and it meant too much. Maybe someday he'd have a child of his own and he could pass the guitar down as a family heirloom. He hoped he didn't reach a point where he had to choose between eating and selling the guitar.

"That eases my worst fears." She grinned at him. "I know this is short notice, but our guitar player might not be able to make it tonight. If he doesn't show, can you accompany me?"

Dave had never played for anyone except himself. He shook his head. "I'm not very good."

"You'd only have to play a few simple chords. Come on, Dave, cut loose." She held her hands out, palms up, and made lifting motions. "Have faith in yourself. Show the world what you can do."

He shrugged and hauled himself to his feet. He could always take a later bus to Hidden Springs. In the big scheme of things, arriving tonight or tomorrow or the next day really wouldn't matter. They locked his things in her car for safekeeping and then crossed the street to the park.

As it turned out, the guitar player showed, so Dave didn't have to make his debut. He didn't know whether he was relieved. About the only emotion he'd experienced all day was a sense of sheer, unrelenting defeat.

He wrangled props for the actors and when Lark had a break, he got them coffee and sandwiches from a deli across the street, and they sat on a bench next to Benson's van.

She shifted sideways to face him, her complexion luminous in the dim light provided by a street lamp half a block away. "What's your story, Dave?"

He looked at her with his sandwich halfway to his mouth. She could be interested in him and this was her way of asking if he were seeing someone, but if he made that assumption and he was wrong, he'd come across like a dope. Not that that was anything new for him these days.

She'd lifted one corner of her bread to inventory the ingredients. "Lettuce, tomato, turkey, mustard. Good." She tilted her head at him. "Well?"

"I'm not quite sure what you mean."

"I hope you don't think I'm being nosy, but I'm going to come right out and ask. Why were you sitting in front of the Mailbox Center with all your worldly goods spread out around you? You looked like this year's poster boy for lost souls."

"Oh, that." He rolled his shoulders in a loose shrug. "Markham-Hook foreclosed on my house and they repossessed my SUV while they were at it. I held a big yard sale and by the time it was over, I felt like I'd been picked over by vultures. The worldly goods you speak of are all I have left after a quick rise to prosperity and an even quicker fall to the bottom of the food chain. My girlfriend broke up with me because her help came with a price I couldn't pay."

"So your girlfriend did you wrong."

"To be fair, we did each other wrong," he said without hesitation. "End of job, end of dating beautiful girl. I'd rather sweep the sidewalk in front of the Pyramid Building with a short-handled paintbrush than crawl back to Hidden Springs, where my only prospect is trying to grow crops on Mawmaw's farm, but I have no choice. When I show up at the Hidden Springs bus station, Mawmaw will hug my neck and tell me it's okay. She'll call me sugarbiscuit and lion heart and pretend she needs me. And all the while I won't be anything except a parasite."

He clamped his mouth shut. He needed to stop whining before Lark got sick of him and ran him off. On the other hand, it had felt good to talk about his troubles. He'd gone from hiding his situation, denying that he was homeless, jobless, and out of prospects, to realizing that the real shame belonged to those who were so thirsty for money and power that they'd condemned their fellow Americans to poverty.

"Dave." Her eyes sparkled and she leaned in close to rest her hand on his arm.

He shivered. He realized that other than being manhandled by Markham-Hook security guards, this was the first time in weeks anyone had touched him.

"I'm looking for a roommate. Please say yes. The neighborhood's from hell, but the rent's cheap and you'll be helping out. Plus, I might be able to get you some temp work with a caterer while you look for something better."

Please say yes? Move in with a sweet woman who might even help him find a job? Why not just ask a starving man if he wanted a bag of groceries and a steady income?

◆◆◆

She wasn't kidding about the neighborhood. Dave glanced over to make sure the door was locked as she piloted the car past abandoned stores and houses on the verge of falling down in tired heaps of crumbled brick and rotted boards. Young men wearing leather coats, chains, and surly expressions lingered on street corners. He wouldn't have felt safe walking these streets after dark even if he had a cop marching with him every step of the way, gun drawn and police radio transmitting.

He didn't imagine he could offer much protection, if that's what she was looking for. He figured he could throw his body in front of attackers as a diversion while Lark sprinted to safety. Presumably she'd call the cops in to save him. But, hey, he wasn't about to back out on his decision. She was probably scared to death living here by herself and, damn it, though he barely knew Lark, his heart had started going all soft every time he looked at her.

Lark's place turned out to be not an apartment, but a house--a struggling brick structure maybe a little bigger and nicer than most others on the street. It had a garage and basement on the lower level and all the windows in the front were intact, though protected by metal bars. A neatly trimmed hedge bordered both sides of the yard. It was too dark to see around to the back.

As soon as she cut the Nissan's engine, Dave flung his door open and headed toward the garage, figuring to open the door for her.

"No, I park here." She waved him back and popped the trunk.

Together they unloaded most of his things and went to the back door, which opened onto a tiny kitchen--clean, but with sagging cabinets and a faded linoleum floor.

He followed her lead, putting his boxes and bundles in front of the refrigerator and going back for the rest. They'd driven through light fog on the way and now it had thickened into a heavy mist that settled on his skin like a damp blanket.

She locked and bolted the door behind them when they were back inside. Then she leaned against the nearest cabinet and wrapped her arms around her middle.

"I'll bet you're as chilly as I am after slogging through that wet cloud. Coffee?"

"If coffee means I can continue enjoying your company, sure."

He waited for her to make the next move. Just coffee? Coffee and Conversation? Conversation and?

She picked her way around Dave's gear and reached for the kettle on the stove. He was used to fresh brewed, but he'd sold his coffee-maker. Instant was fine, though. Anything she offered was fine. He watched her fill the kettle and pinched his right thigh to see if he were dreaming. It hurt, thank God.

And then, from somewhere in another part of the house, a toilet flushed.

"Jesus, what was that?" He flinched, an involuntary action. Maw-maw used to thump his head every time he used the Lord's name in vain.

"It's just my dad." She twisted a knob on the front of the stove and a blue flame whooshed under the kettle.

Light footsteps sounded behind him, and Dave rotated his body halfway around to see a man standing in the kitchen doorway with his arms folded across his chest. Mid-forties, maybe, and about six feet tall. Dark hair, almost as black as Lark's. Flat stomach. Upper arms bulging with well-defined muscles. Clean white t-shirt tucked into faded jeans. Bare feet. And the expression of a bear that hadn't managed to score supper in about a week.

Lark stepped over to link her arm through Dave's. "Hey, Dad. This is Dave Griffin and his stuff. He needs a place to stay. Dave, this is my father, Joe Tremaine."

Reflexes he didn't know he had took over. Dave put on a friendly smile and what he hoped was an expression of willingness to respond helpfully if called upon. "Hello, sir." He thrust out his hand. Tremaine didn't move.

"You have money for the rent?" The voice was pleasant enough.

"Yes, sir. I, uh, sold most of my things. And after I paid the tax bill for my grandmother's farm, I still have a little money left." He clamped his jaw shut. No need to babble, or spit out useless information.

"Call me Joe. You can have the back bedroom. Just two rules until I think of more. Pay your rent on time. That's one. And two--don't even think about laying a hand on my daughter. You touch her and I'll have to kill you and hide your carcass where even the rats won't find it."

"Yes, sir. Joe." Dave shuffled backward until his legs came up against his stereo box and he would have fallen if Lark hadn't grabbed his arm and rebalanced him.

"For heaven's sake, Dave, you look like you need a blood transfusion. My dad's only joking."

"Yeah." Joe Tremaine stood easy, smiling and looking at Dave like a helpful cowboy who'd just offered to saddle a greenhorn's horse for him.

Of course the man was joking. Dave wondered whether he should start over by offering again to shake hands. But Lark turned her back to tend to the kettle. Before Dave could move, Joe stepped into his space and fixed him with a marble-eyed stare from eyes so dark Dave would have needed a microscope to separate the pupils from the irises. He made his right index finger and thumb into a gun shape and pointed it at Dave's head. Then he mouthed a silent, "Pow."

Joe sat eating toast and drinking coffee at the wobbly formica-topped dining table in a corner near the kitchen. Lark had a job with the caterer this morning. Until she came back, Joe figured he'd have to entertain the stray she'd dragged home last night. College boy, from the look of him. Maybe a year or two out of college. Didn't matter. Kid looked like he still needed an education, and Joe was going to provide him one as a public service.

On the plus side, he'd paid his rent with a check, showing he had enough sense not to carry all the cash he had left in the world in his hip pocket. Joe would have raised the rent a hundred bucks from what they usually charged, but Lark had already quoted the old figure, so he couldn't. Of course, she didn't know about the cost of his medication going up so much, and that he was gradually increasing the dosage until he felt better and got over the headaches and the funny vibes in his head. He was determined she wasn't going to find out.

On the negative side, the new roomie had his eye on Lark, watching her while pretending not to and wearing a dopey expression, as if just sitting in the same room with her meant he'd won first prize in a lottery. Which wouldn't be a problem, except that Joe sensed the curly-haired stray might be just the type of waif who'd appeal to Lark's mother hen side.

Joe wasn't unreasonable. He wanted Lark to find the right man and settle down, give him grandchildren one day; he'd always wanted that. But this kid had no job, and that fancy college degree he probably had tucked away in the bottom of his guitar case wasn't going to mean a thing with all the good jobs gone. There was no point in Lark wasting her time.

And then there was the kid himself. In the few minutes Joe had spent talking to him last night, he'd come across like a half-baked piece of cookie dough. At his age, Joe was married and had a child--and he'd already killed a man. Joe had been on his own since he was sixteen and couldn't remember a time when he didn't know how the system worked, how you couldn't assume other people would follow the rules you thought were right. Kid must have been brought up in a fantasy world where the good guys always won and no one got away with stealing your ice cream cone. He looked like he still slept with a teddy bear.

He heard the clank of pipes as the water in the shower stopped running, and a few minutes later the kid, what was his name--Dave--padded down the hall and stopped in front of him. His tousled hair was still wet, dripping onto his shoulders.

Joe made his lips into a skinny line and shook his head. Jesus, was he for real? Dave carried his whole life story in his eyes. He wouldn't have lasted thirty seconds in the FBI.

"Sit down." Joe used his foot to shove a chair out from under the table. Blood vessels throbbed in his temples, signaling another headache. He'd have to take another three or four aspirins and take them soon or he wouldn't be able to function for the rest of the day. Things would settle down, though, once he got the money for the church; he knew it would.

"Where's Lark?" Dave didn't budge, other than to tighten the muscles around his jaw.

"I told you to sit." Kid might need more training than Joe had figured.

"I'm not a dog."

Joe could have shot out of his seat and had him in a chokehold before he could blink. Instead, he threw back his head and laughed until tears rolled down his cheeks. Even his headache seemed marginally less painful.

"You know what I could do to you if I wanted to?"

"I've got a pretty good idea, but I don't believe you will." Dave crossed his arms over his chest.

"And why is that?" Joe deliberately made his voice sound like gravel. He flexed his biceps a few times.

"Lark would get mad at you?" Dave made it a question, but he still looked Joe in the eye without blinking.

Joe had to give him credit. Dave had come up with an answer, even though it was a stupid one. And he'd stood his ground. But he still needed tutoring, if he was going to work out as a successful human being.

"Grab yourself some coffee, toast if you want it, and sit at the table. Lark's got a catering job this morning for a bunch of former cheerleaders having a reunion." Joe flicked a toast crumb off the front of his shirt. "She's going to talk to her supervisor about getting you some part time work setting up tables, carrying trays, and maybe washing dishes. That okay with you?"

"Of course."

"Yeah, don't tell me. You'd do anything to earn money, you're practically a Boy Scout. I'm not to make the mistake of thinking you're too good to do manual labor."

Dave grunted something Joe couldn't make out. He watched him get toast and coffee. He figured Dave would rather eat alone than join him, but Joe wasn't going anywhere this morning. He hadn't had any repair calls for two days, though he'd promised to make a bid on a job this afternoon. And he had a couple more details to work out before he went to see the loan shark.

"Lark tells me you used to be a programmer at the big conglomerate downtown till they brought in some cheaper boys from China."

"India." Dave made a face like he wanted to throw up, but was too polite.

"What are you going to do about it?" Best way to find out about a man--throw some hard questions at him and wait to see how he responded.

"You mean about them giving away my job?" Dave smeared butter across his toast. He was giving the bread his full attention. Even so, his lower lip was getting seriously chewed up.

"Of course, that's what I mean. You going to whine and sit on your ass while they get away with treating you like disposable goods? Is that the kind of wimp you are?"

The blue eyes darkened and became the sky gearing up for a tornado. They locked gazes with Joe's black eyes.

"It doesn't make a man feel good about himself to whine. Or to sit on his ass." Dave had made an effort to keep his voice controlled and polite. Joe could tell by the little twitchy muscles on the sides of his jaw. "I tried complaining to the government. I called everybody I could get phone numbers for. Then I went to Washington to speak personally with Senator Drake. And when that didn't work, I crashed a party at Markham-Hook and showed my version of the Markham-Hook as a good corporate citizen video. If you're wondering how that worked out for me, I'll just say I was an ant going up against an elephant. If my life were a movie, I'd go back and do something like hack into their system and bring the whole company down, but this is real life, and I'm just one helpless person, not a superhero. You satisfied? Or do I still qualify for wimphood and ass-sitting in your twisted little book?"

Joe cocked an eyebrow. He was right about Dave being half-baked. Any idiot should have known the only language that counted in Washington was money. On the other hand, Joe knew senior citizens who'd gone their whole lives without getting a clue about stuff like that. And Dave had shown a lot of guts crashing the conglomerate shindig.

"You're right about that movie hero stuff. I'll give you a couple of points for effort, but you've got an awful lot to learn. People who are running the country now don't care about anything but money. Dang, I've seen newborn lambs got better survival skills than you. Tell me, boy, what are you going to be when you grow up?"

"Why don't you get off my back?"

"Hell, don't take any of this personal. I'm just a good old boy trying to make conversation." Joe leaned back in his chair and yawned.

Dave snorted. "You're a whole lot more than the lazy, mean-tempered, southern boy you're pretending to be. And I may have given up, but I don't think it's good for this country to give away all the jobs. I just don't know what to do about it. That make you happy?"

Joe picked up a bread crust from his plate and crammed it in his mouth. He took his time chewing, pretending a deep interest in the toast while he evaluated Dave's potential, finally concluding that Dave was exactly what he was looking for. They'd beat him down to almost nothing, but he still needed money. He'd said last night he'd spent most of what he took in from his yard sale to pay his grandmother's tax bill and that if Lark hadn't offered him a place, he'd have gone back to Hidden Springs to the farm.

Wouldn't be long and he wouldn't be able to come up with the rent. If he turned down Joe's offer, he'd soon have to beg Joe not to kick him out and he wasn't about to do that. Dave sure didn't want to go back to Hidden Springs, where Joe had read that the unemployment rate since the mill closed was fifteen percent.

"I almost like you, Dave. But you still can't touch my daughter."

Yes, Dave was going to be the helper Joe needed at the church. After he got the money, he'd need people to run the bingo, lots of people, but just Dave to start. His headache jabbed him and he winced and then blinked his eyes against a spray of orange sparkles that danced in his vision. Where the hell were the aspirins?

Relieved to be finished sharing breakfast with a self-esteem vampire, Dave pawed around in one of his packing boxes. He was sure his Mental Giant, with its latest to do list safely encoded on the miniature CPU, was around here somewhere. It wasn't as if he had a huge area to search. The house was about one-fourth the size of his home in Eden Acres. Former home, he corrected himself. And last night, other than the size, the first thing he'd noticed was the time-warp decorations taking him to the 1950's--the crocheted doilies flung here and there on the arms of chairs and the beat-up coffee table that fifty years ago would have graced the show window of any furniture store in the nation. He'd actually been surprised to see a color TV in the living room instead of a black and white set.

He sat on the wooden floor and looked around. With the metal-framed single bed and its dingy pancake mattress and the bars on the window, the ten by ten room could have doubled for a prison cell. A faint smell of mildew floated in the air, but was overpowered by the odor of stale cigarette smoke that clung to the bed.

The rest of the furniture consisted of a wooden chair with uneven legs and a chest of drawers that was probably originally meant for an infant. A blue sheet served for a curtain over the window on the back wall. Last night, he'd looked out, but it had been too dark to see.

He got up and walked to the window, figuring the back yard wouldn't offer much of a view, but he at least he could get an idea of the surroundings. He pulled the sheet aside, disturbing a tangle of cobwebs manned by a single spider that waved a couple of legs at him before it scurried away. He peered out through the metal bars and saw a small expanse of grass and then, directly behind the hedge that framed the yard on three sides, a thick stand of underbrush on a lot that was vacant except for the shell of a burned-out house. What had he expected?

He'd unpacked last night, leaving his laptop on the wooden chair. There was no room for the contents of a couple of the boxes, so he stacked them at the foot of the bed. He put his guitar in the corner opposite the chest of drawers.

Lark had given him sheets for the bed and a couple of threadbare towels. She'd said they belonged to the former roommate, but he wasn't coming back. Dave had spread Mawmaw's afghan across the bed on top of the sheets. His moving chores finished, he'd crawled into bed and fallen asleep instantly despite the coffee Lark had made for him and that he'd quickly gulped, so he could get to his room and not have to put up with any more of Joe Tremaine and his icy stare.

But maybe he ought to reconsider about unpacking the boxes. There had to be a way to organize his stuff. His Mental Giant wasn't in the top box, so he slid it out of the way and knelt on the floor to open the second box. The PDA was there under a book. He picked up the book--his one-month anniversary gift from Beth. He waited, expecting the usual twinge of regret that sprang up when he thought of Beth. Nothing.

Someone rapped on the door and he turned to see Lark in the open doorway. She was wearing a white blouse and black skirt, black fishnet hose, and black shoes with low heels, the uniform for her catering job that he wouldn't have noticed on anyone else. Inky strands of hair had slipped loose from the clip on top of her head and spilled across her forehead like a wild pony's forelock.

"Hey, Dave, I'm really sorry for not telling you about my dad when I offered you a room. You looked like you were having cardiac arrest when he first walked into the kitchen."

"It's okay. Unexpected, but not a big deal." Her father was shaping up to be a pain in the ass, but he'd made a promise to himself to tough things out in Avalon. "Your father and I had breakfast together. We bonded."

"I'll bet." She laughed, and her eyes crinkled at the corners and became almost almond-shaped. She was so damned pretty, Dave suddenly wanted to kiss her.

"Room okay?" She gestured toward the bed with both hands as if she were demonstrating the top prize on a game show. She'd asked him last night and he'd told her it was fine, anything was better than sleeping in the street.

"The room is good."

"You're exaggerating. Anyway, this morning I talked to my boss about giving you some work. She says there's nothing right now, but she'll keep you in mind."

Dave shrugged. He was disappointed, but when he'd made his list last night he'd included a reminder to himself to put in applications at every fast food restaurant, convenience store, and other place of business on the bus line. Someone was bound to hire him at minimum wage.

"You poor thing, don't look so dejected. My father wants to take you out with him this afternoon. He says he can use you on a repair job he's got lined up. Mini-job, Dave. Better than nothing."

"Your father? Listen, Lark..." How could he put this without hurting her feelings or offending Joe the Terrible? "That's nice of him, but I've got a plan of attack for a job search mapped out."

He dropped the book and grabbed the Mental Giant. He waved it back and forth. Take note, interested parties. Dave Griffin has his whole day mapped out.

"Been hunting all over for you." Joe appeared behind Lark. "You said you'd take any job, and I'm offering one. It's a baseboard repair out near the stadium. We're leaving in twenty minutes."

"Thanks, but there's no need to invent work for me. I'll find something on my own. Making sandwiches. Emptying trash. Cleaning toilets." Dave wasn't fooled by the Mr. Congeniality act Joe put on when Lark was around.

"After we finish, I'll take you around to apply wherever your little soul chooses. Now quit moping and get your shoes on." He smiled tenderly in Dave's direction, looking exactly like a loving father trying to prod his rebellious son into doing what was best. But Dave was sure that as soon as they got in the truck, he'd turn into the bully whose new hobby appeared to be centered on kicking Dave while he was down.

He reached for his shoes, his teeth grinding together so hard it felt like he was about to snap a filling off. Joe had promised him half a day's work. He'd made a promise to Mawmaw that he wouldn't turn down honest work and he was going to keep that promise--even if Joe hauled him off into the woods somewhere and murdered him.

God, where had that thought come from? He'd been down so long, he didn't recognize up when it happened along. The man was just trying to be nice, even if he was lacking in social skills.

Chapter Fourteen

Joe didn't really have a job lined up for this afternoon, all he had was a woman needing an estimate, but what better way to evaluate Dave's potential as an assistant than to spend a few hours of quality time together driving around Avalon? Besides, he needed to get out of the house for a smoke and he wasn't about to leave Lark and Dave home alone.

"Where we headed?" Dave asked as Joe turned the truck off Oak Street and aimed it toward the beltway. He sat scrunched into the passenger seat between the door and a pile of Joe's work tools, his feet resting on a toolbox.

"Out and about." Joe stuck a cigarette in his mouth and lit it. "It's a pretty day--might as well enjoy it. You ever been down to the river? Lots of trees and shady spots, nature and stuff. Good fishing, too, if you've got a boat. Most of the land is private, so you need a boat--no access except for the public dock."

"I've been by there a few times, but the river doesn't really hold much interest for me. Mostly I've been out to the lake."

Of course he had. Joe knew that people like Dave weren't interested in fishing or in lazy days spent meandering down the Avalon River, which was notoriously narrow and winding. They liked fast boats and jet skiing on the lake. But the river held a great deal of interest for Joe, and he was going to swing by before they did anything else. It was a recent habit, born of his desire to find a way to get revenge, combined with a restlessness that seemed to have come into his spirit with the lessening of his depression. Anyway, they had time. His potential customer wasn't expecting him for another couple of hours.

He slanted a glance to his right. Dave was frowning, no doubt realization dawning that they were headed out of town into what passed for country in Avalon, the poster city for suburban sprawl.

"I thought you said this job was near the stadium." He put his hand on the dash to steady himself as Joe took an exit and whipped the truck around a curve, the bad tires whining against the pavement.

"Later. First I want to show you something."

The road quickly narrowed to two lanes, curving between stands of trees that stood thick and proud, having never known the buzz of chain saws or the roar of logging trucks. Another five miles and a single lane driveway led off the road to the left and toward the river, where a wood frame house painted white was just visible through the trees. Joe bounced the truck on past. Then less then half a mile farther on, a dirt road appeared, a pale line just barely noticeable between tufts of underbrush. He turned off, slowing the truck to a crawl as branches scraped the sides and the top like brittle fingers trying to poke their way inside.

"Dave, look through the mess on the seat and find the binoculars. We're parking in the clearing just ahead and walking about a quarter of a mile toward the river to a spot where we can hide in a thicker stand of trees. And stop looking at me like you think I'm going to knock you over the head and dump you from the Officer Culhane Memorial Bridge on my way back to town."

Dave grunted. He sat still as a little statue in his corner, his face frozen into the blankest expression Joe had ever seen. He was probably wishing this was all a bad dream and he'd wake up in his cubicle in the Pyramid Building with his fingers pounding away on his keyboard. Joe could almost work up some sympathy.

"Boo!" Joe made a sudden movement with his right hand, and Dave jumped halfway out of his seat. Joe laughed so hard he almost steered the truck off the road.

Dave shot him a dark look and turned sideways to stare out the window until Joe parked the truck and they got out. He led the way down a path that was more of a thin line in the underbrush than a clear place to walk. A couple of rabbits bounded out from under a tangle of blackberry bushes. Cottontails flashed and they disappeared behind a log. Not surprising. Dave was making enough noise for a regiment. You'd think he'd been born and raised in the city instead of coming from farm country.

A bare wisp of a breeze sprang up and ruffled Joe's hair. The only sound was the high pitched warble of a bird in the tree closest to him. He sniffed. He smelled dank river mud before he saw the water. They pushed on and reached the stand of trees, and he signaled Dave to get on the ground next to him. They lay on their stomachs, and he handed Dave the binoculars, pointing in the direction he wanted him to look. When he was sure Dave had seen the bench and the wooden dock with the rowboat tied to a piling, he took the binoculars back and studied the scene for himself. Then, motioning for silence--habit only, since there was no one around--he got up and led them back the way they'd come.

When they were back in the truck, Joe reached automatically for a cigarette and then remembered he never took the chance of smoking while he was out here. It would be too easy to drop a butt and leave evidence. They could even get your DNA from cigarette butts these days. Not that he'd done anything wrong by conducting surveillance. They were on public property as long as they didn't pass the line of trees where they'd lain down and looked through binoculars. But you couldn't be too careful when it came to senators. Too full of self-importance, they were liable to squeal like cornered hogs if they felt threatened.

He leaned against the back of his seat and stretched. He felt blood zinging through his veins with the old excitement. "What did you think?"

"River. Bench. Dock and rowboat. Can we go now?" Dave rubbed a line of sweat off his forehead. His heart was skittering in his chest. He wasn't one bit happy about being dragged down to the river for show and tell. A place this far out of town with nothing around except for a few rich people's homes would be a great spot to commit a crime where you could be sure there would be no pesky witnesses to spoil your fun. And something about Joe Tremaine didn't seem right, though Dave couldn't figure out what the problem was. Right now he trusted Joe about as far as he could hurl the Behemoth--if he still had the Behemoth.

"Wiseass. I brought you here for a reason. You know who owns that little patch of land next to the river?"

"No idea."

"Friend of Senator Buford Drake. Drake owns an estate in town, but his friend lets him use this place like it was his own. He comes here for privacy, if you know what I mean. That's his friend's cottage we passed just before we turned off the main road. White frame place, looks like it belongs in a magazine. Glassed in sunroom around the back. Course you can't see much from the road. I know what it looks like, though. Been there."

"Am I supposed to be awed and humbled at the sight of Senator Drake's good fortune?" If so, Joe was going to end up disappointed. As far as Dave was concerned, if Senator Drake dropped out of the next senate race, he'd be doing a service for his country.

"Nope. I'm just trying to educate you about what goes on in the man's life when he isn't in Washington thinking up ways to send this country down the toilet. What you didn't see--because the Senator isn't here today--is him strolling along on the walking path. He goes out to his bench, carries his fishing pole and his red tackle box with him, sits down like he wants to admire the mist coming off the river and maybe take in the smell of honeysuckle floating on the breeze." Joe paused and closed his eyes. He drew in a deep breath and sighed, demonstrating how the Senator reacted to the honeysuckle and the mist. "Man, that smells so good. I surely do enjoy my friend's home on the river."

"Your point is--"

"Shut up and listen. Sometimes he gets in his rowboat and goes fishing, comes back with a whole mess of little bass, too small to be legal, but he's a senator and nobody tries to stop him from killing baby fish. But sometimes a woman, not always the same one, comes along and she, too, is practically knocked on her ass by all the sights and smells of raw nature. She's looking around, gaping her mouth like an oxygen-starved guppy, and she's carrying a fishing pole like she's just out to snare a few bass. She spots Senator Drake on his bench and she stops like she doesn't expect to see him. They greet each other, casual, people just being friendly. She sits down and they talk. From where I am with my binoculars, I can't tell what they're saying, but I can imagine. Few minutes later, they take their fishing poles and head off toward the Senator's place. Later the woman comes out and walks back the way she came. Once in a while he brings one of his young ladies out here with him. Most of the time, from what I can see, they arrive on their own and go back the same way."

"You're saying the Senator cheats on his wife? Am I supposed to call the cops and report what he's doing?"

"Dave, I just figured this was something interesting I could show you since we're roommates and friends. I thought you might get a kick out of seeing how the Senator lives and how he doesn't respect his marriage vows, and him married to a real nice southern lady and all." Joe patted his shoulder and gave him the kind of smile that he usually reserved for Lark's benefit.

Roommates and friends? Dave didn't have such a great track record lately at brilliant thought and wise decision making, but he'd have to be in a coma not to figure out that Joe had more than a passing interest in Senator Drake. He'd have to remember to stand clear when Joe did whatever he planned to do.

"Besides," Joe went on, "if I ever had anything to report on the Senator or anyone else, I could manage without the Avalon cops. I don't suppose I told you yet, but I used to work for the government."

"Doing what?" Dave didn't for one minute believe the government would have anything to do with Joe Tremaine. Joe spoke like an educated man and he obviously had street smarts, but in the few hours Dave had known him, he sometimes gave the impression of a gun about to go off and take out a lot of innocent bystanders.

"Can't tell you exactly. Let's just say I have a lot of special skills and training."

"Such as?"

"Such as, I know how to handle guns, conduct surveillance, and take people down."

What kind of crap was this? Joe must think he was a kid who'd be impressed by his line of bull. "I suppose you got burned out leaving all those bodies lying around and decided to come back to Avalon for early retirement."

"No." Joe jammed the key into the ignition. "Some twisted son of a bitch who should have been in prison threw me off the roof of a two story building. Bounced off a cherry tree and that broke my fall. Ended up with a bad knee--I'm sure you noticed the limp--and a brain seizure problem from getting my skull cracked all to hell. Government didn't have any use for Joe Tremaine after that. Let's head back to town. I'll buy you a cup of coffee at the McDonalds closest to the house and you can put in a job application."

Joe was pleased with himself. He'd shown Dave the bench by the river and gotten pretty much the reaction he expected. Dave wasn't shocked or anything over the Senator, though he was probably raised as one of those little Bible thumper boys who'd walk ten miles out of their way to return a quarter to the rightful owner. But he was sure of one thing. Dave's recent baptism in the unemployment font had taught him that sometimes you had to get creative when it came to survival. Yeah, Joe knew Dave was finally giving up the idea that he'd bounce back into corporate America and figuring out that when the rules favored the big guys, he'd have to change the way he played the game. The kid would do just fine for running a bingo hall. He was sure Dave wouldn't raise objections when he told him they'd keep the charity money for themselves. After they left McDonald's, Joe drove a few streets over to a prospective customer who needed baseboards repaired and had asked for an estimate. He underbid the job, saying they could do it right away at that price, so Dave wouldn't think he'd made up the story about having a job for him. At first he thought the old lady would turn down the bid. Anger flared in his chest, so Joe had to keep telling himself it was no big deal. A headache was crawling up the back of his neck, despite the fistful of aspirins he'd downed after breakfast. But then the woman suddenly waved her hand and said to go ahead. He had to make a quick trip to the truck to smoke a cigarette and to wipe sweat off his face with a dirty rag before they started the job. Then he backed the truck up closer to the house so they wouldn't have to walk so far to reach the tools.

Dave waited for him in the yard, his hands on his hips. "You've got a taillight out on the truck, Joe."

"That right? Guess I'll have to go to the vault and take out money to fix that and get myself a new set of tires while I'm at it. Hell, might as well get enough to buy myself two or three new trucks." He was gratified to see Dave's face flush red before he turned away and busied himself studying the ground.

Dave swung a hammer like it was a flyswatter and he wasted more nails than he used, but when they were through, Joe gave him a couple of dollars. Probably the first money he'd earned since he lost his computer job. Joe sneaked a glance as they pulled out of the driveway. Hard to say, but the corners of that downturned mouth might be moving north just a little.

On the way home, Joe swung past the Quick Buy and stole a carton of cigarettes. Dave stared at him openly, watching from where he'd planted himself by the door. Joe would have to teach him better. He had to learn some cool before they set up the bingo business.

Lark had already left for the park by the time they got back. Dave put on a pout about not seeing her. He didn't say anything, but Joe could read every expression that flitted across his too-open face. He let Dave help him fix a pot of spaghetti, so he could keep him around instead of letting him sit in his room thinking of reasons why he didn't like Joe Tremaine and how easy it would be to get a bus ticket back to Hidden Springs.

Joe used a fork to shove the meatballs around the pan to brown them evenly. He motioned for Dave to stir the spaghetti and said, "You've got a college degree, right?"

"Computer science and business minor. What about you?"

"What makes you think I have an education?" Meatballs were done enough. Joe dumped in the sauce and turned up the gas flame on the stove.

"The government job you told me about. Or was that just a fairy tale?"

"Political science, but a degree isn't worth the match to burn it, if the government fires you and no one's hiring. Reason I was asking is that I've had in mind for some time to set up a--let's just call it for the moment, my own company. You studied business. You must know about tax laws and finances, right? And you know all about computers and how to set up files. And I'll bet you can do a pretty good job of designing brochures and flyers and printing them off." The bingo hall wouldn't earn squat if they didn't advertise.

"Of course." Dave furrowed his brow, and Joe could almost see little wheels wobbling in his head as he tried to get his thoughts up and running. "But what about your home repair business?"

"That's not working out." Joe leaned in close and lowered his voice. "Don't tell Lark, because she'd just worry herself sick, but I barely make enough to cover my expenses. I'll have to kill you if you say anything."

"I know. Leave no marks, hide the body from the rats." Dave rolled his eyes. "You know something, Joe? I'd like you a whole lot better if you didn't keep threatening to kill me."

"I'm not trying to win a popularity contest. You want the job? Set up the books, do the advertising, be my right hand man?"

"What type of business?"

Joe used a fork to wrap a wad of spaghetti around a big spoon. "Here, taste this." He pushed the spoon at Dave.

Dave jumped back. "Ow. I burned my tongue."

"You ought to know better than to let somebody shove a hot spoon in your mouth. What do you say?"

"What kind of business is it?"

"I'm telling you, if you'll just shut up and listen. That's a big fault with you, Dave--you keep interrupting while I'm trying to explain things. This business I'm trying to tell you about is church. It's all about me being a preacher and you being my assistant."

"Church?" Dave's voice cracked. "No. Absolutely not." He backed up against the refrigerator and crossed his arms over his chest. "I'd rather deliver pizza."

Joe walked to the kitchen window and made a big show of peering outside, looking in every direction including up. "I don't see the pizza delivery recruiters lining up for you in the back yard. Maybe you ought to reconsider."

"No way."

"Why? Is helping out a preacher against your religion?"

"You're no more a preacher than I am. You'd just be scamming money off poor people and keeping it for yourself, and that's no better than being a thief."

"Wrong on both counts. I am an ordained minister of the non-denominational Sweet Jesus Church of Love. The love offerings collected in the Sunday basket will be returned to the poor in the form of charity works. Money brought in through other fundraisers will provide a fair salary for me and my assistant. I don't see why you don't jump on this opportunity." Joe sighed deeply and stared off toward the living room as if he were seeing angels and saintly figures that only a man of God could perceive in the dim light of late afternoon.

"The Sweet Jesus Church of Love? Don't tell me. You bought your preacher credentials off the Internet." Dave had started pacing between the kitchen and the living room, sure sign that Joe had him at least thinking about giving in.

"Nothing wrong with that."

"The whole scheme stinks. I'm picturing a dingy, rented rathole with Church of Joe in neon over the door."

"That would be tacky, Dave. I'm planning a class operation. All I have to do is get up the money to rent the church building and buy some fund-raising equipment."

"I don't see it happening. I'll settle for a restaurant job and you can find some other flunky to knock around. Besides, you don't have the money to set up a business."

"What if I told you I can get the funding? A job's a job, you said so yourself. I get the money, you take the job. Deal?" Joe was flying now, sure that he could do anything. Those rich old ladies had money and he was going to take it from them. All legal. "It's not like you've got computer jobs to pick and choose from."

"I'm wondering how you intend to make money running a church."

"Fundraisers." When Dave still looked blank, Joe added, "Bingo. Sweet little blue-hairs with rich husbands to give them lots of money to spend gambling."

Joe lifted the spaghetti pot and carried it to the sink. His heart was pounding in his chest and his breathing was too quick, making him feel like the spicy smell of the sauce was pouring down into his lungs and gumming his airways up. Must be the aspirins. He'd have to look around the house and see if he could find something else for the headaches. Anyway, he'd given Dave the idea and now he just had to be patient about letting him think things over. He'd have his answer by morning and he was one hundred percent certain what that answer would be. Dave still hadn't lost that "my world is shattered" expression he'd been wearing ever since Joe met him.

Tonight, after supper, Joe would go to his room and drag out the Bible he had in there somewhere. If his mind would stop sending him squiggly signals, he'd practice writing a sermon and later he could read it to Dave to prove he really was a minister. He'd work up something Dave would appreciate, such as how God smited down the enemies of the righteous--or was it smote?

Dave lay on his back in bed, his hands behind his head. He'd survived a day of being shepherded around town by Joe Tremaine, local sociopath, and he'd even survived Lark's announcement at supper that she was going out tomorrow night with Steve, one of the musicians from the park. He'd already figured Lark had to be seeing someone. But he'd sort of counted on having her around in the evenings, at least part of the time, to serve as a buffer between him and Joe. And he had to admit he was disappointed. Despite Joe's warnings, Dave had intended to ask her out himself.

He still planned to keep putting in job applications at restaurants and stores, but until someone called, he supposed he'd have to go along with Joe and his church bingo scheme. What else could he do? Joe was right about one thing--the employers of the job world weren't exactly strewing rose petals in the path of Dave Griffin. What it came down to, he supposed, was that when you got knocked down to a place where mere survival remained your only option, you kept lowering your expectations until the unthinkable finally became the obvious solution.

Chapter Fifteen

In the morning Dave slid out of bed and stood in front of the cracked mirror on his bedroom wall to practice lifting his chin and looking self-confident and prosperous. After five minutes of effort, he figured the best he'd accomplished was the expression of a slightly bewildered crime victim.

Lark wasn't working today and she joined them at the table to share a platter of biscuits that Joe proudly announced he'd made to showcase his breakfast cooking skills.

Dave tasted and he had to admit the biscuits were first class. "Very good, Joe. Points on. And you will be happy to know I'm accepting your job offer."

"What offer?" Lark looked from Joe to Dave and back again. Too late, Dave realized he shouldn't have said anything in front of her. "Dad, do you have enough repair work to hire Dave?"

"No, sweetheart, I'm putting my preacher credentials to work-- starting a church. Dave will set up the books, do the advertising, help me out with the fund raisers."

Lark put both hands on the table and levered herself halfway out of her chair. "Dad, we talked about this already. You don't have a religious thought in your mind." Her voice took on the tone of someone delivering a lecture to a naughty child. "Besides, you can't just put up a tent in a vacant lot. You need a building and money."

"All taken care of. Dave has enough cash to get us started and he's generously offered to invest in the Sweet Jesus Church of Love, Avalon congregation."

Lark sent Dave a startled glance. He didn't blame her. He would have sent himself a startled glance if it had been possible. He didn't need the murderous glare from Joe's onyx eyes to know enough to keep his mouth shut.

"We'll start out small. Advertise to get church members, run some fundraisers, and soon we'll have enough coming in to move away from Oak Street forever. Trust your father, Lark. Haven't I always taken good care of you? I'm excited about the opportunity to spread the word of salvation."

He did look excited, Dave concluded. Coaster sized circles of red had appeared on Joe's cheeks, and his forehead was sheened with sweat, but Dave still didn't trust any emotion Joe cared to exhibit. He'd learned in the day and a half since he'd met Joe--the man was gifted with the ability to change his voice, his manner, and his expression to suit any occasion.

"Dave?" Lark's uncertainty showed in her eyes.

"Your dad and I have an understanding."

"I'd hate to see you lose your money. And in case you haven't already figured it out, my father doesn't care about religion."

"Hey, girl, don't talk trash about your dad." Joe scowled, and Lark patted his hand.

"You know I'm your number one fan, Dad. I just want to make sure Dave doesn't lose what little money he has."

"Don't worry." Dave stared into his plate. "I don't believe I'm risking a dime."

Joe let out his breath in a long audible sigh. Dave knew he'd scored points by not tattling. He couldn't help but wonder what Joe would have done if he'd told Lark the truth.

Lark lapsed into silence. After a few moments of drumming her fingers on the table, she turned her attention to Joe, who was working on swallowing an orange pill the size of a cherry tomato.

"What's that?" she asked.

"My seizure medicine, honey."

"Since when? Dad, your pills are half that size and they're white."

"Good God, Lark, why are you all of a sudden so worried about what color pills I take? You think I'm on street drugs or something? Doctor changed my prescription, is all. These work better."

"Why didn't you tell me?"

"No need. New medicine's working fine; it's called Seizure-Out. I'm cured of having seizures, I'm starting a brand new church, and I feel good about my life for the first time since I got hurt. Now stop trying to put me down."

Lark picked up her fork and used it to poke at the biscuit on her plate until it was a pile of crumbs. Dave wished he could break the awkward silence, but he was sure he'd only make things worse. And he was sure there was something he didn't know, some undercurrent to their conversation, but it wasn't like he could ask, and it wasn't his business anyway.

Dave helped Lark clear up the dishes and then, even though Joe wanted him to start on the church paperwork right away, he took a few minutes to call Mawmaw. She worried if she didn't hear from him every few days, and he needed to tell her about paying the tax bill so she wouldn't sell the farm.

"Sugarbiscuit! You know you shouldn't have. You need the money for yourself, not for paying my tax bill."

"No, Mawmaw, it's not *your* tax bill--it's *our* tax bill. Besides, I won't starve. I found a job."

"You did? I'm so happy for you. Praise Jesus."

"Don't get too excited. It's not a programming job and it doesn't pay all that much." He'd have to remember to ask Joe exactly how much he'd be earning. "I'm an assistant at a new church." He caught Joe watching him from across the room and he turned to face the kitchen where Lark was sweeping the floor. How did she manage to move like a swan gliding across a pond even when she was just doing chores?

"You can't go wrong working for a church. Didn't I always tell you the Lord will provide?"

"That's right, Mawmaw. My whole life has turned around. I've got these two nice roommates, Joe Tremaine and his daughter Lark, a fun job, and money coming in. I've got to hang up now. My boss has some work for me."

"Call me again real soon."

He powered off his cell phone. Joe got up and crossed the room to hand him a notepad. Dave paged through the papers. As near as he could tell, they were notes about Joe's plans for the church written in pen. Dave squinted. Joe's handwriting looked like what might happen if a chicken stepped in ink and walked across a piece of paper.

Joe jabbed his arm. "You'll have to learn how to control the tension in your voice if you're going to keep lying to your grandmother."

"You're one to talk about lying." And stealing, too, but Dave didn't bring that up. He had a pretty good idea Lark was clueless about Joe and his cigarettes.

"Don't get pissy with me. I'm just trying to teach you something."

"If I want schooling, I'll let you know."

"Oh, for heaven's sake." Lark moved between them and put her hands on her hips. "You two sound like an old married couple who never got along. Now go work on your church papers and get out of my way."

Lark insisted that Dave come with her to the park that night. About time something went his way in this household, though Dave suspected she just wanted to give him a break from Joe. Now that Dave had agreed to work for him, Joe acted like the opportunity to found his very own church would vanish into mist if he didn't move at the speed of light. Dave felt like his eyes would quit on him any second if he were forced to keep trying to decipher Joe's writing.

"It's not as if you need him to work, Dad," Lark said. "You've kept him at his computer ever since we finished the breakfast dishes."

"Sure, sure, what am I thinking? Wouldn't want poor Dave to keel over from exhaustion before I even preach the first sermon. You go on and get your things and I'll walk him to the car." Joe put his arm around Dave's shoulders and dragged him outside through the back door before Dave could say he knew where the car was parked and could manage all by himself.

"Keep your mouth shut, okay?" Joe said, leaning down and putting his mouth close to Dave's ear. "Remember, if you say anything that gets Lark upset--I don't have to spell it out for you, do I?"

"Just go back in the house and watch some crime shows or do your nails or something and give me a break."

Joe narrowed his eyes and shoved Dave backward into the nearest bush. "Don't forget who's in charge of this operation, Gomer."

Lark appeared around the corner of the house, and Joe, suddenly amiable as a puppy, hauled Dave out of the bush and brushed dirt and leaves off his shirt. "Damn it, watch your step. You keep falling down in those bushes, they're liable to lose their shape." He opened the car door and gestured for Dave to get in.

"See you two kids later." He stood in the yard and waved as Lark backed the car out of the driveway.

Dave tried to think calming thoughts. Evening with Lark. Beautiful weather, stars plastered all over the sky like silver glitter on a velvet blanket, big pale moon coming up through the trees. More importantly, time away from Joe. He still didn't relax enough to think of a clever conversational opener until they were three blocks away.

"Thanks for getting me out of the house for a while." Okay, not clever. Sounded like he was a dog who needed to go for a run. But really good considering the last few minutes with Joe.

"I know my father can come across like the Terminator on speed. But he likes you."

"You think?" Dave fiddled with his seat belt, finally getting it adjusted to his satisfaction.

"Sure. He told me you have a lot of potential. He never would have said that unless he liked you."

"He's okay," Dave said. "I guess I can understand why he feels so bitter, after the government fired him. It's bound to be tough going from a job as an agent, where he even had to kill people, and suddenly be of no use to his country because some criminal tossed him off a roof."

Lark stopped for a red light, hitting the brakes so hard the car skidded. She turned to look at him, her lips tightening. "Is that what he told you? My dad didn't fall off a roof. He got hit by a car. He used to work for the IRS and there certainly was no shooting going on. He sat at a desk all day checking tax returns. God, I'm sorry he told you all that--I'll speak to him."

Dave shook his head. He should have known Joe was lying. "No. That would just hurt his feelings."

"Of course." Her eyes had gone shiny with tears that seemed to magnify their dark beauty. After a few seconds, she said, "You're sweet to think of being kind to my dad. I hope you don't hold it against him--the lies, I mean. He's been through so much and the job loss has crushed him. But then, you know all about what it's like to lose your job."

The light went green and she eased the Nissan into the intersection. Dave stared straight ahead, watching the taillights on a car far in front of them jouncing up and down on the road. Ever since he'd been fired from Markham-Hook, he'd been feeling like he didn't belong in society, like he was some kind of phantom ghosting around the edges of life with no part to play. Joe, with his seizures and his bad leg, must feel even worse.

"Poor Dad. I can't imagine what he was thinking to tell you he went around killing people. Anyway, he wouldn't even know how to...well, he can probably shoot." She laughed. "Okay, I'm sure he knows about guns. He took me to the shooting range with him once when I was a little girl. In fact, I think he has a gun for protection, but I have no idea where he keeps it. Still, there's a big difference between being some kind of agent or whatever he told you he was and working at a desk in the IRS."

"No problem. I understand he had a head injury." Dave knew better than to criticize Joe to his own daughter.

"That part's true. He fractured his skull when he landed headfirst on the road. His medication controls his seizures and he's fine now, except for depression, and that seems to be improving. I guess he's right about the new medication working--I haven't seen him this interested in anything for a long time. But are you sure you're okay with loaning him money for the church? I know you can't afford to lose it, and you can see he's not a good risk."

"I think he has a building in mind and it's cheap." He turned his head to the side, pretending to be interested in a dog loping along beside the road.

Something inside him went sick over lying to her. He was following Joe's orders to avoid upsetting Lark, though he wasn't quite sure why he should listen to Joe after he'd spent yesterday afternoon feeding him a pack of lies. IRS tax inspector. He couldn't have guessed that was Joe's former occupation, but then Joe didn't look like a government agent, either. On the other hand, government agents weren't supposed to look the part.

He concentrated on his plans for the evening. He'd enjoy Lark's show and he'd enjoy socializing with her friends. He wasn't going to like watching Lark sitting with Steve and, later, leaving with him for their date. But he was sure Joe would have a list of chores lined up when he returned to the house on Oak Street, so he wouldn't have time to brood. He didn't know why he was sticking around anyway. It wasn't like Lark had any interest in him, and his job prospects weren't exactly something to brag about. The roadside vegetable stand he kept picturing back in Hidden Springs was starting to look better every minute.

Joe yanked open the front curtains and stood for a moment in the morning sun, letting it warm his freshly shaved face. He brushed a thread off his shirt and crossed the room to sit on the couch. He picked up his Bible off the coffee table and rested it on his lap. If he was going to pretend to be a preacher, he needed the props. He should probably ask Martha to quiz him to make sure he knew his stuff. He slid his cuff back and consulted his watch. Plenty of time to get across town unless they ran into heavy traffic.

Dave made his appearance a few minutes later, and Joe looked him up and down, finally nodding and letting out a low whistle. "Don't you look nice wearing that jacket and tie? Even combed your hair. I figured you'd clean up real good, even though Lark said she doubted you'd ever look like anything more than a mangy hound."

"Where we going, Joe?" Dave straightened his tie. He was not showing any enthusiasm for the project, but Joe was sure he'd perk up when the money started rolling in.

Joe handed him a manila folder. "Hang on to this until I ask for it. We're going to get the money for the church. Didn't I tell you that last night after you got home moping over Lark going out on a date with someone who isn't you?"

"You said we're getting money. But where and how?"

"Stop worrying. When we go into Nick LaRose's loan office, you keep your mouth shut unless you're asked questions, and then you can explain how you're setting up the business side of things, tell them you're my business analyst. We'll walk out of there with plenty of money to rent a building and move out of this hellhole, too. Trust me."

Dave was going to throw a tantrum when he found out they were getting the money from a loan shark. But he had manners and he was fast developing common sense. He'd discreetly wait until they'd left the presence of the big man and his beefy underlings before he started squawking and threatening to go home to Mawmaw.

By this time next week, they'd be in the building and ready for their first night of business and about time, way past time, and maybe Joe would be able to afford some kind of prescription for his headaches because the aspirins made him feel awfully funny in his head.

LaRose had set up his loan headquarters in a respectable part of town. But Joe had done his homework, courtesy of the loose lips down at the shelter. People who didn't know about LaRose's other enterprises would never suspect he was anything other than an ordinary businessman who just happened to employ oversize men with names such as Billy the Ax and One-Eyed Walt.

Joe parked behind the building under the wide spreading branches of an oak. Dave started to slide out of the truck, and Joe grabbed his arm. "Hey, you forgot the papers."

Dave rolled his eyes and picked up the manila folder. "I suppose it would be too much for you to carry."

"You're the assistant and I'm the Reverend Joe Tremaine." He shoved the envelope into Dave's hands. "Don't get uppity."

He led the way around the front and pushed open the door. Dark, polished wood with solid brass fittings. Nice. The sign near the road said the place housed attorney's offices. No mention of LaRose and his name wasn't on the office directory, but his contact had said the second floor, Suite 2B.

The building, like most of the others on this street, had been renovated at some time in the past from a stately home to offices. The walls of the lobby were decorated with oil paintings featuring seascapes where ships laden with sails battled monster waves. Joe nodded his approval. You could tell what the artist painted, instead of having to decipher dabs of paint that looked like a chimpanzee lobbed them onto the canvas after a hard day swinging through the trees running errands for Tarzan.

The windows let in a lot of light, considering they were on the shady side of the building. The walls were paneled in dark wood and an oriental rug in a red and black pattern covered half the floor. Place smelled of orange blossoms. And money. LaRose was doing all right to afford this building. But then, what loan shark wasn't? Joe nodded at the receptionist, who offered no challenge, and headed for the elevator.

The lettering on the door of Suite 2B proclaimed that this was the office of Sunshine High Risk Loans. Joe smiled. He hadn't expected it to say, Nick LaRose, Avalon Loan Shark, but anything pairing sunshine and high risk loans was like saying Joyous Day Boot Camp. He knew from talking to people down at the shelter that LaRose ran a legitimate loan business and also handled cases like Joe's, cases that were off the books because the interest rates and the collection methods weren't legal. He supposed such loans were rated super high risk-- maybe something LaRose called Double Sunshine High Risk Loans.

They walked into a room that looked more like a prosperous person's well-appointed living room than an office reception area. Dave followed so close on his heels that he bumped into him when Joe stopped.

He surveyed the room, noting the leather upholstered couches and armchairs, the television--tuned to *The Price is Right*--and a stack of business magazines on a glass-topped coffee table. There were two doors other than the entry door, one to his right and one straight ahead.

A man, a six-and-a-half footer who looked like he'd recently been whacked in the face with a slab of granite, bounded up from the couch with more speed than Joe would have expected from a lump his size. He eyed them like they were rotten eggs. He probably didn't appreciate being interrupted while contestants were bidding on a washer-dryer combination.

"Joseph Tremaine?"

"Yes. I have an appointment with Mr. LaRose."

"Who said you could bring someone with you, you stupid son of a bitch? Him, too, whoever he is. He's a stupid son of a bitch."

"Mr. Griffin is my assistant." He kept his voice and his facial expression pleasant, but if Joe didn't need money, he'd have taken this ape down in two seconds.

LaRose's man grunted. He stepped forward and ran a metal detector over them and then frisked them for good measure. After that, he snatched the manila folder out of Dave's hands and looked inside before handing it back.

Dave's eyes had gone big as gumballs. Joe nudged him in the ribs with his elbow. He'd known the kid wasn't ready for prime time. Best way to learn, though--total immersion, just like picking up a foreign language.

"Go through that door." Muscle jerked his head toward the door between the couch and the TV.

Joe had to grab Dave's arm and pull him along to get him started, and then they were through the door and in another office. Nick LaRose stood behind a massive desk that was probably solid cherry. He was a tall man, built like a football lineman. Wiry gray hair stuck up from his head in spikes and his eyes were a soft velvet brown that didn't go with the rest of his appearance or his reputation.

He pulled his chair closer and sat. He had doughy hands that he placed palms down on the desktop. Dual pinkie rings and a wedding ring. Nails polished with clear lacquer.

"You're late, Tremaine." No expression in his low pitched voice.

"Your receptionist held us up. Gave us some lip about our ancestry and then insulted us even more by doing a weapons search."

"That's his job. Who's the baby?"

"This is Mr. Griffin--my bodyguard."

Joe wished he had a camera to record the expressions that paraded one at a time across Nick LaRose's face, ending with a booming laugh that brought tears to his eyes. At least he'd loosened up, which was what Joe intended.

"What's he going to do if I decide to shoot you? Hit me with his rattle?"

"He's bigger than he looks. Now that we've finished with the introductions, I'm ready to talk terms." The headache, which was almost constant now despite his having doubled the dose of the Seizure-Out and the aspirins, jabbed him in the temple and for a few seconds he saw purple flames licking the ceiling. He blinked and they went away. Damn shame about the headache because if it weren't for that, he felt good, better than he'd ever felt, and ready to get back into the business world.

LaRose had kept them standing in front of his desk where he probably had a mini arsenal in his desk drawers in case they misbehaved. He leaned toward them and said, "How much you need and for how long?"

Joe turned to Dave and plucked the folder out of his hand. "I've got the information right here--the amount I'll need and my projected income." He'd added enough extra to the loan amount so they could afford to move right away.

He slid the folder across the desk. LaRose put on a pair of reading glasses and studied the paper, taking longer than he needed to.

"Preacher, huh?" he said, finally looking up.

"Duly ordained and ready to bring the good word to those who thirst for salvation."

"What's a preacher need with a bodyguard?" LaRose glanced at Dave. His face twisted into a smirk.

"These are dangerous times."

LaRose shoved the folder away from him and leaned back, stretching his arms behind his head. "You're proposing a very risky enterprise. You've gotta know that, preacherman, or you'd have gone to a bank. Then there's the fact that you have a reputation in your side of town--Crazy Joe, isn't that what they call you?"

Joe clenched his fists. Shimmering waves of heat flared out from his torso and down his arms and legs. Did everybody in Avalon know what had happened to him? "I had a couple of seizures. All under control now, thanks to the miracle of modern medicine." He didn't know how he kept his voice steady or the smile on his face.

LaRose grunted. "You have to understand my side of things. I got a reputation of my own."

"So I've heard." LaRose's men had mastered the creative use of golf clubs when it came to dealing with people who defaulted on loans. But Joe wasn't going to fail. He had the whole business worked out, he'd sent in his papers, he had Dave to help him with the business side. His whole future, Lark's future, depended on him getting the money, and here he was having to beg from a man whose face had started to melt around the edges. Joe leaned over and gripped the desk, earning him a raised eyebrow from LaRose. No, LaRose's face was fine, it was only the stupid headache making him feel so rotten and he wouldn't have the stupid headache if LaRose would just give him the money.

"I know your terms and I'm willing to deal." Joe's voice came out dry. "Any interest rate you say."

Dave made a sound, might have been a squeak, and grabbed his arm. Joe shook him loose.

"Doesn't matter," LaRose said. "You think I like having to send my boys over to motivate flakes? Roughing you up won't pay my bills. I know about you, how you're a sick man."

"If you already planned to turn me down, why'd you agree to see me to begin with?"

"Just wanted to find out what you're up to. Curious, you might say. Now I know and I'm not interested."

"But, I—"

"Get out of my office, you crazy bastard."

LaRose punched a button on his desk, and the oversized cretin from the outer office peeled himself away from Bob Barker long enough to escort them out the door. Dave didn't take much persuading, Joe noticed.

Chapter Sixteen

True to Joe's predication, Dave waited until they were back in the truck before he kicked up a fuss. He made up for the time lag with a world class tantrum like Joe needed any more trouble today, any more noise with his head about to explode.

"You could have gotten us killed, you maniac. LaRose is a criminal. I'm through with you and your stupid schemes and I don't know why I ever agreed to this."

Joe put his hands to his forehead and rubbed back and forth as if he could rip the headache and the humiliation loose from his skull. Dave was not showing any gratitude to Joe for providing a job and a place to stay. Not only that, but his complexion had gone unhealthily pale, and Joe considered hunting up a paper bag for him to breathe into before he hyperventilated himself into a faint.

"Yeah, I know." Joe gave up on the forehead massage. The light was killing him, strobing in through his eyes and piercing his brain. He found his sunglasses on the truck seat and stuck them on his face. He started the truck and roared out of the parking lot into traffic, causing the driver of a minivan to jam on his brakes and lean on his horn. "You're giving up and going back to Mawmaw with your tail between your legs to build yourself a fruit stand."

"Vegetable stand. And what's wrong with that? If the only job left for me in Avalon is hanging around with you while you hatch up wild schemes involving people who make a living putting bodies in barrels, then I'd rather sit out in the hot sun all day trying to sell tomatoes."

"Hell, boy, you don't know how to build stuff. I saw how you knocked the nails in all crooked when we worked on those baseboards. Didn't your daddy ever teach you anything?"

Dave wrapped his arms around his middle and stared straight ahead. "No. He died."

Joe chewed on his lip for a minute. Damn. It was tough losing your father and Joe ought to know. His own dad had run off when Joe was only seven. Didn't even pretend he was going out for cigarettes, just said he was leaving, and drove off after work one day, his clothes in a paper bag and his new girlfriend sitting beside him in the front seat of a ragged-out Chevy wagon.

"Hey. I'm real sorry about that, okay?"

"I'm still not sticking around. I'm done with you and your lies."

The headache exploded across his forehead. Joe yanked the truck to a stop against the curb, nearly clipping a parked convertible. He shot his arm across the seat and grabbed a fistful of Dave's shirt. "Damn it, how do you think I feel, getting accused of being crazy by a piece of scum like Nick LaRose? Now you're calling me a liar, you pissant?"

"You heard me."

Brave sounding words, but he noticed Dave had unlocked the door and grabbed the handle, slithering closer to escape.

"Nobody calls me a liar and walks away without a scratch." He was damn tired of people thinking he was nothing because he had no job and thinking he was crazy because his head hurt and he'd had some kind of damn seizures. About time he let the world know that Joe Tremaine wasn't going to lie down and be a mat they could use to scrape their filthy shoes on. "Where the hell do you get off making accusations like that?"

"You told me you did secret work for the government like you were this country's answer to 007 or something and then Lark told me you were an IRS tax clerk and that you didn't fall off a building, you got hit by a car. I'll bet you killed a lot of people who tried to cheat the government out of money, didn't you? I'm sure people who claimed their dogs as exemptions or wrote off their groceries as a business expenses got blown straight to hell when you caught up with them."

"Jesus, Dave." Fireflies danced on the windshield. Joe peeled his fingers loose from Dave's shirt and dug around in his jacket pocket until he found a couple of aspirin. He swallowed them dry. Seconds later, flames roared to life in his stomach singeing off a layer of cells. "Just when I start believing you've got potential, you come up with something like this and disappoint me. You really think I'm going to let my little girl grow up scared that her father might end up in a bodybag instead of coming home to her every night?"

"When it comes to you, I don't know what to think."

"You don't have to think anything except that now you have a job, soon's I find the financing for the church." Poor little messed up Dave. His whole safe world had melted away like hot ice cream when Markham-Hook dumped him in the street. He was lucky Joe had come into his life to drag him out of the gutter. He pulled back onto the road, gritting his teeth against the stomach pain. "And for the record, the part about being a government agent and getting pushed off a roof is true."

"Prove it." Dave looked as smug as a squirrel who got all the acorns in the park. Joe was going to have to work on getting some respect out of him.

"I don't have to." Joe said. "Now forget all that and let me handle the tough side of the operation."

"You mean, such as getting money from loan sharks?"

"What are you worried about? I'm the one signing on the dotted line. Anything goes wrong, I'm the one they work over with golf clubs." But that wouldn't happen. His church was going to make him rich.

"Yeah, good luck with that. Sorry I won't be around to see it. That is, if you can find a loan shark willing to take a chance on you."

He went into a pout after that. Joe didn't bother him. He expected he'd have been pretty pissed himself if he were in Dave's shoes.

Joe turned left at the corner and aimed the truck west instead of east. Dave jerked upright in his seat and smacked him on the shoulder. "I said I'm getting my gear and leaving."

"Nobody's stopping you. First, though, I want to run by the building I'm planning to lease, take another look at the place and make sure I still like it. After that, we'll get your stuff and I'll drop you at the bus station. Fair enough?"

"I can't wait."

Dave had waited in the truck while Joe called the building's owner to meet them with the key and he'd had ample to time to cool off and reflect on the morning's events. Seeing an actual building made Joe's plan seem so much more reasonable. He had to admit, the building had potential. Joe had already worked out how many tables and chairs he could cram into the main room. Dave made a quick calculation. Bingo five nights a week times the number of cards per game times the price per card. Subtract a few dollars for prizes. He raised an eyebrow. Not bad. Plenty for the loan payment, even at a double digit interest rate. And once the loan was paid off there was real money to be made--if they could get enough players. He thought they could. Joe would turn on the charm with the lady customers. They'd knock each other out of the way to attend his bingo nights.

Dave figured he wasn't going to like working for Joe, but it was a job. Or maybe he should think of it as a JOB. The state of being employed surely deserved top billing.

Joe led him into the building and opened the door to a room painted robin's egg blue. There were windows on two walls and built-in bookshelves, as well as frilly curtains on the windows. Kind of Laura Ashley.

Joe said, "This is your office. I figured you'd like blue."

Not especially, but it sure beat the nicotine stained yellow back at Chez Joe on Oak Street. And, like Joe said, Dave was not a player as far as loan sharks were concerned. If any problems developed, they were Joe's worry. They were Joe's busted ribs and Joe's bloody face and Joe's bruises. He shuddered and pushed the mental image away. Just because Joe treated him like an especially dumb sidekick, didn't mean he had to enjoy the thought of Joe getting the crap beat out of him.

He didn't say a word, though, when Joe put in a call to someone to set him up with another loan shark, someone named Vin Shelton. He hoped Joe didn't expect him to go along this time to be a target.

When they got home, neither of them mentioned the original plan for Dave to pack his stuff and depart on a westbound Greyhound. He settled himself at the dining table with his laptop and worked on the advertising for Avalon Sweet Jesus Church of Love, while Joe put together a lasagna.

He thought for a few minutes, chin resting on his cupped hand, and then typed in a couple of lines. *Join a fine group of people. Our main concern is the dispensing of Christ's love through charitable works.*

Guilt clawed away at his soul, trying to get a tight hold, and he didn't respond. He'd started to add a line about helping hands, but he remembered Joe had said not to emphasize the charity part. Avalon gangsters and loan sharks wouldn't be swayed by excuses if a payment fell short because all the bingo money went to people in need.

Last year he would have been appalled at the thought of being part of an operation like this, but the events of the last few months had taught him a number of lessons, not the least of which was "adapt or die." And then there was "survival of the fittest." And "don't be a sheep." Not original, these lessons, but they served the purpose.

He hoped he'd be able to adapt to being around Joe. He still didn't know whether the government agent story was true. What Joe had said about not telling Lark made perfect sense, yet he'd seen Joe lie and he'd seen him steal cigarettes. And even if, as Dave suspected, the government had taken one look at Joe Tremaine and said, "no thanks," that didn't mean he wasn't capable of doing serious harm to someone if he got in one of his wild moods.

He heard the oven door slam. The smell of onions and garlic drifted across the room, so strong he could almost see little particles dancing in the air like dust motes. Damn. Now Joe would come in here in to look over his shoulder, offering input that Dave didn't need.

Sure enough, Joe walked into the room, his gait as steady as it could be with his wrecked knee causing him to lurch like a three-wheeled shopping cart. He seemed calmer now, free of the agitation that had gripped him since the scene in LaRose's office. "Lark won't be home for another hour or so. Come on. I want to show you something."

"What is it?" Dave typed in a line about like-minded souls sharing their commitment to a higher power. Damn it, his creative juices were flowing, and he did not want to deal with interruptions.

"You can't see it from here. Come on, take a look. Aren't I going to let you use my truck tomorrow to go put in an application at a Burger King where I saw a sign they were hiring?"

"I don't know. Are you?" What new game was Joe making up rules for now?

"That's up to you." Joe narrowed his eyes and rocked back and forth in front of him, his arms crossed over his chest.

Manipulative bastard. Dave saved his file and trudged into the kitchen. He didn't know if Joe was serious about letting him use the truck, but he knew Joe wouldn't let up until he complied.

"This way." Joe drew a key out of his pocket and unlocked a warped door between the stove and the refrigerator. Of course, Dave had realized when he moved in that the door led to the basement, but he hadn't been curious about checking it out.

Joe flicked on a light just inside the door, and forty watts or so tried, but failed, to make a serious impression in the blackness. Dave trailed him down a narrow set of stairs, just able to see where he was placing his feet. The basement had a concrete floor and cinderblock walls and looked like a vault, except it had a door in one wall that presumably led to the garage. He stopped at the bottom of the stairs. The dank air smelled like a locker room on a wet day and, judging from the webs drooping in feathery tangles and competing for space on every available surface, it was home to half the country's spiders.

"This way." Joe turned right, waving a mess of webs out of his face, and now Dave saw that the room wasn't entirely empty. A stout wooden cabinet stood in one corner, a padlock on the front.

Joe unlocked the cabinet and drew out a wooden box. He opened the box and turned to Dave. "Take a look." He wore the expression of a child showing an A paper to his mom.

Dave peered inside. There was a handgun, shiny and smelling of oil, in the box. Dave wondered if he should be worried. If so, he wasn't doing a very good job. He felt strangely detached and trusting. But Joe had a way of pushing his buttons, so if he wasn't careful, he exhibited whatever emotion Joe called up.

Get Dave angry? Sure, just insult him a little and drag him off to a meeting with a local crime lord. Want to scare him? Act like a gorilla on drugs and threaten to kill him. Or like now. Gain his trust? Just look at him with eyes filled with friendliness and treat him as an equal.

"Keep the gun around for protection. I've got another one upstairs in my room. You know how to shoot?"

"Uh, not exactly. My father taught me how to use a rifle, but not handguns." Dave lifted his shoulders in a motion that was almost a shrug.

"Firing a handgun isn't hard. It's hitting what you want to hit that's the problem. I'll bet you've heard that one before. But we get the church all set up, I'll take you out to the shooting range. And when we get time, I'll show you some stuff about carpentry. That's a skill you can always use."

Dave studied his hands, pretending indifference. He'd like to be able to build things, to swing a hammer and cut wood as easily as Joe did. And he liked the idea of knowing how to use a handgun.

"See, this is what I really wanted to show you. Figured I could trust you not to tell Lark." Joe put the gun back and picked up an envelope lying in the drawer next to the gun box. He pulled a letter out of an envelope and pushed it into Dave's hands.

The letter was from Senator Drake, addressed to FBI Agent Joe Tremaine thanking him for saving the Senator's life. Dave didn't try to hide his surprise.

"What'd you do? Shoot someone trying to kill him?" He had to admit he was impressed.

"Nah." Joe put the letter back and relocked the cabinet. He wiped the key off on his shirt and held it up for inspection before he rammed it back into his pocket. "You probably don't know this because he keeps it private, but Senator Drake's got a bad heart. He had a heart attack and me and another agent, buddy of mine named Sam Marshall, saved his sorry hide. CPR."

"He must have been pretty grateful."

"Yeah, Dave, guess you can see that from looking around at where I live and all. The son of a bitch was so grateful, he let them kick me out of the bureau after I got hurt. Should have let him die, right there on the floor of the men's room where he landed when he fell." He spun around and led the way back upstairs.

The scent of the cooking lasagna made Dave realize how hungry he was. He looked around at his surroundings as if he were seeing them for the first time and catching on that he was in a different world from the one he'd always known, even when he was growing up poor back in Hidden Springs. Bars on the windows. A loud report down the street that almost definitely was a gunshot. The knowledge that there were guns in the house and that he'd agreed to learn to use them. A thought drifted into his mind. What was that corny old saying his Sunday school teacher always came up with when kids complained about things not going their way?

"When life gives you lemons, make lemonade."

Lark couldn't believe Dave had been able to put up with her father all day. He'd driven them both crazy over supper, talking too fast and telling them about fifty times that he thought the lasagna was the best he'd ever made. She didn't feel right about the church; something was wrong with the whole situation, but she was too busy and too tired to feel like getting to the bottom of things. As long as Dave was hanging around with Dad, she'd let him take over for a while, because she simply couldn't handle any more.

She had to admit to a big load of guilt resting on her shoulders. She hadn't felt so free in months, not since Dad had his last seizure, and it was all thanks to Dave being around to look after him while she was at work. After they finished the dishes, she gave in to impulse and said, "I'll bet you haven't been to a movie in a long time. Want to go with me tonight, my treat?"

Dave hesitated, looking at her as if he were wondering, "what's the catch?" He put down the dish towel and carefully smoothed it out, flattening it on the countertop like it was fine linen and needed gentle care.

"Okay," he said finally. "But I thought you and Steve were dating."

"Steve's okay, but we're not a couple and we're not going to be."

Dad pretended to be angry when she said she and Dave were going to the Cinema Twelve. He went into that tough guy act where he snorted and waved his arms and scowled. Looked pretty silly. Then he threatened to toss Dave off an overpass if he touched her.

"I hope you're not taking my dad too seriously," she said when they were on their way. "He makes a lot of noise, but he hasn't killed anyone yet."

Dave turned red and made a choking sound. Now what was wrong? She looked at him sharply and he said, "Sorry."

No explanation offered. There was an awkward silence, during which she started to think going to see a movie was a bad idea. She liked Dave. He was attractive and she felt comfortable around him. She even had to admit she was hoping he felt the same way about her, but as someone to go out with--well, they just weren't clicking, damn it.

As if he'd read her thoughts, he leaned across the seat toward her and said, "Right now, you're probably thinking your act of mercy in taking me to a movie isn't working out and you're wishing you'd decided to spend the evening vacationing on Devil's Island."

"It's not *that* bad." She looked away, hiding her expression.

"The thing is, I feel like I'm shifting back and forth between parallel universes. There's the regular world and then there's the world according to your father. Sometime it takes a few minutes to make the switch." He took a deep breath, holding it until she thought he must be turning blue, let it out in a whoosh and said, "There. Now what movie do you want to see?"

"You choose."

"A comedy. If that's okay with you."

Exactly what she would have picked. They saw a new Ben Stiller movie. Before it was half over, they were holding hands. Lark couldn't remember which of them had made the first move.

When they got back home, she was sure Dave wanted to kiss her goodnight and she wanted him to. But before he leaned in toward her, he glanced toward the front door.

The kiss was everything she'd expected. Still, she couldn't help wondering what he'd have done if her dad had been looking out the window.

Chapter Seventeen

Dave coaxed the truck into a higher gear and glanced out the window. He knew this neighborhood--had driven past on his way to work when he still had work. Edgewood boasted older, well-kept brick homes on large lots, as well as winding streets protected from the sun by massive oaks that met in a canopy over the pavement. Picture book pretty. On a whim, he cut through, dreaming about living here if he ever got back on his feet.

He slowed to look at the scenery. Since he'd been here last, at least a fourth of the houses had ended up with for sale signs stuck in their front lawns. One even had a foreclosure notice displayed prominently on the door.

He'd thought only upscale subdivisions like Eden Acres were in trouble. Then he wondered why he'd believed the rest of the middle class was immune to the jobless recovery, why it should be only those higher up, or those who'd never had much who were losing their homes.

His response was to speed up to the corner and turn in at the Burger King parking lot. He'd already found out he was helpless, and it hurt too much to think about other people in other neighborhoods ending up in the ranks of the homeless.

A line wound out the Burger King door. Big crowd. No wonder they were hiring.

"Excuse me," he said, bypassing the line and walking up to the uniformed kid behind the counter. "I need a job application."

The kid turned and ambled over to the fryers where he lifted a sizzling basket of fries out of boiling oil and emptied it in a tray. Took his time to dump salt on top. Came back to the register and said, "Get in line."

Dave felt like smacking some manners into him. "I'm not here to order. I'm just looking for a job."

"You and everybody else in Avalon." He jerked his thumb toward the door. "That's the line."

Dave turned and stared into the patient eyes of an elderly woman. Behind her were assorted Americans. Teenagers. Middle-aged men and women. Even a man with a cane. At least thirty people in line and no telling how many more had come and gone since the sign went up.

He marched back outside, past the end of the line, and across the parking lot. He wouldn't give the rude kid the satisfaction of seeing him wait around for an hour just to get a piece of paper. Besides, there was no point in even applying when he had about one chance in a million. He hopped into the truck and a second later hopped back out, squinting into the glare of the sun bouncing off an older model red Toyota. Was he seeing right? A female figure in a Burger King uniform and a pair of running shoes had just crawled out of the Toyota.

Dave's internal logic mechanism was unable to process and connect the vision to anything that made sense. Loretta? A former computer programmer at Markham-Hook, working in fast food? Couldn't be. The Loretta he remembered always wore expensive business attire and pointy-toed high heels and enough make-up to supply a modeling agency. He wouldn't have thought running shoes could even shape themselves to her feet, which must be permanently pointed by now. And Loretta driving an old Toyota? She'd bought a Behemoth the same day he'd bought his. In fact, they'd crossed paths at the Spectrum Motors lot.

He waved and called out, "Hey, Loretta."

She was going too fast, jogging toward the back of the building. She zipped past him for a few yards, until she was able to put the brakes on and turn around.

"Dave? It *is* you. Thought I was hearing things." She trotted over and wrapped her arms around him in a hug.

Dave returned the hug. Her hair smelled like chicken nuggets. "How's it going?"

Her mouth twisted. "You can see that for yourself. Masters in Computer Science, stellar performance reviews, and fifteen years of experience and hard work don't mean a thing when your job can go offshore or the damn company can import cheaper workers to replace you. And what about you? You find a job?"

"I came here to apply, but half the people in the state got here first. I've got one other prospect. If my friend can get the financing, I'm the office boy for a church slash bingo hall." He didn't know why he'd added the part about the church. Maybe he thought church office boy sounded more important than would-be Burger King applicant.

"Well, good luck with the job hunt. You deserve it more than anyone I know."

"Sure." He let his face muscles go slack. Loretta was just being polite. She'd always treated him like a pesky underling.

"No, I mean it. Back when Harris first knifed us in the back, we all thought you were crazy to open your mouth and give up the severance. We thought we'd be able to go right out and get new jobs, maybe even for better pay. I don't need to tell you what's wrong with that picture."

"So you're saying--"

"I'm saying I admire the way you fought them. You've got heart."

"Yeah, and I got my ass kicked. I might as well have deliberately rammed my head into the side of a fast moving train. I'm through fighting." Battling a greedy corporation caused you a lot of pain deep in your soul; he knew that now.

She playfully punched his arm. "Don't give me that. I heard about what you did at the programmers' banquet this year. Wish I'd been there to see the look on DeWinter's well-bred face when he watched your version of life at Markham-Hook. Did he actually show an emotion?"

"I'm sure I detected a fair amount of dismay." Now that the danger of being arrested was past, Dave could almost be proud of what he'd done, even though his actions had cost him the early foreclosure on the house and the car.

"You're something. I mean, not only did you show the truth about Markham-Hook, but since he and Beth are an item, DeWinters must have been really pissed to find out you were the one who did it. Double nightmare for good old Ox."

Dave made an inarticulate noise. Beth and Oxford DeWinters? No wonder DeWinters had been so determined to avoid embarrassment for Beth that he'd offered Dave a job--and a permanent transfer out of town. Heat streaked up his face and for a few seconds he swayed on his feet. He finally had to lean back against the truck until the dizziness passed.

Loretta's hand shot up to cover her mouth. "God, I'm so sorry. I thought you knew. I thought that was part of the reason you went to the banquet--to get revenge."

"No." The word was a dry squawk.

"Are you okay?"

"Sure, I'm over Beth. I was surprised, that's all. And I've learned to keep my mouth shut." Funny how a little humiliation and the loss of your home could knock you down and keep you there.

"I'm sorry to hear that, because what you said made a lot of sense. 'Bye now, hon. I've got to run. Only my second day on the job."

Dave watched her sprint across the parking lot. Had he lied when he told her he was over Beth? He inventoried his feelings. Nothing emotional, other than disappointment over being too late to get a Burger King job. Physically, his only feelings were mild discomfort from a rough spot on the truck fender poking into his back through his shirt and a vague desire for lunch. If Beth found someone else, he should be glad for her. But did it have to be Oxford DeWinters?

My, it was hot in the kitchen, ungodly hot if truth be known. Ruby would have opened the windows for a cross-breeze if she weren't leaving. She crammed two foil-wrapped loaves of her homemade banana bread into her bag, along with the new afghan she'd crocheted in shades of pink and cream. She'd intended the afghan for a sale at the church, but her sugarbiscuit had said he was renting a room from a man and his daughter. Gifts were always appreciated and maybe if they were grateful enough, these people would kindly tell her exactly what was going on with her grandson.

She didn't for one single second believe the story about him having a great job. He'd called her again last night and he'd tried to make her think his life was just one big picnic, but Ruby Griffin was born a long time ago. One day David was going to stop making the same silly mistake--trying to deceive her. He only did it to spare her feelings, but Ruby had told him a million times that the end didn't justify the means and she'd tell him a million times more if she had to.

A car horn sounded out front. Millie Banks was giving her a ride to the Greyhound station. David wasn't going to like it when she showed up to check on him. But as his grandmother, she had certain rights. If she didn't like what she saw, he was coming straight back to Hidden Springs with her, even if she had to drag him home by the ear the way she had the time he got into a fight at Sunday school with a boy who stole his cupcake.

She picked up her bag and her suitcase and headed for the door. "Coming, Millie," she called. Goodness, that woman was the most impatient creature on earth. Even Millie's own husband couldn't stand her nagging and had left town with a pretty little schoolteacher. Not that Ruby approved of adultery, but she had a certain sympathy for the man.

She had plenty of time to get to the station and get her bus ticket and plenty of time to read while she waited for the bus. A thrill of excitement passed through her. She couldn't wait to see the expression on her sugarbiscuit's face.

Joe lifted his pillow. The gun was still there--loaded and ready if he needed it. He sat on his bed and stared at the walls. Martha must be right about there being a God because it was clear a higher power was out to punish him. And doing a pretty good job.

There was nothing wrong with operating a bingo hall. After all, wasn't he dealing with the same God who let Martha be a phone actress to keep her and Freddy from starving? So why in the hell wouldn't anyone loan him money? He'd gone to two other loan sharks, after Dave came back with the truck, went alone this time, didn't feel like fighting with Dave. They turned him down like he was no better than a common street beggar. He hadn't heard back from his contact about Vin Shelton, so he figured that was no go. He was so close. So close and his dream was snatched away, and he couldn't understand why God was letting this happen. Joe wasn't such a bad person, was he? God hadn't said, "Okay, Joe, you can run a phony church if that's what you need to do. Better than robbing stores. But I tell you what, I better not catch you borrowing money from criminals."

Now God seemed to be saying, "I don't like your operation and I don't like you. I was just kidding around, letting you think the nightmare was finally over, and now I'm laughing my ass off watching you suffer."

He squeezed his eyes shut and rocked himself back and forth. He was going nuts, hearing lectures from a God he still wasn't sure he believed in. No, he was sane, seizure free, and finally okay, better than he'd ever felt, with dreams and a way to succeed and no more depression like when he was on his old medicine. The voice in his head was only his own conscience. It wasn't real, just like the fuzzy edges around his vision weren't real; they were just caused by the headaches.

For the millionth time he went over his options. Sam would help. He'd promised when Joe left for Avalon, he'd said, "Joe, if there's ever anything I can do." Joe used to have too much pride to even think about calling him, except to exchange awkward hellos a couple times in the past year. But they'd worked together and he'd helped Sam get a promotion. You might even say, if you were being generous, he'd saved Sam's life. Sam was supposed to be the one on the roof that day, the day Joe got pushed off. Sam owed him.

He shoved his hand forward and slid his fingers across the smooth barrel of the gun. No, he wouldn't need the gun, not now. Sam would loan him the money, maybe even visit and check out the church. He'd be shocked about Joe becoming a preacher.

He'd laugh and say, "You crafty son of a bitch. I should have figured you'd find a way to make money."

Joe would answer, "Couldn't have done it without you loaning me the money. Knew I could count on you. Best friend I ever had."

He'd make the call tonight. It would be such a relief to finally have the last piece of his plan fall into place.

※

Ruby wasn't surprised when the cab driver turned onto a street where most of the houses had bars on the windows and trash piled in the yards. And those women on the street corners--goodness only knew what they were up to. Made her blush to think of it. She'd known David Robert was lying when he said he lived in a nice place. In a few minutes she'd find out what other lies he'd told her.

The cab stopped at a brick house with a blue car parked out front. Older model car, but well kept up from what she could tell. And at least the yard was clean. The cab driver helped her up to the front porch with her overnight bag and her purse, and then she rang the bell. She heard footsteps tapping inside, but she still used her cane to bang against the door.

The curtain at the front window moved aside, and she caught a glimpse of a young female face. Cautious, weren't they? Needed to be in this neighborhood, though, Ruby could see that.

The door opened and she saw a pretty young woman standing in front of her. Ruby's hip hurt after climbing the steps. She leaned hard on her cane and said, "Hello. I'm looking for David Griffin."

"Come on in. I'll bet you're his grandmother. He has your eyes." The girl smiled warmly.

"He does. Unfortunately, he doesn't share either my good sense or my devotion to the truth--which is why I'm here." Ruby snapped her mouth shut. She'd intended to start off with a few social niceties.

"Let me help you with that suitcase." The girl took the suitcase and stepped aside. "Please come in. I'll get Dave."

She didn't have to. He chose that moment to wander into the room. He looked like he'd found his clothes in the discard bin behind a thrift store and he was way past due for a haircut. Ruby pressed her lips together.

His expression was everything she'd anticipated and more. "Mawmaw?" His voice came out in a schoolboy squawk. His hands rose to the top of his head to scrub around in his hair as if he could find answers among the curls.

"Come give Mawmaw a kiss, sugarbiscuit. Then introduce me to your friends."

He stumbled over and pecked her on the cheek. She could feel the heat coming off his face. Next time he'd know better than to tell her stories. On second thought, probably not. He hadn't learned yet, though he'd been given ample opportunity.

"This is Lark." Then he indicated a man sitting in a battered recliner across from the couch and added, "And her dad, Joe Tremaine. Uh, Reverend Joe Tremaine."

Reverend Joe Tremaine, amusement lighting his lean face, got up and limped across the room. He shook her hand. "I'm so happy to meet you. I'm sure you know that Dave talks about you all the time. Nothing but good, of course. Could I interest you in a cup of coffee or maybe some tea?"

"Tea would do me fine, thank you." My, the charm positively rolled off that one. Handsome, too, in an understated way. Ruby would have to keep an eye on him.

A look passed between Lark and David before they went into the kitchen together. Ruby lifted an eyebrow. Something going on there.

⁂

Joe sighed from the bottom of his lungs. He had enough problems without adding someone else to the mix. On the other hand, he didn't mind the entertainment. Dave should have listened to him about lying to his grandmother instead of getting smart-mouthed. Now the old lady was here to see what was what, and the look on Dave's face when he spotted her standing in the doorway was something that ought to be photographed, framed, and handed out to every little kid in America who thought he could get away with fooling his elders.

Mrs. Griffin--no, she'd insisted he call her Ruby--had brought banana bread and she'd given Lark an afghan that she'd crocheted. Nice lady. Dave was way out of his league, though, and was liable to give things away with his stammering and his evasive answers to her barrage of questions. For God's sake, did he have to repeat everything she said, like he was a friggin' parrot?

"Church assistant? Safe neighborhood? Nice church building?"

After he'd lied to her on the phone, Ruby had raced to Avalon on what was no doubt the fastest bus in the Greyhound fleet. But there was no point in alarming her with talk of loan sharks. Joe would have to help Dave out of this one. Ruby could stay overnight and then, Joe having eased her mind, he'd personally put her on a bus back to Hidden Springs.

He waited until Dave and Lark finished their banana bread and told Ruby how great it was and then he surprised the two of them by asking them to run out to the grocery and pick up a chicken for tonight's supper.

Dave shot him a suspicious look. Joe read his mind and knew Dave was wondering what he was up to because Joe was not in the habit of providing ways for him to be alone with Lark, especially not since she'd taken to looking at Dave moon-eyed the same way he looked at her. As soon as they left, Joe moved from his recliner to sit beside Ruby on the couch. He'd get her thinking his way, then it would be, "So glad I met you. So glad you're taking care of sugarbiscuit for me. See you again some time, Joe."

"I know David has probably told you he's dead set against moving back to Hidden Springs. Feels he'd be a burden on me."

"Boy's a hard worker. Wants to take care of himself." Joe nodded and smiled, resting his hands in his lap to mirror Ruby's body language.

"Maybe so, but I'm going to tell you, the same way I'm going to tell him. Things have changed a lot back home. Developer came along and he's putting in a bunch of houses. We're getting a new grocery, a motel--a big one--and a fancy, sit-down restaurant right off the interstate exit."

"That so?"

"There's jobs for people who don't mind doing yard work or making burgers. If things don't work out at the church, sugarbiscuit can come on home and find him a job. Won't pay much, but it's honest work."

Joe wasn't going to let that happen. Not until he got the church going, anyway. He leaned forward as if to take her into his confidence and said, "I can see you're worried about Dave and I can see why. The boy grew up without a father and he doesn't have a lot of street smarts. I just want you to know, the church is going to work out fine. I'm taking real good care of him."

"Are you?" Ruby directed her gaze to the bars on the living room window. She looked back at him and cocked an eyebrow.

"Sure, this is a dangerous neighborhood. I never would have moved here if I had a choice. Times have been tough, but praise the Lord, I found the calling. We'll be moving into a new parsonage once the money starts coming in. We'll find something on the nice side of town, real safe, plenty of good people."

"Umm-hmm. Let me tell you something. I've lived on a farm all my life. I learned a long time ago to tell the difference between flowers and manure. You are most likely a lot of things and you might even have a piece of paper that says you're a preacher. But you do not have the calling. Tell me exactly what's going on here or I'll get it from my sugarbiscuit."

Joe's mouth dropped open and hung that way, until he realized he must look like a dead fish. He frowned and tried to think and wasn't sure he could do both things at the same time. The sleepless nights and the worry were tearing him up so bad he couldn't even operate well enough to convince Dave's grandmother of the truth of a few simple misleading statements. How was he going to start up a bingo hall and pretend to be an honest man of God if he couldn't even fool an old lady?

Her gaze didn't waver; bored into him like she had augers for eyes. "You did understand what I said, didn't you?"

He rubbed his chin, did some serious throat clearing and then put on his most charming smile. "Okay, you got me. I used to work for the IRS. Got hurt in an accident on the way home one day, so they dumped me. I've been out of work for more than a year, except for odd jobs, and my pension's not enough to bridge the gap. My doctor switched me to a new medicine that costs more per ounce than gold, but it's working real well, I feel terrific. Finally thought up a way out of this mess, after sitting on my ass for months hoping for a visit from the death angel. I got the idea off the Internet--the preacher credentials, too. The church is a cover for a gambling operation in the form of bingo. I haven't got the funding yet, but I will. A good friend owes me a favor and he's going to loan me the money. And that's all of it, the whole truth." If his Bible were handy, he'd have put his hand on it and sworn.

Ruby slowly shook her head. "Last year I would have torn into you, Joe Tremaine. But I don't think in black and white any more when it comes to survival. I'm not going to say a word against you or your bingo hall. Just remember--you let any harm come to my grandson, I will hunt you down."

Joe took both her hands in his and after a moment, felt her relax. This time his strategy had worked. He'd mixed the truth in with lies so cleverly that she'd believed it all, even the part about him working for the IRS. Damn, he was good, getting back on his game.

"I'll make it a priority to see that Dave doesn't get into trouble. In fact, I look after him like he was my own son."

"I appreciate that. And if your church doesn't work out, you and your daughter are welcome to come back to Hidden Springs with David and stay at the farm with us. You've helped my grandson and I'll gladly return the favor."

Joe thanked her and carried on like she'd offered to put him up at Buckingham Palace. But he couldn't picture himself wandering around in a field watching corn grow or tending to a pen full of hogs, while Lark stayed busy learning the fine art of quilt making from a bevy of country women. The church was going to become reality even if he had to rob a bank.

Chapter Eighteen

Joe somehow managed to keep from telling Ruby any more lies. Even so, it was clear she still had her doubts about his chances for bingo success. She didn't make any secret of her reservations the next morning at the bus station, when she counted out a few dollars, argued down Dave's protests and said, "This is your emergency money. If you get down to where you have no job, no money left, you get yourself a bus ticket and come on back to Hidden Springs. I will not have a grandson of mine homeless and starving in the streets, maybe having to beg or steal to survive." She looked pointedly at Joe, and he put on his most charming smile and was sure he hadn't fooled her. "Promise me you'll use this money to get home, sugarbiscuit."

Dave turned all the shades of red Joe had ever seen and even invented a few new ones, but he finally tucked the money away in his wallet and said, "I promise, Mawmaw. Emergency use only."

Joe laughed and teased Dave about being a sugarbiscuit, but he kind of wished he had a Mawmaw of his own to go home to. He'd never met his father's mother and his other grandmother, the only one he'd ever known, had a tongue like a viper and was prone to slapping him halfway across the room every time he got close enough. She'd made him call her Jacqueline and fetch her beer and cigarettes.

※※※

Lark had rushed through ironing her work clothes and dressed as quickly as she could without putting a fingernail through her pantyhose. Kathie had called at the last minute with a job when she was practically out the door with Dave to take his grandmother to the bus station. Too bad. She liked Mawmaw and she was always glad of the chance to spend time with Dave. Since their movie the other night, they'd been practically inseparable, despite her father's dark looks.

Today's job had been a couple of hours working a luncheon, but she couldn't turn down the money, especially since Kathie had recently expressed concern about work slacking off. Something about summer and people being away on vacation. But any person who had to call in a caterer at the last minute was going to host the party from hell. Lark had dragged herself home and walked into the kitchen feeling like a dishrag. She was going to soak in a hot bath and then nap for a few hours until she had to leave for the park.

She wished Kathie had been able to find something for Dave, but that wasn't likely now with work slowing. Besides, his grandmother wanted him to move back to Hidden Springs. He didn't want to leave, though, and she was glad. Just thinking about Dave, her heart swelled with feeling and a soft smile tugged at the corners of her mouth.

As soon as Dad's church...she paused in the middle of hunting in the refrigerator for the bottle of juice she was sure was hiding on the bottom shelf. Something was going on. More than once, Dave and her father had suddenly stopped talking when she walked into the room. She figured there had to be a problem with the church or they'd have already gotten the building and the equipment. But Dad would never tell her and Dave was going along with him. She'd just have to let things play out. A vague feeling of unease took hold of her and she shoved it out of her consciousness. Worry never did a bit of good. Lark knew that better than anyone.

Where were they anyway? She needed to tell them to be quiet, so she'd be able to sleep. She found the juice, turned to get a glass from the cabinet and spotted a note on the counter from Dave.

They'd gone out to bid on a repair job. How thoughtful of him to leave a note. Dad didn't often think to let her know where he was going, and sometimes she'd been frantic when he came in late and her imagination had run away with her, telling her he was tearing through Avalon screaming he had the formula to save the world.

Funny how those fears wouldn't shake loose from her psyche. It had been months and Dad was finally feeling better, and she still didn't trust that he was okay. She wondered if she'd ever feel safe again.

The phone rang and she reached across the counter and grabbed it before the second ring.

"Joe there?" A deep voice rumbling in the bass range.

"No. May I take a message?" Maybe the repair business was finally picking up.

"Yeah, sweetheart. This is Vin Shelton. You tell Crazy Joe the answer is no on that quick loan. And while you're at it, tell him don't waste my time. And I mean that."

The receiver clicked in her ear. Her heart pounded and she put her hand to her throat, feeling her pulse throbbing under her fingers. Vin Shelton. She'd heard the name before, but couldn't remember where. He was trouble, though. That was obvious from what he'd said and the way he said it.

Her jaw tightened. She'd been right. Dad was up to something, something that was going to get him in a lot of trouble. She paced to the front window and back. This was all her fault for letting down her guard and trusting Dave to ride herd on her father. Why hadn't she been paying attention?

She fumbled a notebook out of a kitchen drawer and ran a finger down a list of names and phone numbers. Dialed the fourth number and waited till someone picked up.

"Hello." Martha's voice was sultry.

"Martha, this is Lark Tremaine." Even to her own ears, Lark sounded young and excited and she hadn't wanted to bother Martha. But Martha would know the answer to her question. "I need a favor. Could you tell me about Vin Shelton?"

Long pause. "Lark, honey, you don't want to go messing with that one."

"I just need some information--who he is, what he does. He called here with a message for my father."

"I won't hold back on you." Martha made clicking noises with her tongue. "He's a common thug. A drug dealer. A loan shark who likes to beat people up."

Lark twisted the phone cord around her fingers until the wire bit into her flesh. "I should have known."

"Is your dad in some kind of trouble? I've already got him on my prayer list, but I suppose I could find time to pray harder." Martha already spent half her spare time in church, and as far as Lark could see, it hadn't done much good for her and Freddy.

"Thanks. But I think he's okay. This Vin Shelton person called to have me tell Dad the answer is no." She forced a laugh. "Your prayers must have already worked."

"I hope so. Your father's a good man, just needs a lot of looking after. You call me if you need help. I'm always glad to do whatever I can for my friends."

Martha was sweet, a kind Christian lady who really meant what she said when she put people on her prayer list. But all the prayers in the world weren't going to help her father when Lark got through with him. Dave, too, if he was in on this. Retribution wouldn't be long in coming, either. She'd heard the truck door slam out front right after she hung up the phone.

Dad sauntered in looking like he'd found a million dollars in the back yard. Dave trailed in behind him, not a care in the world. Did they think she was stupid?

"We got a gutter repair for next week, Lark." Dad plopped down on the couch and yanked off his work boots.

"That's nice. Think you could take time out of your busy schedule to not bother Vin Shelton?" She crossed her arms over her chest and watched the play of emotions on her father's face and the look he exchanged with Dave. She didn't need to see the red flush across Dave's cheeks to know he was involved.

"Baby," Dad pasted on a look of tenderness, little lines creasing the corners of his eyes. "I don't know what you--"

"Stop lying." If she'd had a cushion handy, she would have hurled it at his head. Two cushions. One for Dave. And to think, she'd had feelings for him, thought he was special. All the while he was deceiving her just like her father did. "You, too, Dave. Dad said you were loaning him money for the church, and you let me believe that. The truth is, you have no money and the two of you have been trying to get money from loan sharks, like we don't have enough trouble."

"Loan sharks?" Joe held up his hand. "We haven't talked to loan sharks. You've got this all wrong. Lark, you're jumping to conclusions."

When would her father learn to stop treating her like a kid? At least Dave had enough respect for her to look away and blush and at least he wasn't trying to keep up the pretense.

"I worked the whole thing out and I'm putting a stop to it right now." Her heart thudded against her ribs. What if she were too late? What if thugs came to the door and dragged her father outside and beat him to a pulp or set the house on fire?

"I'm sorry," Dave said. "I shouldn't have lied to you."

"A little late to be figuring that out." Her voice shook and she knew she was seconds away from bursting into tears. Damn it, why did she cry when she was angry? "I should have known better than to trust you. Men always lie and say they're protecting women, but the truth is, they're only trying to save their own sorry butts."

Dave looked like he wished he had some kind of machine to instantly transport him out of here to another time and place. Too bad it hadn't been invented yet.

"I really am sorry, Lark. Your dad thought you'd only worry if you knew the truth."

Joe hauled himself to his feet and balled up his fists. "Hey, don't go blaming me, farmboy. Big kids make their own choices."

"You're right. I listened to your bad advice and look where that got me." Dave sighed deeply. He put his hands together as if he were praying and said again, "I'm sorry."

When she didn't answer, he added, "Maybe I ought to listen to Mawmaw and go back to Hidden Springs." His voice had turned flat and his face held no expression.

"Yes, maybe you ought to do that," she said in clipped tones. "You're certainly not doing me any favors by helping my father get into trouble." That's it, cut and run. Leave her stuck with her problems like all the other men she'd ever met. Everyone, except her dad. But right now, *he* was the problem.

Dave could run off if he thought so little of her that he didn't even want to work things out or stick around until she cooled off and was ready to forgive him. She was just glad she hadn't let herself fall in love with him. Now the tears came, stinging her eyes and spilling down her hot cheeks.

She stumbled down the hall to her room and flung herself across her bed. A few minutes later she could hear Dave moving around in his own room. She realized he was packing his things. She rolled over on her back and stared at the ceiling. Told herself to get a grip. She was working tonight at the park and she couldn't let her friends down. And there was still Dad to look after. He was out of control and now she wouldn't have Dave to help. She tightened her jaw. She'd managed before Dave showed up and she'd do just fine without him.

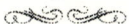

Dave rammed the last of his clothes into a box, raw despair eating away at his heart. He was stupid. He deserved a trophy for screwing up. Mawmaw had told him a million times that a person of integrity didn't lie, and he'd still let himself be sucked into Joe's scheming. Now he'd messed up his chances with Lark, right when he was coming to the realization that he was crazy about her, and that maybe there was such a thing as love at first sight--or second sight. Whatever. He pounded his fist into the mattress. No, it wasn't fair to blame Joe. He was responsible for his own actions. And Joe hadn't been the one who'd lied to Mawmaw, telling her how great he was doing so she'd come up here and caught him. You'd think he'd have learned.

He needed to get back to Hidden Springs where he could spend the rest of his life wondering what would have happened if he'd been honest. The next bus west didn't leave till after ten tonight, but he sure wasn't going to stick around here and make himself sick thinking about her being so close and how she was through with him. He'd take a city bus to town and wait on a hard bench in the station, the clock slowly ticking away all those long hours until he could leave Avalon forever.

Lark sure was in a snit when she roared out of here heading for the park, angrier than he'd seen her in a long time, and Joe knew it was because Dave had left. Too bad Dave didn't care enough to stick around and soothe her feelings. He'd pined over her since the minute he moved in and then he'd run out at the first little disagreement. If he cared, he would have gone out to the corner store and got her flowers and a card and then he would have begged forgiveness as many times as it took, until she finally gave in. Obviously, he didn't care, and Lark was lucky she found that out before she got her heart broken. Joe had been right from the start when he figured Dave wasn't good enough for her. And he would point that out when she was ready to listen. Meanwhile, he'd have to find someone else to help with the church.

He went into the kitchen and looked up the number. Okay, he didn't have to like it, but Sam had said he'd do anything. Sam had plenty of cash--the money wouldn't mean much to him. He might have to wait to trade in his latest car, but he'd be happy he had the chance to do something for Joe. It didn't matter that they'd talked only a few times since Joe had moved back to Avalon. Distance couldn't erase the bond of friendship.

He grabbed the phone, quick before he changed his mind, juggled the receiver so he had to lunge forward to make the catch, and finally managed to punch in the numbers with fingers that felt like globs of dough on the ends of his hands. That had happened a couple of times recently--the numb fingers--and might be a side effect of his medication. He made a mental note to check at the library or the pharmacy when he had the time. On second thought, why bother? He felt great; he was finally getting his life back on track after the long months of depression.

On the tenth ring, someone picked up.

"Hello." Sounded like a voice coming out of a tunnel. Sam must have been up all night, probably working a case.

"Hey, it's Joe. Thought I'd give you a call and see how life is treating you in the big city."

"Yeah, you came up on caller ID. How you doing? Must be four, five months since we talked."

Right. Not since shortly after his last seizure, when Joe wasn't completely himself. He hoped Sam wouldn't hold it against him, the way he'd acted, telling Sam he was a fool for working for the government after the way they treated his best friend.

"I'm a changed man. Fully recovered. Got plans, found a way to make a living." He grabbed a pencil out of a kitchen drawer in case he needed to work out some figures for Sam. Sam would want to know every detail before he committed.

"I admit, I was worried about you, buddy. Glad to hear you're well again."

Was he? Sam couldn't have sounded flatter if an elephant had sat on him.

"Reason I'm calling is I remembered your promise, how you said you'd do whatever you could to help me out. I need a favor, a big one. You know I wouldn't ask if I had any other options. I'll pay you back with interest, so it won't cost you a cent."

"A loan? I'm in no position…you have to understand, I'm thinking of buying a vacation home."

Joe could picture Sam's gray eyes darting from side to side the way they always did when Sam tried to find a way out of something. The eyes had practically danced out of their bony sockets that day, until Joe gave in and went up on the roof while Sam covered the back door. The day Sam got a commendation and Joe got a fractured skull.

"You can't lose. Sam, I'm a preacher now, got a real diploma. I'm starting my own church. Lots of money to be made on bingo. Haven't you heard about all those buses that take people to gamble, whole convoys of warm bodies with money to burn? It's going to be like that with my church."

A long pause on the other end of the line and Joe should have known, but he kept his hopes up. Good friends always helped each other.

"Church? Sounds like big start up costs for a building and all. Why not get yourself a regular job and save up, start out small, build the congregation up gradually?"

"A regular job? What's that? You think I'd be on the phone begging you to open your damned wallet for a friend who saved your life if it was that easy? Haven't you heard that all the white-collar jobs have gone offshore or to cheaper imported labor? Guess I'll have to get a job in the booming service industry, only first I'll have to get in line with all the millions of other Americans who want jobs sweeping floors. Maybe I ought to kill about half of them, so I'll have better odds. What you think?"

"Come on, Joe, stop being so damned dramatic. The economy's in recovery, getting stronger every day. Didn't you listen to Senator Drake's last speech? Corporations are poised to hire millions of new workers."

Joe held the receiver out from his ear and shook it. When he spoke again he made no effort to keep the volume down. "Poised to hire? That's about as useful as saying 'getting ready to shit.' Did Senator Drake also announce that he just formed the Trading With Friends Caucus to promote the offshoring of even more American jobs? And that he used taxpayer money to fund it and he's using more taxpayer money to pay for a junket overseas to schmooze with the job thieves."

"You sound so bitter. Listen to me, Joe."

Joe slammed the receiver against the counter and let it drop, dangling on its cord toward the floor. After a minute, he retrieved it and dropped it back in its cradle. A sledgehammer was working him over between his eyes. He ought to name the damned thing, the headache. It had become a permanent fixture of his life. Where were his pills and his aspirins? Missing again. He should chain them to his head so he could find them without having to paw through every corner of the house five times a day.

He found the pills on the nightstand in his room beside the aspirins. The aspirin bottle, anyway. It was empty. He turned it upside down and shook it over the bed and then heaved it at the wall next to the window, not caring where it landed or what it hit. He supposed he'd have to hunt through his wallet to see if he had enough money left for more painkillers if he couldn't find any in the kitchen. But didn't Lark have a bottle of codeine or something left over from when she broke her wrist? He remembered her saying at the time that they'd given her enough pain pills to drug a rhino.

He rummaged through the bathroom cabinets. Nothing except some expired vitamins. Looked like something green growing on them. He swallowed a Seizure-Out and put the bottle down next to the sink. If Lark had any codeine left, it would be in her room. Damn. He didn't want to look though her stuff; what if he found birth control pills? But this was an emergency. The pain in his head was so bad he was sure he'd wreck the truck if he tried to drive down to the drugstore for more aspirin.

Lark's room was the best one in the house. She had real curtains on the window, white with little pink and yellow flowers splashed all over the material and a matching bedspread and some kind of room perfume, lavender, he thought, in a jar on the dresser next to all her make-up.

He pushed aside tubes of lipstick and jars of nail polish, pink and scarlet and crimson. Nothing even close to being pain pills. He didn't want to, but he pulled open the top drawer, pushed aside some frilly bras and a satiny purple nightgown, and then his probing fingers located a prescription bottle.

He pulled it out of the drawer. Read the label. Tylenol with codeine.

He went to the bathroom and took two. He probably needed to take some Seizure-Out. Had he already taken one? No, he didn't think so. He found the bottle and downed another of the big orange lumps. Those pills were any bigger, they'd have to be lubricated to get them down.

The pharmaceuticals better start working soon. The top of his head felt like it was going to fly off into space and, damn it, his ex-friend Sam was to blame. Couldn't help Joe. Too busy spending his money on himself. Didn't give a damn that Joe had nearly died because of him. Needed to buy a vacation home so he could…no, it wasn't Sam, Sam was his best friend. It was goddamned Senator Drake who told the lie about the economy being so fantastic that people were falling all over each other on their way to the bank to put in their money. That's why Sam wouldn't help him.

"Go right out and get a job, folks. Plenty of work and don't forget me at election time."

Bastard. Joe him ought to burn down his fancy house, provide some work for local contractors. He wished there was a way the Senator could experience for himself what his trade deals and his trading caucus had done for his fellow Americans. Sent the country right down into the third world. Let *him* live on Oak Street for just a week. He'd learn that…

His thoughts came to a fork and he stopped, pondering which way to go. Stopping like this, deciding he could control things, it was insight, was what it was. He wasn't going to circle uselessly back to the beginning like he always did. Oh, no. Not now.

He went into his room and pulled the Luger out from under his pillow. It was heavy and cold until he wrapped his long fingers around it and then it molded itself to him, becoming a part of his hand. All his senses had sharpened, so even the air in the room seemed to be visible.

He gave himself a moment to sort his thoughts. The Senator might be at the river this weekend. It wasn't as if Joe could call someone and find out. But he hadn't been there last weekend and he didn't often miss this time of year. This was Friday. If he were going to show, he'd be there already. If not, Joe could try again next week or the week after, until the Senator finally arrived in town.

His hands trembled and the edges of his vision fuzzed up like a camera lens going out of focus. When he looked at the clock to check the time, he could make out the red numbers doing jumping jacks. Eight o'clock. Lark wouldn't be home till after eleven. Plenty of time to do what needed to be done.

Chapter Nineteen

Lark wandered all the way around the stage and then to the end of the block and back. Other than street vendors and a couple walking a Doberman, the park was deserted. She sat on the edge of a bench. It hadn't rained yet, but the seat was clammy, and she could feel dampness seeping through her jeans. She'd give her group another five minutes and then call Steve to find out what was going on.

"Hey, Lark." Someone grabbed her shoulder from behind.

She yelped and nearly jumped off the bench. She turned to see Benson looming over her. "Next time give me some warning."

"Sorry. Didn't mean to scare you." He wore the apologetic look of a spaniel caught soiling the carpet.

She took a deep breath. "How come everyone's late?"

The air felt wet and a breeze had sprung up, whipping her hair into her eyes. She rolled down the sleeves on her shirt to cover her arms all the way to her wrists and felt only marginally warmer. Off to the side, she could see the street vendors packing up. A couple of popcorn bags broke loose from a clip and the wind tumbled them down the sidewalk, popcorn spilling out of the bags like confetti.

"Don't you watch the news? There's a storm moving in." Benson pointed at the sky where lightning forked across dark clouds.

Lark shrugged. No, she hadn't watched the news. She'd been too busy fighting with Dave and yelling at her father.

"Steve and the others have already left. I waited to tell you we canceled for tonight, because I wasn't sure you knew. Your phone was busy when I called your house, and then I called again and no one answered. I figured you'd already left."

"My dad is supposed to be home. He probably stepped out for something. Anyway, it was sweet of you to wait." She hoped her father wasn't out stealing cigarettes again or talking to loan sharks. If he was, she'd--well, she didn't know what she'd do, but maybe his doctor could adjust his medicine.

She turned to leave, and Benson said, "Lark? Want to get coffee? Or maybe something to eat?"

"I really ought to go home. My car doesn't travel well through water, and you know how the roads flood once you get outside the beltway."

"It's not exactly an upcoming hurricane. Rain and a little wind, that's all. I thought you might want to talk and, to be honest, you look like you could use a friend right now."

"I do?" Were her emotions written across her face? Maybe she was sending out some kind of "tonight I hate men" vibe. After all, if people could give off love pheromones to attract each other the way all those studies claimed, they could probably give off hate pheromones.

"Do I detect a hint of a smile?" Benson moved closer. "You could tell me your troubles and I could nod sympathetically and maybe even offer some worthless advice."

She considered for a long moment. She'd make herself sick if she worried all the time about what trouble her father was getting into while she wasn't home. He was perfectly fine and he wouldn't dare do anything for the next few days, now that she'd caught him lying. Besides, Dave was still at the station waiting for the bus. If he had second thoughts and decided to apologize, she wouldn't be home and she wouldn't be at the park. Let him wonder where she was.

She linked arms with Benson and smiled up at him. "Why not?"

Joe parked the truck and got out. Darkness had fallen early thanks to a massive bank of storm clouds that had moved in over the past hour and now dangled in the sky like a woolen blanket on a clothesline. He nodded his satisfaction. He didn't need moonlight to showcase his activities to witnesses lurking in boats on the river, that was for damned sure, not that people were likely to be boating during an impending storm.

He'd already checked at the Senator's river house and seen no one around, though a slick little black Porsche was parked around back. If the Senator wasn't at the dock, Joe would go back to the house and ring the bell and try to talk his way inside. Witnesses? Didn't matter. Once the Senator understood how things were, he'd make it all right and he'd be grateful as hell.

He fingered the gun in his jacket and then he slipped into the underbrush, making more noise than he should, as much noise as Dave would have, but figuring no one could hear over the sound of the wind that was vibrating the treetops like tuning forks.

He angled to the right of the Senator's bench, keeping to the underbrush. Long minutes passed while he wriggled between half grown pines, standing under the protection of bigger trees. When he got closer to the river, he came to a tangle of blackberry bushes blocking his path like razor wire and he veered right. Place was an obstacle course and his breathing was coming funny--fast and shallow, while his stomach was a raw nerve. He was more out of shape than he'd thought. A moment later and he was at the path, farther down than he'd originally planned, but not so far that he couldn't look back and see the recognizable form of Senator Drake. Alone.

The Senator had his back to him. He'd just picked up his tackle box. Probably figured his date wasn't going to show in this weather and he might as well get back to the house before the storm broke. Joe broke into a shambling trot, best he could manage on his bad leg. When he was maybe fifty yards away, the Senator turned. His expression was wary, but controlled, and he raised his hand in a half salute.

"Hello. You live out this way?"

Like Joe could afford the neighborhood. His faded jeans and his shirt with the hole in the front ought to be some kind of clue, even for Senator Drake. He waved back and slowed to a walk and closed the distance between them, finally stopping a few feet away. He was still breathing a lot harder than he should have been, the air hitting his lungs like ice water. By now faint alarm showed on Senator Drake's face. He was maybe figuring it hadn't been such a great idea to ditch his taxpayer-funded protection back in Washington for a weekend at the river with some hot chick.

The Senator went into a power stance, hands on hips and feet braced apart. Looked funny on such a small man. "Don't I know you?"

Joe couldn't believe Senator Drake wasn't running for his life. But then, arrogance could do that to a man, could make him think he was so special no one would dare harm a hair on his precious head.

"Damn right, you know me." Joe smoothly drew the Luger out of his jacket. "Let's go."

The Senator's stance didn't change, but Joe was gratified to see his expression had turned into a mask of disbelief. "What do you think you're doing?"

"You can stay right where you are and let me shoot you, or you can let me show you something you need to see. I don't care which one you choose 'cause I'm Crazy Joe, thanks to you." Joe heard himself saying the words and he felt like he was outside his body watching a bad movie. But he didn't know where to find the off button to Crazy Joe and he wasn't sure he wanted to.

He jabbed the air with the gun. "Move it or I'll blow a hole in you a car could fit through."

The Senator slowly raised his hands. Joe moved the gun, this time pointing it directly at Senator Drake and he scurried to step off the path winding up the hill where Joe indicated. He walked behind the Senator, watching the back as straight and stiff as a flagpole. Hadn't given up yet. But then, he wouldn't. The Senator was used to being treated like a man who was better than everybody else. Joe directed him across the clearing and through the trees to the truck and had him get in on the passenger side after using duct tape to secure his hands behind him. Now see how much fight he'd show.

"You won't get away with this." Voice had gone from arrogant to whiny.

"Think that's one of my worries?" Funny how the Senator seemed only about half his normal size now that a crazy man had him in custody. Joe chuckled.

The Senator's face had lost most of its color, and Joe could see he was struggling to draw a normal breath. He put on his "lie to American people smile," as if Joe was too stupid to know what he was doing, and said, "Let me go and I'll forget I ever saw you. I imagine you're a person had a few setbacks and you're under a lot of stress. Most of my constituents think I can solve their problems, but what it comes down to is making laws for the greatest good. Of course, I can listen to your case and put in a word, help you out with whatever it is has you so upset. Be glad to. I've got a great understanding of the troubles people can run into, just day to day, and I'll speak up for you. Health problem? Money worries? We have all kinds of government agencies waiting to step in."

"Shut up and listen. You're going to do a lot of listening for as long as I want you to." Joe slammed the door and walked around to the driver's side and yanked the door open.

"What do you want with me? Money? My people can pay ransom. You just state your terms." He forced a laugh.

"It's not that easy." Joe backed the truck around and guided the wheels onto the dirt road. The Senator sat still, shooting him questioning looks, no doubt trying to size him up and figure what to offer next. Didn't have a clue that it was way too late, that Joe was in charge of his life for at least the next week or so, and by the time he got back home he'd be a changed man. Educated. Newly compassionate.

When he got to the highway, Joe stomped the gas pedal, fishtailing the truck. He was still outside himself, fading in and out of his body, flickering like a candle. Lark would approve of what he was doing. Every American would approve. Senator Drake was a traitor, caring only for his own enrichment and for the foreign lobbyists who'd given him money to betray his fellow Americans. Joe would get a medal when he was through reprogramming Senator Drake.

"If not money, then what?" The Senator's voice, high-pitched and trembling, broke into his thoughts.

"You ever stop to think about what you've done to ordinary Americans with your fool trade laws? You can spout lies all day long, but truth is the whole thing is just an experiment, it's not working, and you don't give two seconds of your time to even think about it because you're raking in the cash from business interests and foreign lobbyists. You're too busy reading reports from free trade 'think tanks,' where smug, self-righteous rich boys get paid to print off the garbage you use to justify your actions. Meanwhile, Americans are losing everything they ever worked for."

"But I…" Something lit up in the Senator's face. "Joe Tremaine. Now I remember you." As if all his problems were over now that he knew who he was dealing with, words tumbled out of his mouth. "Listen, Joe, I understand you had a head injury. You're not responsible for getting a little out of hand. I'll tell them that, see that you get some help and some government aid. You'll be good as new, maybe even better than new."

"Yeah, right. Kind of help you mean is me locked up for the rest of my life and you still free to hand over American jobs to whoever gives you money." Joe's mouth was so dry he'd have drunk out of a mud puddle if there'd been one handy. "I'm going to tour you around Avalon, show you how people live when they don't have jobs. Then I'm going to take you to my house and give you dinner. You like leftover spaghetti and water? That's all I can afford most nights. After you eat, I can tell you about people still paying on their student loans, while the only jobs they can get are sweeping the streets or running the register at a convenience store. And that's only the ones who have jobs. Rest of them spend their days down at the homeless shelter, feeling useless, begging for food, while you sign more anti-American trade deals and then go home to your mansion. I'll bet you have solid gold bath fixtures and window panes made out of diamonds."

The Senator started to say something, coughed, made a gargling sound and then apparently opted to keep his mouth shut. He slumped against the door and let his head droop. Good. Finally ready to listen. Besides, Joe wasn't interested in any lies the stupid bastard had to tell. If he said one more thing, Joe was liable to crack him across the mouth like he deserved.

The road had started wriggling from side to side like it didn't want the truck driving on it, so Joe had to use all his concentration to keep from sliding onto the shoulder. That was the Senator's fault, too. If Joe had his bingo hall, he'd be too busy working to be out kidnapping the Senator. What was it like, he wondered, to have the sickness of greed-- greed so deep and so ingrained that a man would sell out his own country to get more money than he could spend in a hundred lifetimes? He felt his stomach heave.

He glanced sideways and then forced his gaze back to the road. Left on Foster Boulevard, scoot past the restaurants and theaters that were lit up like a mini Vegas strip, left again onto Graham Road where well-kept older homes had somehow started to glow in the edges of his vision like leering jack o'lanterns. Then another mile and two turns onto streets that meandered past houses that got progressively more ill-kept, until he got to Oak Street.

"This is where I live. Nice, huh?" He braked to a stop in the middle of the road. "You see the drug dealers and the working girls on the corner? Hey, at least they have jobs so they can support their families, right?"

The Senator ignored him. His mouth hung slack and a wad of thick drool had run down his chin. His half-open eyes stared straight ahead like he might be expecting Superman to show up and pluck him out of the truck and fly him back to safety.

"Be that way. I don't want to listen to any more of your lies, anyway." Joe passed the house, turned left at the next corner, accelerated past the speed limit and eventually picked up the outerbelt to circle back toward Avalon. On the other side of the city, he could show the Senator the empty mills and the rows of foreclosed homes where the mill workers used to live. He looked to his right and saw Senator Drake still cowering against the door. He pressed the truck's accelerator and roared on into the darkness.

⁂

As if she were reading tea leaves, Lark peered into her cup where a patch of dark liquid lay at the bottom. She swirled the liquid and said, "No, thanks."

Benson had just offered another refill. But two cups of coffee in the evening was more than enough, though they'd been here for a couple of hours, sitting in a back corner. Benson had encouraged her to talk about what was bothering her and then, before she could decide where to start, he'd gone on to tell her all about his parents who couldn't understand why he didn't have a real job and his problems finding a decent car on a budget that didn't include much room for car payments.

She didn't mind. Not really. She'd been able to nod and make sympathy noises at all the appropriate times, and Benson had seemed satisfied. She'd ended up numbing her mind, hadn't thought of Dave more than a hundred times or so.

But coffee had taken a lot longer than she'd planned. At least the rain had slacked off for now. The wind was gusty and lightning flashed in the distance toward the river, streaking across the sky every few seconds. Maybe the rain would move on to that side of town and stay there. She and Benson said their good-byes in the parking lot, and he waited till she drove out first and was on her way before he left.

She got off the beltway and took it slow until she saw that the flooded streets had already drained. A surprising number of cars, considering the weather, were still clogging the roads. With a sudden sense of urgency, she sped up, weaving between vehicles all the way to Oak Street where she finally slowed when she reached their block. The house was dark when Lark pulled into the driveway. She drew her brows together. Dad never went to bed until she was safely home.

She got out of the car and hurried through the rain to the garage and lifted the door. His truck was gone. Damn it, if he'd gone back to talk to the loan sharks after she told him not to, she'd kill him. She unlocked the front door and shoved it open.

"Dad?"

She flicked on the living room light and went in. He wasn't in the kitchen or the living room. "Dad, you home?"

She strode down the hall. His bedroom door was open. And so was hers. Why would he have gone in her room? She stood in the doorway and looked, but couldn't see anything out of place. She shut the door and went to the kitchen to look for a note, not that she really expected one. She even went downstairs to hunt in the basement, though that dark hole gave her the creeps and she scurried back up as soon as she saw it was empty.

She ought to relax and wait for him to return, but how could she? He never went out at night when she wasn't home. Never. What if he'd forgotten to take his pills? She thought back, trying to remember if he'd taken one this morning. She was almost positive he had. Now where did he keep them? In his room usually, but sometimes in the bathroom. She'd check, not that she expected to be able to tell how many pills should be in the bottle.

She didn't see the pills in his room. She tried the bathroom. She flicked on the light and stood in the doorway and saw the bottle on its side in the sink. She didn't know how she'd missed it earlier. Only a couple of pills left. She thought there should be more, a lot more. How many was he taking anyway? She looked down and something on the floor caught her eye. It was another prescription bottle. She picked it up. It was the bottle for her pain pills from when she broke her wrist. Only two tablets remained. The bottle had held at least six tablets when she'd seen it last, she was positive.

She rubbed her hands across her cheeks and tried to think. It couldn't be good to mix medications. Her dad might be in real trouble now, out of his head and, even worse, he might be driving, might have already crashed his truck. No, she needed to stop imagining trouble. Very likely he was at the shelter or even over at Martha's. Or he might have told Martha where he was going. She'd just drive around the neighborhood, see if she spotted his truck, check with Martha. If she didn't find him, she'd return to the house and see if he was home yet.

Surely, though, he'd be back before eleven when she was due in from the park. She was worrying herself over nothing and she ought to simply settle in with a good book, but it couldn't hurt to make a quick circuit of the neighborhood to reassure herself. She grabbed her keys and dashed out the door.

⁂

Joe pulled into the garage and went back to haul the door down. He walked around to the front of the truck and yanked open the passenger door. The Senator slumped into his arms like a sack of laundry. Joe shoved him away, and, held up by the shoulder harness, he slumped like a rag doll in the other direction.

"Get out." Sweat trickled down Joe's chest. "Didn't you hear me? Get the hell out of the truck."

No response. Was he waiting for an engraved invitation? Didn't Senator Drake remember that Joe had a gun? His vision was finally clearing, sharpening its focus, but the headache was ramping up again. He rubbed his forehead against his shirtsleeve. He needed more codeine. First he had to...had to what? Get Senator Drake out of the truck and lock him in the dank room under the kitchen so he could teach him what it was like living every day afraid you wouldn't have food or a home for tomorrow. Teach him what it was like to have bill collectors call and threaten to take what little you had left. Teach him about the soul wrenching shame you felt when you didn't have a way to earn a living. What in the hell was wrong with the idiot that he couldn't figure out he'd hurt people and now it was time to pay the price?

"Lesson time. Move it." Joe prodded him in the ribs with the gun barrel and then shook him. The Senator's head rolled back and forth like a balloon on a stick, shaking loose the glob of drool Joe had noticed earlier. "Senator Drake? Move, before I blow your sorry ass to hell."

The head flopped down against the chest. Joe frowned, something flickering in his mind, trying to get his attention. He thought for a moment and finally put his hand on the Senator's neck, feeling for a pulse. He moved to the wrist, then tilted the Senator's head back and looked into his blank eyes.

Son of a bitch. Senator Drake was dead as the bass he'd left in a bucket back at the river. Joe leaned across the body and unhooked the seatbelt. He dragged the Senator off the seat and hoisted him over his shoulder to carry him to the back of the truck where he placed him on a tarp. He rolled the body to one side and yanked the duct tape off the Senator's wrists.

He stepped back and looked at the body. He had to think what was happening and why. The thoughts that had warped through his mind earlier, the voices telling him what to do and how to do it had deserted him. But now the headache was back and he had to take something, more pills, and then he could think what to do about the Senator. They'd fry him for this. What the hell had he been thinking? Where had the voices come from anyway? Oh, God, please don't let it be another seizure. He'd taken his medicine, as much as the doctor had prescribed and more.

He went upstairs, found his Seizure-Out bottle in the bathroom, and took another. There was only one left now and God only knew where he'd find six hundred dollars for another bottle, and hadn't he had that thought enough times so that he wanted to punch somebody out? He supposed he'd end up robbing a bank.

Two more codeines for the headache and in a few minutes he couldn't remember why he'd been so worried. Oh, yeah, the Senator, but that was nothing, they'd give him a medal. He needed to take the

Senator...where? To a television station, maybe? Show them how he'd done the country a big favor? His skin was on fire. Maybe he'd take a cold shower first.

⸎

Dave shifted uncomfortably on his seat. Wouldn't you know the bus would be late? At least they'd finally gotten on their way and he told himself that the closer he got to Hidden Springs, the better he'd feel. He tried deep breathing to help him relax, but the deep breaths tasted more like diesel laden fog than the sweet air of freedom he craved.

He peered out his window. They'd just gone through some little town, nothing but three or four churches and a gas station. He estimated they were a good thirty miles out of Avalon. He looked at his watch. Eleven o'clock. Maybe he could sleep on the way to Hidden Springs.

No, he was kidding himself. He wouldn't be able to sleep or even rest. All he could think about was Lark and how he'd deceived her and how he'd never see her again. He was running home to Mawmaw instead of sticking around to make things right.

The bus rounded a turn, the engine whined into a higher gear, and they picked up speed, streaking through the night. Even so, Dave reckoned they had six hours ahead of them. The bus, nearly full, would have a hell of a time working up speed once they started the long climb into the mountains.

Chapter Twenty

The front door slammed and with effort Joe redirected his focus. Lark stood in the living room. Droplets of water on her jacket twinkled like a million stars forming constellations all over the front of her. So pretty he felt like crying.

She hung her keys on a hook by the door and then put her hands on her hips. Her rosebud lips had formed into a pout. "Where have you been, Dad? I've been worried sick, out looking for you all over this side of town." She might be worried, but her voice was controlled. She was tough. She wasn't going to let on how bad she felt, but he knew.

He went to the kitchen and filled a glass with tap water. He gulped it down. The dry mouth, maybe from the codeine, was making him feel sick and the water didn't help.

"Dad?" Lark had followed him to the sink. She put her hand on his arm. "You okay?" Her pout turned into a mask of concern. "You feel so hot--you're burning up. And you've taken a bunch of pills. I was home earlier and found the bottles. Now tell me where you've been and what's going on."

She was something, his daughter. She had to be hurting over Dave's desertion, but she was sparing all her worry for her dad. He'd soon have her feeling better.

"Of course I'm okay. And I've got good news, I've been counting the minutes till you got home. You know how Senator Drake's the one wrote up all those bills to ship our jobs out of the country and even import workers to take our jobs? Well, he can't do it again. Not ever. He's dead in the garage, baby, they're going to give me a reward."

The concerned expression slid off her face, until nothing was left but blankness. "He's what?"

"Dead. In the garage. Jesus, my head hurts." Joe put his hands over his face and kept them there even as Lark led him to the couch. He could feel her hands trembling. How could he get her to understand that everything was going to be okay now?

"Dad, what did you do?" She pulled his hands down and stared into his eyes.

"I didn't do anything, baby. Got a bad headache, though." She should be telling him how happy she was. "Senator had a heart attack."

"Let me get you some ice." Still helping him, even when she was exhausted. Damn that Dave for running out. He should be the one getting the ice while Lark rested.

Gratefully, he waited and let her put an ice bag on his head. Heard her say, "I'll be right back." Heard the basement door open and a moment later heard Lark scream. He wished she wouldn't. His head hurt too much.

―――

The bus pulled into a station, another town with a name he didn't recognize. Dave shifted in his seat and stared at his hands. Each mile seemed to stretch out like a rubber band that eventually gave way to yet another and another in a never-ending series. Now he had to sit here even longer, till luggage was loaded and slow-moving people got around to climbing on the bus. All he wanted was to get back to the farm where he could pretend the last few years never happened. He supposed the rest of his life would be like the road, stretching out in front of him, empty and without real meaning, his life over before he was thirty. He sighed. He hadn't felt this down since the Markham-Hook job loss announcement.

He watched a young woman climb on the bus and take a seat near the front. She was a redhead, but something about the way she moved, her easy grace, reminded him of Lark. He suspected it would be a long while before he stopped seeing Lark in every pretty woman, but there was nothing he could do about that.

The bus jolted into motion and lurched back onto the highway. Dave had nothing better to do than to keep staring out the window and allowing himself to sink deeper into misery. But, damn it, why was he giving up? Had the long weeks of unemployment turned him into a complete wimp? It was as if the company had taken a part of him when they took his job and his home and he'd wandered around ever since like someone who'd been knocked in the head with a two by four.

Images from his past swam through his head like dreams-- Mawmaw brushing dirt off his clothes after he'd been in a fight. The eyes on the giant Lincoln in Washington looking at him with deep understanding and somehow communicating sympathy and courage and hope for the future. Loretta praising him for trying to fight back. He didn't deserve any of it, not any more. But why should that be?

A surge of adrenaline burned through his veins, and he raised his head and thrust out his chin. He'd wandered around in a daze long enough. He cared about Lark and he was going to let her know how he felt. It didn't matter if Joe got in the way, he was still going to tell her. After that, if she didn't want to forgive him, he'd leave. He'd be hurting, but he'd go to Hidden Springs knowing he'd be able to live with himself.

He got to his feet and staggered down the aisle to the front of the swaying bus. The driver glanced at him in the mirror, then aimed his eyes back at the road.

"Something wrong?"

"I changed my mind. I've got to go back to Avalon." The bus hit a bump and Dave grabbed the back of a seat to keep from falling.

"Should have got off at the last station. Next stop isn't for about fifty miles."

"Isn't there a small town a few miles ahead? You can let me off there or just put me at the side of the road." He wasn't sure, but he thought it might be illegal to keep someone on a bus against their will. If not, maybe he could kick up a fuss so the driver would call for the cops to take him off the bus. No, that wouldn't work because they'd take him to the nearest jail and he needed to be in Avalon, not arguing with a mean-natured deputy about how he was in a heap of trouble.

"I have to get to Avalon. Like a couple of hours ago. I don't see why that's such a big deal." Then he added, "I'll lose my girlfriend if I don't go back tonight."

A middle-aged man in the seat behind the driver chuckled and said, "Come on, let him off. Can't stop true love."

"You have a fight with the young lady?" The driver smoothly changed lanes and passed a couple of slow moving cars.

"Sort of, but after a few miserable hours spent thinking things over, I see where I was wrong and if I tell her how sorry I am, she might forgive me." Dave knew that practically everyone on the crowded bus had been listening in, and now other passengers started cheering and whistling and he heard a few shouts of "let him go back to his girl."

"I can let you off at a gas station a couple of miles ahead, but I can't unload your luggage."

"That's okay, it's tagged. Just leave it at the station in Hidden Springs."

He was already moving toward the door before the bus came to a stop. Passengers hung out the window offering encouragement and advice.

"Get on your knees and beg forgiveness."

"No, give her a diamond ring."

"You'll be sorry. Ain't no woman worth this much trouble."

He looked back over his shoulder and waved, and the bus burped blue smoke and then was nothing more than taillights. When the way was clear, he crossed the road and stuck out his thumb. If he didn't get a ride, he'd have to walk back to Avalon. Probably take him the rest of the night and all day tomorrow, unless he could get to a station they'd already passed and catch a bus east. Didn't matter. Even if it took him a month, he was going home to Lark.

She couldn't stop shivering. There had to be a way out of this without causing trouble for Dad. She ought to get him to the hospital, and the only way to do that was to call an ambulance, but even though he'd stopped speaking for now, what if he started blurting out that the Senator was dead in the garage? The hospital people would send the police back to the house and find the body. Dad would be locked away forever, pining for freedom, and it wasn't fair; he hadn't done anything. The Senator was nothing but evil, so her father shouldn't have to suffer because of him. Maybe if she waited, Dad would be okay eventually, but she had no way of knowing if that was true. And if she waited, he might die and that would be all her fault. She had to call someone, get help. Right. As if one of her co-workers or friends would get involved in something like this. Even Benson wouldn't want to help. He'd look at her, startled eyes gazing down that long nose of his, and tell her that he was sorry and all, but her father had committed a crime and he had to pay.

Dad let out an especially piteous groan. He was suffering. She had to get him to a doctor and she'd pray he kept his mouth shut until she could think what to do and…her thoughts were interrupted by the sound of a car in front of the house. She slipped to the window and moved the curtain just enough to give her the merest glimpse of a car speeding away down the street. A familiar figure was marching toward the steps.

She yanked the door open and Dave looked up. They locked gazes. She wanted to go to him and couldn't move. He ran up the steps and into her arms. She lowered her head and sobbed against his chest, relief washing over her.

Dave held her tight. Thank God he'd had sense enough to figure out he'd made the wrong move. She missed him as much as he'd missed her and she'd forgiven him already.

He squeezed her thin shoulders. "Lark, it's okay. I'm sorry I lied to you and I'll never do it again. I'll do anything for you. I never should have left." He'd thought about promising her the moon and the stars, but that sounded corny.

She sniffled and lifted her face to look at him. Her eyes were enormous. "You have to help. Something's wrong with Dad. First he kept saying Senator Drake had a heart attack and he's dead in the garage, and now he won't talk at all. He keeps moaning and shaking. His head hurts him bad. I can tell it does."

Dave let go of her. "He must be having trouble with his medicine. Have you called an ambulance?"

"I can't."

"Why not?" Dave glanced at the couch. Joe was curled on his side with his arms wrapped around his head. He knew Joe had been troubled by headaches--he'd gobbled aspirins like popcorn ever since Dave had met him.

"The Senator really is dead in the garage." Lark clasped her hands together. "He's in the back of the truck. Oh, God, Dave, I don't know what to do."

Dave's heart dropped down somewhere around the level of his navel. He whirled and raced through the kitchen and down the basement steps two at a time, missing the last step and falling to his knees at the bottom. He stumbled up and plunged through the connecting door to the garage and then skidded to a stop. He felt shivery, like a kid afraid something in the dark might grab him. He tightened his jaw. No such thing as ghosts. He stepped over to the truck to look in the back. His stomach wove itself into a tight knot. Dead senator all right. No signs of blood or violence that he could see. With a curious feeling of detachment, Dave marched back upstairs.

"Okay, Lark, I don't know what happened to Senator Drake, or why he's in your father's truck, but we have to call the police." He picked up the phone, and she snatched it out of his hands.

"No! Dad didn't kill him." She paced, wringing her hands. "He says he just brought him home to show him the way poor people live. It isn't his fault the stupid Senator dropped dead on the way. Senator Drake had a bad heart. It could have happened anywhere, in Washington, or in bed with one of his girlfriends, or driving his car."

"But it happened in your father's truck and your father kidnapped him. That's a crime, Lark."

"What are you, a cop or something?" She glared at him. "Look at my father. He's not a killer, you know that. He might have had seizures, but he's not a killer. They'll put him in prison forever if you tell the police."

"What do you expect me to do?" Dave crossed the room and knelt by the couch to peer into Joe's eyes. It was hard to see the pupils in eyes so dark, but Dave could make them out and see they were hugely dilated and the whites of the eyes were red, webbed with dozens of tiny, swollen veins.

"Look." Lark came up behind him and he turned. She held up the prescription bottles, shaking them. "This is what he took. His new seizure medicine and codeine. He shouldn't have mixed them."

Dave thought codeine and other drugs made your pupils go to pinpoints. Maybe Joe was different. Or maybe Lark was right and the mix of drugs caused a weird reaction. He ran his hands through his hair. Who cared about the side effects of a couple of drugs? Lark was asking him to commit a crime, and he couldn't do that.

"If what you say is right, that the Senator just had a heart attack, they won't do anything to Joe."

"Sure, Dave. They'll only lock him in a mental ward until he's back to normal and then they'll throw him in prison and never let him out. I know Dad has been kind of rough on you, but is that any reason to let him die in jail for something he didn't do? Hasn't his life been unfair enough?"

"Am I supposed to haul Senator Drake down to the local landfill? Maybe I should package him up like a to go order and leave him on the doorstep of the funeral home."

"If you aren't going to help, you can just go right back to town and follow through on your original plan to take a bus to Hidden Springs. I don't need you or anyone else." She lifted her chin and stared at him. "All you have to do is keep your mouth shut."

He sighed. Lark's loyalty to her father was going to get them in big trouble. The thing was, he knew that if he had a father, he'd feel the same way.

He looked at Joe again. Nobody home right now, and that made for a pretty scary situation. He liked Joe, at least he liked him okay during the times he'd acted sane. And Joe had even been good to him, promising to teach him to shoot and help him learn carpentry. But that didn't give Joe the right to get away with kidnapping a senator.

"I can't, Lark." He didn't turn around to face her.

"You can't keep your mouth shut? You're going to get me in trouble for helping my father?"

"No. I meant--I don't know what I meant." What if Lark was right? Why should Joe, or anyone else, have to go to prison because Senator

Drake died in their truck--even if he shouldn't have been in their truck to begin with? Jailing Joe wasn't going to bring the Senator back. And if Joe hadn't been sane, hadn't known right from wrong when he kidnapped Senator Drake, then he wasn't guilty of a crime. But would the government see it that way? Not likely.

What would Joe do if their positions were reversed? He didn't know, but he did know he couldn't let Lark face this alone. He leaned forward, fumbled in Joe's jacket pockets and found the Luger, but no other weapons. He took the gun into the bedroom and put it in the drawer of the nightstand. When he returned, he said, "Give me fifteen minutes head start and then call an ambulance."

"You mean it?" Her voice was low and husky.

"This is probably the dumbest thing I've ever done in my life and there's some pretty stiff competition for the number one spot." He kissed her. "Move your car so I can get the truck out of the garage."

Dave didn't know where he was going. Much as he disliked Senator Drake, he couldn't stomach the thought of abandoning his body where it wouldn't be found for months. He pulled the loose part of the tarp over the corpse and anchored it down with Joe's ladder. He didn't believe he could possibly hide the body where it would never be found. Dumping at sea would be a good plan, but then there was the guilty conscience to factor in. Besides, he didn't have a boat.

He realized he'd let himself become so detached in the last few moments that he was thinking about disposing of a body as calmly as he might be choosing the color of a new car. Maybe that made things easier.

He backed out of the garage and waited for Lark to pull her car inside and close the door before he headed out. After a few minutes, the truck seemed to have a mind of its own, turning onto Graham and then onto Foster Boulevard without him making a conscious decision. The river. Sure. Take the Senator right back where Joe found him.

Chapter Twenty-One

It was cool out. After the earlier storm had passed, more clouds had moved in and were reluctantly letting loose a spattering of drops every few minutes. Dave kept under the speed limit, cars passing him like they were auditioning for the Daytona 500. He wasn't breaking any traffic laws, not tonight, no way. He glanced in the mirror. Then why in the hell had a patrol car slipped in behind him, flashing its lights and hugging his bumper? He tried to remember if there was a protocol to follow when cops stopped you while you had a body in your vehicle.

Mind gone to mush. Heart slapping against his ribs with every beat. He flicked on his right blinker and pulled smoothly onto the shoulder of the road. Even with the ladder on top of the Senator, the tarpaulin wrapped bundle still looked suspiciously like a body.

At least in prison he wouldn't have to worry about where his next meal was coming from and they might even give him one of those prison laundry jobs where you earned eight cents an hour. Okay, he had to pull himself together and act like a grown up. But how? He was facing the end of life as he knew it. It was one thing making an adjustment to being jobless and homeless. It was quite another being the new guy on the cellblock for getting caught with a dead senator wrapped like a burrito in the back of your vehicle.

A uniformed sheriff's deputy approached in a measured walk, clipboard in one hand and the other resting on his belt an inch away from his holstered gun.

Dave rolled down his window. He watched TV and movies. He knew the script for this part. He was supposed to say, "Good evening, officer. What seems to be the problem?"

"Hey," he squawked. Very good, Dave. Just tell him what size handcuffs you wear and assume the position.

"Driver's license and registration, please." Pleasant voice, which didn't go with the face that could have been transplanted from a bulldog.

"Yes, sir." Dave shifted onto his left hip until he could free his wallet from his back pocket and extract his license. Then he leaned across the seat and flipped open the glovebox, dislodging a heavy lump with a rag wrapped around it. The lump was about the size and weight of a gun. His stomach plummeted, but when he reached under it, the rag fell open to reveal a greasy wrench. Dave released his tightly held breath and gripped the stack of papers in the glovebox, his fist closing around them like a crab's claw. No fine motor control, but that wasn't exactly his main problem at this point.

He shuffled through assorted invoices and a bill for lumber and finally found the registration. Handed it over, managing to keep his hand from shaking, but couldn't do anything about the sweat squirting out of little pores all over his body.

The officer handed back the license and studied the registration, silently mouthing the words as he read. After what seemed an hour, he said, "Who's Joe Tremaine?"

"Uh, friend of mine. I work for him. Small home repairs." Carefully neutral expression. Voice holding steady.

"Sir, did you know your left taillight is out?"

Of course he knew. Damn Joe for not getting it fixed after he told him about it, money or no money. If he could steal cigarettes, he could steal taillights. Where were his priorities?

"Is it? Sorry, officer. I didn't know."

The officer handed back the registration along with a warning ticket. "Get it fixed, okay?"

"Yes, sir, I'll take care of it first thing in the morning. And thanks for letting me know."

He'd make sure it got fixed, if the officer would just go back to his patrol car without hanging around to see what Dave was hauling. He watched in the rear view mirror as the cop played a flashlight over the bed of the truck. Back and forth and then sideways, dancing the beam over the tarp like he was putting on a light show. Dave leaned against the back of the seat and sweated out a few more gallons of precious moisture. Just when the cop leaned into the truck to get a closer look, the radio in the police car crackled. The cop rammed the flashlight into the holder on his belt and headed back to his car.

Dave gulped. He must have aged ten years in the past ten minutes. His face would probably be covered with little worry wrinkles by morning and he could almost feel his arteries hardening up from stress.

He wanted to sit still for a while to regroup and get his breathing back to a point where he didn't sound like someone on a respirator, but that would only invite suspicion and besides, he had a body to get rid of. He waited until the cop pulled out before he eased his way back onto the road.

He'd keep his mind on the goal. Get the body to the river as soon as possible, unload, and get back to Oak Street to curl up and forget this ever happened. He passed the exit he used to take to get to his home in Eden Acres. Only a few more miles to go.

By the time he got to the River Road turn off, his hands gripped the wheel so tightly he figured he'd have to pry them loose when it was time to get out of the truck. He glanced at the sky. There were no stars and no moon. The sky was solid dark, no doubt still covered with storm clouds he couldn't see. He'd only been here the one time with Joe, but he recognized the Senator's driveway when he rolled past. So far he'd only seen one other vehicle since he'd turned onto River Road, a Cadillac headed toward town, and he silently begged the body-dumping gods to keep up the good work.

The dirt road to the dock, showing as a lighter smudge between the black clumps of the underbrush on either side, appeared on his left and he turned in, bumping forward until the truck was brought up against a line of trees. The wind had been fierce earlier in the evening, had died down, and now picked up and lashed the treetops while lightning flashed across the sky.

It was maybe half a mile from here to the dock. He scurried around to the back of the truck and slid the ladder off the tarp. He wiped his mouth on the back of his hand, hoping that whatever was trying to boil up his throat would go back down. He'd never touched a corpse before. But he didn't have the luxury of being able to wait around until he actually felt like touching dead human flesh.

He opened the tarp and slid the Senator's body forward, close enough so he could pull the upper half of the Senator up and tilt the body over his shoulder. Everything he'd ever read about dead weight was true. He fell back for a few steps until he could steady himself against the trunk of a pine tree. Then he staggered forward, bent low under the weight. From a distance, he'd look like a mad scientist carrying a lab built android to the top of a hill so a lightning bolt could trigger it into life.

He decided on his way across the clearing that he'd leave the Senator on the bench. That is, if he made it as far as the bench. He tripped over a rock and barely kept his balance. His lungs screamed for mercy and his leg muscles burned. Why hadn't he spent more time working out at the gym when he still had a membership? But then, Avalon Fitness only had equipment for lifting weights up and sensibly putting them back down, not for picking up a slab of meat and hauling it half a mile in the dark while wind threatened to blow him off his feet. He had to keep stopping to rest his trembling legs.

When he finally reached the dock, he stumbled forward and dropped the Senator on the bench. After his breathing went halfway back to normal, he arranged the body in a sitting position and then let it slump sideways, chin resting on chest. Looked natural enough, like the Senator had been out here enjoying the river when fate overtook him. No one had to know that fate was named Joe Tremaine.

Big drops of rain the size of ping-pong balls had started to pummel down in the past few minutes. Dave wanted to run back to the truck, but his legs couldn't do more than drag him in the general direction like he was a hundred years old. Before he was halfway back, the sky opened up, rain gluing his clothes against his body and freezing the exposed parts of his skin.

He stumbled the last few feet through the underbrush, got to the truck and hauled himself shivering behind the wheel. He started the engine and experienced a few seconds of panic when the truck's wheels slipped in the dirt that was quickly turning to mud. He'd noticed the tires were bad--Joe couldn't afford new tires either. The truck finally grabbed traction and lurched backward. He stopped in the clearing, reversed, and roared back to the road.

Rain was pouring down on the windshield like heaven's main dam had sprung a leak. The wipers thwacked back and forth, failing to make much difference in the amount of road he could see ahead of him in the truck's lights. He leaned forward to peer through the windshield and slowed to a snail's crawl.

He ought to be feeling some major guilt, but right now all he could summon was relief, glorious relief, the sense of security that belonged to a man riding the roads without a dead senator in the back of his truck.

※

Dave woke up on the couch where Joe had been curled in agony last night. The first thing that made him realize he was conscious was the fiery jabs from his aching, knotted muscles. He peeled his eyelids apart with his fingers and studied the numbers on the clock over the TV. Ten-thirty. Usually by this time of morning the sun was streaming through the front windows. Not today, though. It was still raining, water thundering on the roof, sounding like a herd of buffaloes galloping toward a salt lick.

He sniffed. Coffee.

Lark walked out of the kitchen with a cup in each hand. Her face, childlike without her make-up, was the color of gardenia petals and her eyes looked puffy and red.

Dave sat up. "How's Joe?"

"They admitted him. The doctor said it turned out he was allergic to his new seizure medicine. It made him hyper and caused severe headaches, but Dad didn't notice because he was so happy not to be depressed anymore, he kept taking more and more until he overdosed. Then when he mixed in the codeine for the headaches, he went completely off the planet."

Dave wondered what Joe was like when he was on the planet. He realized he'd never known Joe when he wasn't taking his medicine.

He rubbed his chin. "Uhmm. Did he blurt out anything about--"

Lark shook her head. "No, thank God. They're going to let him come home this afternoon. Dave, you have every right to be upset, but Dad wants to see you. It's okay. He's fine now that he's off the drugs, though it's going to take him a while to fully recover."

How fine was fine? He was afraid to ask. He took the cup she handed him and leaned back against the couch cushions, deliberately blanking out his mind.

When he finished his coffee, he ate a bowl of soggy cereal and then borrowed her car to pick up Joe at the hospital. He'd avoided turning on the TV and the radio all morning. But when he got to Avalon Medical Center, a special news report on the TV in the lobby played on the screen and he had to look. A woman newscaster announced that Senator Drake, apparent victim of a heart attack, had been found dead near Avalon River where he was spending the weekend.

With a start of guilt, Dave glanced around. Eyes were glued to the TV; no one was paying any attention to him. If the cops were going to get suspicious, maybe start looking for a red truck seen on River Road last night, he'd know soon enough, though.

Joe was dressed and sitting in a chair when Dave walked in. The pupils of his eyes had gone back to normal and his expression was pleasant enough.

"Hey, Dave. You can stop staring at me like I'm a pit bull wants to take your head off. I've had a drug to kill the effects of that poison messed my mind up, though it's going to take a few days to wash all of it out of my system."

"That's good, Joe." For lack of anything more constructive to say. How did you relate to someone who'd gone crazy and threatened to kill you before he got around to kidnapping a senator?

"Doctor did some tests this morning. Seems like my brain has healed up some since my accident, so I'll only need to take pills if I start having problems." He was watching Dave, studying him like he was waiting for a reaction.

"That's good news." If Joe was okay now, Dave was prepared to start all over. But he wasn't going to set himself up for more trouble. "Ready to leave?"

"Hell, yes, I'm ready. People around here give too many orders and ask way too many questions about body functions."

Joe walked with him to the car, commented on the weather, which any fool could see was still wet, and plopped down in the passenger seat, squirming around until he had his long legs folded into the space in front of the seat. After Dave pulled out onto the road, he finally asked the question.

"Did I dream what happened last night? About wanting to put Senator Drake through some kind of Joe Boot Camp, so he'd mend his ways?"

Dave kept his gaze straight ahead, looking at the drops of water running down the windshield between beats of the wipers. "You know it wasn't a dream."

"Guess I do. Unfortunately, it never is. How did you solve the problem, or do I have that to deal with when I get home?"

"Didn't you watch the news this morning?"

"Too busy getting my head examined."

"Seems they found the Senator's body at the river." Dave told him the rest, not leaving out the part about the broken taillight. He half expected Joe to jump all over him for attracting the unwelcome attention of a cop.

Instead, Joe leaned forward and flipped on the radio. Dave hunched his shoulders toward his ears. But he couldn't live the rest of his life in a state of denial. The news announcer said the doctors suspected a heart attack. The autopsy was scheduled for later in the day.

Joe nodded. "Exactly what I figured. Good thing it rained so hard last night. Washed away the clues, not that they'll be looking for any. You can start breathing again, get some oxygen back in your blood before you pass out and run off the road and kill us both. Even if they decided it was something else, they'd never connect it to me."

Dave glanced at him. He appreciated the way Joe said "me," taking responsibility, instead of trying to pin something on him. "I didn't get rid of the tarp," he said.

"I'll take care of it. Hide it where even the rats won't find it."

Dave couldn't help grinning. Then he said, "Uh, Joe, Mawmaw told me if you and Lark want to come to Hidden Springs with me, she's got plenty of room at the farm."

"Yeah, she told me the same thing. That's mighty nice of her."

"What do you say? I haven't mentioned anything to Lark yet, thought I'd ask you first."

Joe reached across the seat and squeezed Dave's shoulder. "Come on, sugarbiscuit. Let's go home."

Epilogue

Fall in Hidden Springs had brought an unusually pretty burst of reds, golds, and yellows to the trees that crowded the mountainsides. Now, with winter a few days away, the trees had suddenly dropped their leaves, blanketing yards and clogging gutters. A cold front promised for the end of the week was predicted to bring snow. Dave wondered if the county would plow the roads all the way out to the farm. Most likely. The town's mayor had recently bought property out near the farm and he'd make sure he had a clear path to the local grocery. And if the power went out, the mayor would have that seen to right away. Dave didn't want the power to go out--he was working on a website about job losses.

"You going to take all day to get the floor cleaned up?" The skinny figure standing in front of him cast a narrow shadow across his table.

Dave blinked. He couldn't even get away with having his own thoughts while he was on his lunch break.

"Sir, no Sir, I'll get right on it. As soon as feeding time's over." He tapped his watch. "Fifteen more minutes, Mr. Wilson."

Wilson grunted. He worked his mouth like he wanted to come out with a clever comeback, but nothing happened between his brain and his voicebox. Dave didn't bother teasing him.

His new boss, who insisted on being called Mr. Wilson instead of Chris, was the manager at Hidden Springs Burgers. He was twenty-one years old and he'd emphasized when he hired Dave that if Dave worked hard, he might make assistant manager in a year or so.

The poor sap was on salary and that meant he got to work sixty or seventy hours a week for the princely sum of twenty-three thousand dollars a year. Dave was earning a lot less--only a dollar above minimum wage--but he was glad for the job.

In the six months since he'd returned to Hidden Springs, the jobless recovery had deepened until bankruptcies and foreclosures were running at record highs. Dave figured, that being the case, people should be able to get jobs as collectors. He pictured a scene in a busy call center, the phone lines throbbing and heating up from overuse, and employees dropping from fatigue.

On one side of the call center room a gaunt man wearing tattered jeans and an Avalon Grizzlies tee shirt, punches in a number and watches a woman a few desks away pick up.

"Hi, Marlene. You going to make a payment on that obligation? Your car payment?"

"Oh, hell, Bill. Left my money bag at home." They both cackle. Then Marlene goes, "I need a payment from you on that credit card. These debts don't just fade away, Bill." More cackling. They both hang up and dial other co-workers.

Dave would have laughed at the scene playing out in his mind, except that it wasn't really funny. Even the call center jobs had been outsourced to countries with cheaper labor.

Someone pushed open the door on his right, and he glanced up to see Joe limp inside ahead of a couple of tourists. Joe came over to his table and held out a copy of the Hidden Springs Gazette. "Figured you'd be on break about now. Got a few minutes between jobs and came over to show you something might brighten your day. Seen today's paper?"

"This isn't about Senator Drake, is it?"

After the autopsy, the official cause of death had been listed as a heart attack, but the news articles all screamed headlines about unanswered questions and the conspiracy boards on the Internet were lit up with speculation. Dave didn't know if he'd ever stop looking over his shoulder.

Joe rolled his eyes. "Sure, Dave, a couple of deer hiding in the bushes saw the whole thing and decided to turn us in for the reward money. Stop worrying and read." He sat across from Dave and pushed the paper across the table.

Dave quickly scanned the article. For a second he felt almost lightheaded. Someone had called in an anonymous tip to the SEC. The investigation had just gotten under way, but already it seemed there was ample evidence that John Victor Harris had schemed to defraud stockholders of hundreds of millions of dollars through insider trading involving companies Markham-Hook had bought. He'd been arrested last night.

Markham-Hook, its stock price plummeting, was self-righteously denying all wrong-doing. John Victor Harris, of course, had been immediately fired, but Dave doubted he'd been escorted from the building toting a cardboard box. A picture of Oxford DeWinters, looking CEO-ish, accompanied the article. If it weren't for the damage to the stock price, Dave could almost believe DeWinters had been the one who turned in Harris.

He looked around and grinned. At least his own life was going okay since his last day at Markham-Hook. More than okay--he and Lark were engaged. She'd found part-time work at the Hidden Springs library and she'd formed a local theater group. They were opening in a musical next week. Joe had a handyman business and he helped out at the farm, repairing the barns, making plans to put in crops, and fixing up the house for Mawmaw. In the evenings he did online readings for a psychic hotline. Tarot, crystal ball, or just picking up vibes, Psychic Joe would tell you anything you wanted to hear about your love life or your finances.

Mawmaw kept saying, "You'll be the death of me, Joe Tremaine." But she and Joe had bonded like a long-lost mother and son, and Dave knew she didn't really mean it when she threatened to put Joe on a bus back to Avalon if he didn't mend his pagan ways.

Joe left and Dave tossed the newspaper into the nearest trashcan. Flipping burgers and mopping floors for Hidden Springs Burgers wasn't his dream career, but it would do for now. He had his website about job losses and he hoped people were finally coming to their senses. Yeah, one day the country would return to government of the people, by the people--Dave just had to hang in there and keep fighting.

He looked up and caught Wilson glaring at him from behind the counter. Dave waved like he was greeting a cherished friend and picked up his mop. He moved over to a corner and started sloshing gray water back and forth across the greasy floor, his arms moving like a metronome in time to the country music playing on the jukebox. In a few minutes, the lunch crowd, mostly day laborers from the new highway project, started wandering in a few at a time to order the cheapest burgers on the menu.

Printed in the United States
37661LVS00004B/250-273